The Soldier's House

The Soldier's House

a novel

Helen Benedict

 Red Hen Press | *Pasadena, CA*

Book design by Mark E. Cull.

Library of Congress Cataloging-in-Publication Data

Names: Benedict, Helen, author
Title: The soldier's house: a novel / Helen Benedict.
Description: First edition. | Pasadena, CA: Red Hen Press, 2026.
Identifiers: LCCN 2025034386 (print) | LCCN 2025034387 (ebook) |
ISBN 9781636282787 paperback | ISBN 9781636282794 ebook |
ISBN 9781636284835 library binding
Subjects: LCGFT: War fiction | Novels | Fiction
Classification: LCC PS3552.E5397 S65 2026 (print) | LCC PS3552.E5397 (ebook)
LC record available at https://lccn.loc.gov/2025034386
LC ebook record available at https://lccn.loc.gov/2025034387

The National Endowment for the Arts, the Los Angeles County Arts Commission, the Ahmanson Foundation, the Dwight Stuart Youth Fund, the Max Factor Family Foundation, the Pasadena Tournament of Roses Foundation, the Pasadena Arts & Culture Commission and the City of Pasadena Cultural Affairs Division, the City of Los Angeles Department of Cultural Affairs, the Audrey & Sydney Irmas Charitable Foundation, the Meta & George Rosenberg Foundation, the Albert and Elaine Borchard Foundation, the Adams Family Foundation, Amazon Literary Partnership, the Sam Francis Foundation, and the Mara W. Breech Foundation partially support Red Hen Press.

First Edition
Published by Red Hen Press
www.redhen.org

To the children who have lost life, limbs, family, and a future to war.
And to the hope that the powerful will stop killing you.

Last night
I rinsed my mind with geniality
And dyed my heart with departure
I left my fingers and took my bag.
—Omar al-Jaffal, "My Soul" (2014)

How can I live comfortably in a country
where swords are sharpened for our people.
—Lamea Abbas Amara, "San Diego (On a Rainy Day)" (2015)

PART I

1

I was not born into this world knowing how to be an exile. Who among us is? We enter life prepared to be one with kin and tribe. Even those of us delivered into a circle of outcasts—Kurds, say, Palestinians or Jews, or any other people history has deemed pariahs—sense nothing of this as infants. No, my first years on this earth revolved only around Mother, her milk my nectar, her lap my haven; Father, with his weary eyes and scents of tobacco and mint; and my baby brother Zaki, his belly as soft as rising dough. I could not know how soon each of these loves would be taken from me, any more than I could know what it is to be rescued by my enemy.

Our airplane touches down with a jolt so violent it flings my heart to my throat. For nearly three years we have waited for this moment, counted the minutes, endured the days, yet my little one misses it entirely, being sound asleep. I try to wake him, tell him, "Tariq, *habibi*, we're here. We're in America at last!" but he is too depleted from our twenty-six hours of flying and layovers even to stir. I have to carry him off the airplane, my shoulders wound with all three pieces of our hand luggage, while my mother-in-law hobbles behind, declaring herself incapable of managing anything more than her handbag and his crutches. Tariq is heavy, as the sleeping always are, although not as heavy as he should be. My son weighs at five what he weighed at three.

Bearing him down the ramp into the glassy cube of the airport, its lights so bright they sting my eyes, its air frigid, I look over the people around me. The American soldiers promised to meet us here, but I have no idea where to find them. Nor am I sure that I will recognize the soldier-girl Kate, seven years having passed since we met. As for Sergeant Donnell, I've never even seen a picture of him. Had my husband, Khalil, brought home so much as a photograph of an American soldier in his phone, all of us could have been killed.

At the bottom of the ramp, I search again for our hosts. I assume they will be in uniform but can see nobody in military dress, or anyone who seems to be waiting for us, only a clump of irritated travelers waiting to board the airplane we have just left.

"Mama, what do you think we should do?" I have fallen into the habit of calling Hibah "Mama" in lieu of my real mother. She, I was forced to leave behind.

"We should retrieve our luggage, that's what," she snaps. Hibah is never so imperious as when asked for advice.

We follow the signs for Baggage Claim down a series of long corridors, looking about in the hope of hearing a greeting. I cannot help but notice the stares—at my mutilated child; at Hibah, small and wasted inside her black abaya; at my own scarred face and non-Western clothes. I lift my head so as not to see.

When at last we reach the baggage area, suitcases cycling by on conveyor belts shaped like tongues, I glance around once more for the soldiers. Not here.

"Mama, would you mind sitting here against the wall? I need to put Tariq down." She scrutinizes the floor with the haughty disdain of her earlier days and pronounces it far from clean, but as neither of us can see a bench or chair, she sinks onto it anyway, reaching for Tariq. He is so deeply asleep, his mouth slack, his curls damp with sweat, that his little body drapes across her knees like a coat.

Standing by the tongue under our flight number, my veins coursing with equal measures of excitement and apprehension, I clutch myself against the air-conditioning and watch, hypnotized by the suitcases spinning away on their endless loops. Pink blue black brown. Pink blue black brown. But as bag after bag appears and reappears until it is claimed, none of them ours, a knot forms in my throat. In those suitcases are the few possessions we collected during our limbo in Damascus with which to make a new life. *Please,* I pray to the baggage chute, *please don't swallow the last of what we have.*

The chute, of course, is not listening. Every one of our suitcases is gone.

"I won't stand for it!" Hibah cries when I tell her. "Go complain!"

"Mama, please, don't make such a racket. Wait here." I hurry over to a sign bearing the words, *Operations Center Lost and Found*, under which a balding man with the face of a tortoise stands behind a counter, gazing into a mobile phone with the same bored impatience I used to see on Baghdad bureaucrats.

"Good day to you, sir," I begin, pausing to collect my English. "My luggage, it is not on the loop. You have it here?"

He looks up, his watery eyes stopping at my scar, as eyes so often do. "We don't have no baggage here, lady. Nothin' but lost kids and umbrellas." He waits, grinning. When I fail to react, he shrugs and pushes over a form for me to fill out. It asks for a home telephone number I do not have, a cell number I do not have either, and the address to which we are going, which at least I do have, although it means little to me: 533 Sugarhill Road, Slingerlands, New York.

"Call and we'll tell you when it shows up." He hands me a copy of the form and a small square of paper reading, "*Redeemable Coupon, Free Shoeshine!!!*" I glance down at my sneakers.

"My family, we are being met. Where—"

"You gotta go through Baggage." He squints again at my scar.

Shaken by this exchange, which seems to me sinister, I return to Hibah. She is now as deeply asleep as Tariq, her head leaning against the wall, her withered face pallid inside her hijab. Her mouth has fallen open, revealing a discolored front tooth and a missing canine. She is not yet sixty-nine, but the trials of the last few years have made her look and move as though she were eighty.

Prodding her awake, I heave Tariq to my shoulder, while she uses his wooden crutches to lever herself to her feet. "Stay calm, Mama," I say as quietly as I can, "but I am sorry to tell you that our suitcases seem to have disappeared."

"*Ya Allah*, help us!" she wails instantly, her voice rising.

"Shush, please." I scan the room. More stares. "Come. Let's find the soldiers."

Having gone through hours of interrogation and delays by immigration when we first landed at Kennedy Airport, we are not required to do so again here in Albany. Nonetheless, as I carry Tariq past the customs officials, Hibah grumbling beside me, I know how conspicuous we must look, three obvious Arabs without a single suitcase between us. A familiar dread washes through me, an iced finger on the spine. After all, we are from a country with which the United States is still at war.

As I feared, an officer calls us over, a paste-colored man with stiff yellow hair and milky gray eyes. "Bags."

"Sir, all our luggage, it is lost."

His eyes flicker to my scar and then to Hibah's hijab. "Passports."

I present these quickly, along with our visas and the sponsorship form from Sergeant Donnell, all of which the officer examines for so long the ice creeps to my throat.

"Proof of lost luggage," he barks then with the same lack of civility common to all those in the uniform of authority. I hand him the copy of my report and the coupon for the free shoeshine. He squints at them for another interminable stretch. "OK. Go." Thrusting the papers back at me, he stares at Tariq with open distaste.

I pull my little one to my chest and hurry away. I am always so careful to close up his trousers on the left side, to cut the empty leg short and sew it into a tidy seam, so as to protect him from just such looks as this.

On the far side of Baggage Claim, I search the hurrying crowds again for the soldier-girl Kate but see nothing of her. A man is looking at us, though, tall and broad-chested, with glaring white skin, cropped black hair and a military bearing. Even from this distance and behind his brown-framed glasses, his eyes gleam a preternatural blue. He isn't in uniform, only jeans and a brown T-shirt, but as he marches up to us, I know it is him.

"Are you *Oum* Tariq?" He has a mild voice, middling in tone, slurred in that American way. A surprisingly gentle voice for a killer.

"I am."

"I'm Jimmy Donnell. Welcome to the US! So relieved you made it at last."

I peer behind him. "Your wife, where is she?"

"She . . ." He shakes his head as if to put his tongue back into place. "She couldn't come. I'm sorry."

Kate Brady promised to be here. Surely this soldier doesn't expect us to enter his car without his wife. "But . . . so she is waiting for us at your house?"

"Uh, no. Sorry."

"But she will return soon?"

"I don't know—I'll explain later. So sorry . . ."

Three times already he has apologized. And each time has only brought bad news.

"You must be totally bushed," he says then, stepping up to Hibah, whose head barely reaches his elbow. "You're *Oum* Khalil, I know." His Arabic is slow and ungainly but at least he knows to address her in the proper way, as Khalil's mother, as he also addressed me properly. In a few more mangled Arabic phrases, he adds, "Peace be upon you. Your son, may God have mercy on his soul, spoke of you all with such love."

Hibah wishes him peace in return, her dim eyes moistening.

"So this is little Tariq, huh?" the soldier says next, returning to English. He bends to peer into my son's sleeping face. "Khalil talked about him so much I feel like I know him."

I turn to shield Tariq from his invading eyes. "The airport, it has lost every piece of our luggage."

"Shit, you're kidding! Did you report it, fill out one of those forms?"

"Of course I filled out the form! I have done nothing but fill out forms for years!" I draw in a breath and try to master myself.

"So that's why you were late." Ignoring my outburst, he glances at Hibah, her face gray with fatigue. "Listen, why don't you both sit on this bench here and I'll pull the car up. It's time to get you ladies home."

2

Tariq props himself in the bedroom doorway, a twig of a boy balanced on one crutch, his single leg poked into an oversized sneaker like a stick in a bucket. "Jim-Jim! Football!"

Sitting up with a start, a spasm twanging through his neck, Army Sergeant Jimmy Donnell, seven-year veteran of the war in Iraq, cups his hand around the pain, gropes for his glasses and squints at the clock: 05:30. "Jesus Christ, kid, it's way too early." He yawns, which only hurts his neck more. "Listen, go down to your mama. Aren't you supposed to be saying your prayers or something?"

"No football?"

"Later. Promise."

Tariq fixes his eyes on Jimmy a moment, his narrow dab of a face somber. Then, with a twist and a scoop, he swings out of the room and disappears.

"Fuck." Throwing off his sheets, Jimmy stands and stretches—muscled, naked, pale as salt—and crosses the bare wooden floor to the window. Leaning his forehead against the glass, he gazes through the gauze of the insect screen at the front yard below. The sky is slipping from twilight gray to a spangling blue, late May flowers winking under the dew webbing the grass, which is severely in need of mowing. It's going to be a bold, hard-lit day, offering nothing in the way of cover. Kate's absence knocks against his ribs like a trapped bird.

Down in the kitchen, Naema pushes up the heavy wooden frame of the window and rests it carefully on a stick, the catch broken like so much else in this ramshackle house. Four days now she has been in this northeastern corner of America and still she cannot accustom herself to its dazzling effusion of green.

Squinting against its glare, she leans her elbows on the windowsill to watch Tariq out in the front yard. It is hard for her to believe that her son can play alone under the sky like this, with nothing to fear but bees.

He is sitting beside the flowerbed with his back to her, his whole leg folded beneath him, his stump nestled into the grass. Leaning forward, neck stringy, shoulders sharp, backbone a line of knobs under his oversized T-shirt, he plunges his hands into the weed-netted soil. The previous morning, Naema heard the soldier tell him the flowerbed was full of treasures, and Tariq has already unearthed a miniature rusted car and a tiny white plastic horse. "Generations of kids've played here," the soldier said. "Me, my brothers, Mom, Granny, we all left our crap behind. Whatever you find, bud, it's yours."

Tariq already worships this soldier. He does not understand.

Behind her, Hibah is searching the kitchen for flour. "Naema, come help," she commands, peering into a cupboard of cereal boxes, a drawer of dried pasta. She wants to cook pancakes the way Sergeant Donnell showed her because ever since they arrived here, Tariq will eat nothing that isn't eggy or white. He adores all that sugary mush the Americans call food. She intends to make pancakes for the sergeant, as well, to show her gratitude, but Naema remains stubbornly at the window. "Why must you be so ungracious?" Hibah grumbles. "Come!"

"We're not his servants, Mama." Naema speaks without turning around. "I don't know why you insist on being in his kitchen at all. We should stay in our own room and mind our own business."

Hibah glances at her. The long neck, the thick braid of black hair dangling to the small of her narrow back, the stubborn set of her shoulders. Her daughter-in-law has changed so much since Khalil brought her home as his bride. A gracious girl she was then, face smooth, figure slender, eyes the gold of a tiger's, so in love with him that no one in the family could resist her. Now she has grown brittle and sharp; body too spare, mouth too sour. That star-shaped scar etched into her right cheek.

"'Cast no dirt into the well that yields you water,'" Hibah mutters. Giving up on the flour, she fills a saucepan to make tea.

Jimmy stands in front of his closet mirror, scrutinizing himself with the same severity he had used to inspect his platoon. Cheeks scraped. T-shirt spotless. Jeans ironed. Desert boots brushed. Glasses polished. Back at the start of the war, he'd been the barefoot, scruffy type on his furloughs home, the unshaven, beer-with-breakfast type. But the events of his last tour knocked all that out of him and now he's pure army. Five hundred push-ups every morning. A twelve-klick speed run around Slingerlands. An hour lifting weights in the basement to ear-crunching heavy metal. And the long and vigorous shower he needs twice a day to scrub out the black airgrease, the burnpit poisons, the moondust deep inside his every pore—that desert grit he still feels grinding away inside him when he runs, when he breathes, when he shits and when he thinks, even after twenty months stateside.

Down at the kitchen door he hesitates, uncertain of what to say, how to move. Kate's sudden desertion has left him unbalanced, just as these new women in his kitchen make him feel an invader in his own house. Clearing his throat so as not to startle them, he murmurs, "*As-salaam aleikum*" before forcing himself to walk in.

Naema ignores him, still at the window, but the old lady replies in kind and gestures to the frying pan.

"No, no, let me do it." He offered them the run of his kitchen because theirs is nothing but a tabletop burner and a knee-high fridge, while his is roomy and bright with red cabinets, a hickory-planked floor and a brick fireplace wide enough for a spitted sheep. But that doesn't mean he wants them to cook for him. He pulls out a chair. "Sit, *Oum* Khalil. I'll make us breakfast."

Hibah mumbles something, her face inside her black hijab a disk of wrinkles. Khalil once told Jimmy that his mother had been a distinguished figure before the war, hostess to intellectuals and poets. But here, with no English and that black abaya draping her from neck to feet, it's hard to see her as anything but an old-world peasant.

"Let her cook, this is what she wants," Naema tells him without turning around. "We are making tea. You will take some?" Her English is impressive for someone who has never lived in the West, but her accent unmistakable. The rolling r's, percussive t's and d's.

"Uh, sure. Thanks." He glances down at the old woman, her mouth as puckered as a pecan. "Tell her she can cook another day if she'd like. It's just that I got us some French toast ready last night."

Naema remains at the window with her back turned, her small frame engulfed in a shapeless gray sweat suit that belongs to Jimmy's brother, Patrick. Tariq, too, is in somebody else's clothes—Jimmy's own childhood soccer shorts and a navy-blue T-shirt, a single shoe disinterred from the attic—their suitcases still somewhere in limbo, their own clothes in the wash. Jimmy would have lent Naema some of Kate's outfits if Kate hadn't whisked away every last thread when she vanished.

"Want me to get Tariq?" he asks. No reply. Taking this for consent, he heads outside, holding his head up gingerly as he steps off the front porch. He's only thirty, yet the bones in his neck feel as frail as balsa wood, ready to snap at any second, thanks to his years of ricocheting off the ceilings of Humvees as they jounced over the Iraq desert. His neck still hurts just from sitting up in bed that morning.

Crossing the yard, noticing not one but three new groundhog holes perfectly designed to swallow a crutch, he squats beside Tariq, still wrist-deep in the flowerbed. The boy is humming one of those wavering Iraqi songs that Jimmy finds so wrenching, his little kid voice reedy and wistful.

"Any luck, bud?"

Tariq lifts his head. Under his black curls, he has a fine-boned face, acorn-colored and big-eyed, tapering to a pinch. Jimmy can't look at him without seeing Khalil, the warmth in his gaze, the kindness nestled in the curve of his mouth. The sorrow twists, a flint in his chest.

"Yes, luck!" Grinning, Tariq hands him a miniature yellow tractor caked in soil. When Jimmy's brothers were small, they used to play at burying their toys in this flowerbed to make treasure hunts, only to lose interest and leave them there forgotten. Those same brothers he raised mostly by himself till he went to war. Who haven't visited him once since Kate left, not even to meet Naema.

"Wow, look at that!" The tractor must have been buried there at least ten years, from back when his mother was still well enough to garden. The flowerbed has grown into an impenetrable jungle since then, grapevines choking the rosebush, wheatgrass suffocating the peonies, yet the tractor hasn't lost a single wheel. Jimmy considers telling Tariq that an elf has been keeping it in good shape, changing the oil and tires so he can plow his tiny fields. But, although Naema has taught her son an admirable amount of English, he probably wouldn't understand a story like that. And then, Jimmy has no idea if an Iraqi would even know what an elf is.

"This is a tractor. Track-tor. Now you say it."

"Trrractorrr."

"Awesome!" He rubs Tariq's head, the curls tickling his palms. Naema glowers at him whenever he touches her son, but he can't help himself—that bloom of affection each time he looks at the kid. "The tractor's yours now. Let's go in. Time for breakfast."

Handing it back, he reaches to lift Tariq up, but the boy shrugs him off, seizes one of his crutches and pulls himself upright. Moving across the yard in a rapid series of lurches and swings that avoids every groundhog hole in the grass, he grabs the porch banister, hops up the steps and disappears inside, leaving Jimmy to carry the other crutch in after him.

"How dirty you are, *habibi*!" Naema exclaims, leading Tariq to the sink, where he has to balance on his crutch and stretch his arms up one at a time to reach. She rinses off the toy and scrubs the soil from his hands, his little palms hard and calloused, fingers as fragile as sparrow bones. She kisses each one in turn, her lips lingering.

"Stop, Mama!" Snatching the tractor back, he swoops over to a chair and throws himself into it, dropping his crutch to the floor with such a crash that Naema and Hibah both jump, hands flying to their chests, a familiar terror flooding their veins.

"Tariq, I told you not to do that," Naema snaps.

Jimmy leans the second crutch beside its mate, opens the refrigerator and stares into it, waiting for his own nerves to calm. What was he doing? Oh. Taking out the bread he left soaking overnight in egg, milk, cinnamon and vanilla, the way Kate taught him, he fries it up with a peel of butter and a sprinkle of nutmeg, its eggy fragrance permeating the room. Once everyone is settled around the table, he serves Tariq and Hibah a slice each, but Naema waves hers away. "I have my yogurt."

"You sure?" Disappointment cuts through him.

"Help yourself, Sergeant, and sit."

He obeys, joining them at the same scratched-up wooden table where he ate as a boy, his brothers Patrick and Rory squalling and scrapping on one side, his mother loopy or hungover on the other. She's gone now—four years in and out of mental hospitals and buried these past six—just as all his previous life seems to be gone.

Hibah mumbles some kind of prayer and nods at the others to begin, while Jimmy opens the bottle of maple syrup Kate bought from a local farmstand as a welcome gift for their guests. "They better like this stuff, given what that fat fuck charged me," she said with no hint of her plans to flee. Jimmy drizzles some over Hibah's toast and then Tariq's.

"What is?" The boy peers at it before cautiously touching it with his tongue. He looks up in delight. "*Sukar*!"

Naema glances at him with a rare smile but rejects the syrup with the same aversion she did Jimmy's toast. He avoids it as well, his taste for anything rich and sweet undone by too many years of MREs and T-Rats, not to mention all the unidentified Iraqi bugs partying in his guts.

Silence drapes over the room. Naema stirs her yogurt, nibbles a spoonful, stirs again. Hibah moves her toast around without trying a single bite. Even Tariq, his face only just peeking above the tabletop, takes no more than four mouthfuls before pushing his plate away in favor of driving his tractor along the table's edge. Jimmy glances at his guests' downcast eyes and barely touched food. *This is never going to work, Khalil. I'm such a goddamn idiot.*

"Sergeant?" Naema raises her eyes to him, their golden irises darkening to amber in the kitchen's weak morning light. "We need today to find clothes." Her hair has loosened from its braid to fall in a curtain over her scarred cheek, making her look almost girlish. How old is she? Jimmy wonders. His own age? A couple years younger? Khalil never said. But her tight-lipped expression is so forbidding it pushes his eyes away.

"I could buy you some stuff at Kmart if you like," he offers, looking at *Oum* Khalil instead. "It's cheap."

"No," Naema replies for her. "We do not wish for you to spend money on us. I shall buy the clothes myself."

"But I'm happy to get you some." Naema has almost no money, he knows that.

"No."

He stares down at his plate. Was she this fierce with Khalil? "I know where we can get some for free, if that helps."

She draws herself upright, her slight shoulders squaring, high-boned face stern. Folding her hands on the table, fingers long and worn, she regards him steadily. "These clothes, they are new?"

"Uh, no. Hand-me-downs."

"Pardon?"

He raises his eyes to her. "I mean, like, worn before? By other folks? But we can wash them, no prob. What d'you think?"

She hesitates, the distaste visible on her face, and looks over at Hibah, who is clutching her tea glass and staring into the dormant fireplace, the tea trembling.

"Very well. My mother-in-law, she will not like this, but it will do for now. We wish not to be in your debt, Sergeant. And, *insh'Allah*, our luggage, it might arrive any day." She pushes her yogurt aside. "There is something else also. This morning we must meet our appointment at the Refugee Resettlement Center in the city of Albany, receive our social numbers and find a school and a doctor for Tariq. There is a bus we can take?" Naema isn't sure where Albany is, only that it's a city some distance away that contains the airport, whereas the soldier's house seems to be in a village.

Jimmy shifts in his chair. "That's probably more than you can fit into one day. But you don't need a bus, I'll drive you. I have to go into town anyways."

"It is not necessary. I am able to drive."

He takes off his glasses and polishes them with the hem of his shirt. He knows something about Iraqi driving. "I'm afraid that's not a good idea till you get your New York license." He drops his eyes again. "I'm sorry."

Naema tenses. He said it again. Sorry. He says it a dozen times a day and each time the word glances off her skin like a stone.

She studies him a moment, this hulking stranger to whom she is so bound. Neck bent, gaze fixed on the table, massive shoulders hunched. The three violent loops of barbed wire tattooed around his inflated left bicep, the bayonet and grenade etched into his right forearm. The scars shining over the backs of his hands. The face long and candle-white, cheekbones a ridge under his eyes. And the eyes themselves the color of empty sky, the color of nothing. This is the man her husband claimed to love as a brother?

Naema turns to Hibah. "Mama," she says in Arabic, "would you mind getting Tariq ready while I wash the dishes? Our clothes should be dry now. The soldier is taking us to the city."

Blinking out of her daze, Hibah glances up. "Which city?"

"The one where our airplane arrived. We have to take care of our resettlement papers there."

Hibah places her knotted hands on the table and, with an effort, levers herself to her feet. Passing Tariq his crutches, she caresses the tender stalk of his neck. He is so like his father was at this age. The same dense curls, sharp chin, soft chestnut eyes, although Tariq's are far more troubled. For a moment, Hibah allows herself to believe that Tariq is not her grandson but her son, as she has secretly been doing ever since Khalil was murdered. Her way of unspooling time.

Once she and Tariq have left, Naema looks again at Jimmy, who is moving his own uneaten food around his plate. "Sergeant, if any of the people we meet today, they ignore me as usual and talk to you as though I am deaf, please tell them that I speak English."

"Uh, sure. Of course." He is about to plead with her to stop calling him sergeant when they both hear a car pull up outside, so he stands to look out the window. "Well, what a surprise, it's Pat. One of my long-lost brothers. Wanna meet him?"

Naema backs away. "Not while his clothes, they are on me, no." She hurries out of the room.

3

I know the soldier and his missing wife have always believed that the bombs were what drove me and my family from Baghdad, but this is not the case. No, we stayed all the way through the American attacks they called "Shock and Awe" and much of the mayhem that followed as well, hoping, as so many in war do, that soon it would all end and life would return to normal.

Baba made a shelter for us in the basement, equipped with snacks and water for our bellies, blankets for our beds, candles for our lights. "Down!" he would shout at the first whistle of an incoming mortar or whine of a warplane, and we would drop whatever we were doing and scramble down the stairs, each of us trying not to reveal the terror that gripped our hearts.

Zaki would bring his guitar and play for us while we hid, a mix of the old Iraqi tunes Baba insisted he learn and his favorite Western pop songs, one I remember about a blackbird, another about peace. Mama would smile at his off-key warbling, or perhaps at the naivete of the words, and nod her head to the beat, a little off herself, her long hair straying out of its bun, worry carving lines across her forehead. And all the while each of us would be listening for how close the bombs came—for whether it was our neighbor's turn, or our own.

Most of the time those days, we had no electricity in our house and very little food. The tap water tasted like burnt rust but we drank it anyway. We lived on rice, bean soup and chickpeas because to buy bread we had to dodge the bullets of snipers, while meat was to be found nowhere at all. We squabbled, made up, played cards, listened to the battery-powered radio, wrote in our journals and stared out of the windows when we dared, our thoughts circling as relentlessly as the military helicopters above. I will never forget the menace of those giant black hornets, the loud *thwack thwack thwack* of their blades, the terrifying roar of their engines.

"Fellow inmates," Zaki would say with mock gravity on those days we felt most cooped up, "today we are packing our bags for the journey to the bedroom." Or, "Fellow inmates, I'm selling train tickets to the kitchen."

After each round of bombing faded away and the sky fell quiet at last, we would climb to the roof to survey the damage, clutching our scarves to our mouths against the stench of burnt buildings and bodies. Our playmates across the street, five sisters, dead under the rubble. Palm trees scorched to blackened sticks. Cars reduced to charred skeletons. Apartment buildings sheared in half as if by an enormous saw. Mosques and shops and food stands smoldering under shattered bricks and twists of rebar.

"Why are we still here?" Mama said to Baba one day as we gazed down at the destruction. "Why don't we go stay with my mother?"

"Baghdad is all of our mothers, Zaynab. We cannot desert her now."

Mama could say nothing to that. Six years earlier, Saddam's henchmen had arrested Baba and thrown him into Abu Ghraib, where they tortured him for writing a poem they said had "committed an irreverence towards His Excellency" by portraying the death of a soldier as tragic rather than heroic. The real reason was that Baba had refused to join Saddam's Ba'ath Party. But Baba remained faithful to his vision of a free Iraq, even under the torture. It was this vision that kept him loyal to Baghdad and it was this vision that made it impossible to defy him.

March crawled through the bombs to April and then May, when a new phase of war began, this one from within, because once the Americans had dismantled our army, police and even our civil services, not to mention the electric grid that ran traffic lights and burglar alarms, there was nothing to prevent the city from falling into chaos. Soon, hundreds of young men, tired of poverty, or simply angry, bored or frustrated, were swarming through the streets like locusts, stripping shops, libraries, museums, theaters, offices. I would look out the window and see a boy running down the road with a broken lamp, another with a seat from a film theater. What use had they for these things? But no matter, anarchy had seized the day. And all the while, the American soldiers lounged on their Humvees in their bulging uniforms, helmets and sunglasses, sweating under the sun, snapping selfies, smoking cigarettes, not lifting a finger to help.

As the havoc spread unchecked, the criminals grew emboldened. They snatched children off the street for ransom. Dragged girls and women away to rape. Murdered boys for a portable phone or a pair of shoes. It became too dangerous for Zaki to go to school or for me to attend my classes at Baghdad Medical College. We had grown more afraid of our fellow citizens than we were of the enemy.

After three weeks of this, Baba made an announcement over breakfast, his voice as gray as his face. "Children, it breaks my heart to say this, but it has finally become necessary to leave. Your mama and I have agreed that it's too dangerous for you here. We'll go live with Bibi Maryam, as your mother suggested. You may each pack a single bag only. We depart, *insha'Allah*, at dawn."

"You mean tomorrow?" Zaki scrambled up from the floor in a panic. "But I need to say goodbye to my friends. Can't we wait a day?"

"No, *habibi*, we can't." Baba drew him close and kissed the top of his head. "For six hours yesterday, I sat in a queue waiting to fill our car with petrol. Each hour we delay is another hour closer to never being able to leave at all. Now go pack, and please, don't make this any harder by arguing."

Baba sounded firm but I could hear the shame seeping through his words. Had he not been a husband and father, he never would have abandoned his beloved city at such a time.

Zaki spent all night trying to decide what to pack. Two sets of guitar strings or one? His favorite sneakers or his football shoes? His bootleg CDs or his pirated tapes? His green shirt or his white one, his blue socks or his brown ones? The pile on his bed grew higher and higher, while the duffel bag Mama had given him to use seemed to shrink. "I don't know how to choose!" he wailed, pulling frantically at his overgrown hair. "And what about my pigeons? I'd leave everything if I could bring them. But Baba said no." Poor Zaki. He had spent much of his young life raising and training those pigeons. He kept them in a coop on our roof, giving each its own name, learning its favorite spot to be tickled. Zaki was only thirteen and small for his age, his head large atop a scrawny body, his face bony and wide-mouthed. In so many ways, he was still a child.

For me, the packing was not so difficult. The objects I possessed were nothing compared to everything else I was about to leave behind: my studies, my plans to become a doctor and, above all, Khalil.

As soon as Khalil heard that we were leaving, he rushed over to see me. We had been courting for two years by then and had plans to marry and, once we had our medical degrees, to open a clinic together for the war-wounded and sick, he as the internist, I as the pediatrician. How young we were then, Khalil twenty-four, I twenty-two; how young and full of dreams. "I'll die a little every minute until we can be together again," he said, his arms around me, his hands holding my head to his chest. Khalil was upright and slender in those days, not battle-hardened and stooped, the way he became only a few short years later. "This war will end soon, *insh'Allah*, and then we'll be free of Saddam and free to open our clinic in the new Iraq. Right, *ayuni*?"

"God willing," I murmured into his shirt. But even then, I did not believe him.

Baba came into the room to tell Khalil politely that he must go and let me finish my packing. Baba liked Khalil, as did Mama, and he liked them. I wish they'd had more time together.

As Khalil prepared to take his leave, I couldn't bear to watch. I could not stand there while he turned his back to me, opened our door and passed out of it, perhaps forever, for who can know what war might do to time or to our intentions? Before he could even say goodbye, I rushed out of the room.

At dawn the next day, Zaki and I carried our bags down to Baba's old car, once red but now worn to rust, stuffed them into the already crammed trunk and climbed into the back without a word. Mama huddled in front beside Baba, weeping; I sank into my grief over Khalil; Baba sat silent and grim. Zaki squeezed in beside me, hugging his guitar as though he expected it to be snatched from him at any moment, and, indeed, Baba had tried to make him leave it behind. "We don't have room, *habibi,* not even for a pin." But Zaki had clung to it with such desperation that Baba had been forced to relent.

"Goodbye Leena, goodbye Farida, goodbye Halima," Zaki chanted under his breath, naming his pigeons one by one, his lips trembling.

"Try not to look back, any of you," Baba murmured as he pulled the car away. "It'll only hurt more. And when this is over, Allah willing, we shall come home."

We all knew it was necessary to hope.

The drive out of Baghdad was slow, hot and perilous, every intersection clogged by an impossible tangle of cars, bicycles, carts, donkeys, mopeds and buses, pedestrians darting between them like panicked mice. Each turn we needed to take seemed to be blocked by a military checkpoint made of either a concrete barrier, a Humvee or a tank, while American soldiers shouted at us and waved their incomprehensible commands, their faces scared, angry and sunburned all at once. At one point, those soldiers directed Baba to drive through a market and, just as he did, one of their vehicles tore past us, mowing down stalls and fruit, baskets and carts, a mother and her two small daughters, blood and dismembered limbs everywhere. Zaki thrust his head out of the window and vomited. I closed my eyes.

Four hours it took us to get free of Baghdad, a drive that used to take thirty minutes. Mama stopped weeping at last, her slender back straining forward as she peered through the dust-caked windshield. Baba said not a word, only hunched his shoulders and gripped the steering wheel, his glasses grimed, the back of his shirt blackening with sweat. Zaki laid his head on my lap, quaking, while I held him close and stared out the window into the dangers beyond. The bloated carcass of a donkey or dog could mean a hidden bomb, as could a discarded plastic bag. A military convoy could result in our arrests or deaths. A movement behind a palm tree could turn into an ambush. Even a cluster of ragged children might be lethal, for one of them could dash under our wheels at any minute to beg for a piece of bread. I pulled my gaze back to my frightened family, and that is the moment I first understood the full weight of my future. Baba was crushed by cruelty and heartbreak, Mama weighed down by loss, Zaki a child. It would be up to me and me alone to fight for our survival.

When we arrived at my grandmother's house in Umm Qasr, a village on the southern border near Kuwait, we were shocked to see how much she had deteriorated in the few months since we had last visited. Anxiety and fear had withered her body and scribbled over her face until it was as lined as the pit of a peach. Worst of all, her salty wit had grown dull, her good nature cantankerous. This is what war does to the old, as I was to see later in Hibah. Yet, for the moment, I felt relief. At least, I told myself, we are safer here than we were in Baghdad.

A few nights later, everything changed again. We were eating a supper of rice and wild herb soup, the only food we could find at the time, discussing how Zaki and I were to keep up our studies without school, when we were startled by a furious shouting outside and a hammering at the door. "Open up!" voices bellowed in American English. "Open up now!"

Soldiers.

Mama leapt up, white-faced, grabbed my arm and tried to drag me into the back room, but I twisted out of her grip. And before anyone could stop me, I ran to unlock the door. Perhaps if I speak English to these invaders, I thought in my naivete, I will make them understand our innocence and they will not hurt us.

"Naema, don't!" Baba cried. Too late. I had already slid back the bolts.

Three soldiers burst in, looking like alien monsters in their padded uniforms, helmets and night goggles, instantly filling the house with their angry stink and shouts. Batting me aside as if I were no more than a gnat, they rushed at Baba and knocked him to the ground. "Baba!" Zaki screamed, running to help him. We all knew how frail Baba was, how his legs had been smashed again and again by Saddam's torturers, his heart cracking open with the pain.

One of the soldiers turned to Zaki then, little Zaki, barely tall enough to reach my chin, kicked him in the stomach and threw him face down on the ground next to Baba.

"Stop, please!" I cried in my English. "He is only a child!" But still I had no effect. I was nothing to them. Nothing and nobody.

Bibi was wailing now, no doubt back in the moment when Saddam's thugs had stormed into her house just like this and dragged her husband to his death. Mama was shouting curses at the soldiers, her words as ineffectual as mine. One of the soldiers turned his rifle on us then, pinning us against the wall while his companions pressed their filthy boots down on the necks of Zaki and Baba, ground their faces into the floor, tied their hands behind their backs and pulled black hoods over their poor, vulnerable heads. I could hear Baba choking, Zaki whimpering in terror. "Stop!" I cried again. "This is a child; my father is sick. They will suffocate! Please!"

As if I had not spoken a word, the soldiers hauled Baba and Zaki to their feet and, jabbing their enormous guns into their backs, pushed them out of the door. I ran after them just in time to see the soldiers throw my father and brother into the back of a truck like sacks of rice, surely bruising their flesh or splintering their bones. I heard Zaki cry out. But Baba made not a sound.

"Please don't hurt them!" I pleaded again. "Please!"

The soldiers jumped in the truck and roared away, leaving me standing in the road, choking on dust and fury.

Before that night, I had never talked to an American soldier, having always regarded them as something not quite human. I rarely saw a pair of eyes behind their sunglasses, a patch of skin beneath their helmets and scarves, heard a word that wasn't a command or an obscenity. But the morning after Zaki and Baba were taken, I knew the time had come to speak to these people face to face. If people they were.

"Mama, I'm going to the American prison," I announced, pulling on a brown abaya. "*Oum* Ibrahim told me that's where they keep all the men they arrest. She said she'll take me with her."

Mama plucked at her fingers, hands trembling, eyes darkened by fear and sleeplessness. "No, stay here, *habibti*, please. It's too dangerous! I can't risk losing you, too."

"I have to go, you know that. We can't just sit here and do nothing. I have to find out what they've done with Baba and Zaki. You look after Bibi. The prison's only four kilometers away. I'll be back soon." And after wrapping my head in a blue hijab, I left Mama and her pleas behind.

Several others joined *Oum* Ibrahim and me on the walk, most of them women. *Oum* Ibrahim herself, a tall, grim-faced widow, had three sons in the prison, leaving her with nobody to help her with her farm. Little apple-shaped *Oum* Rayya, whose two older boys had died fighting in the Iran war, had been forced to watch the Americans snatch her only remaining son away in the night, just as they had Baba and Zaki. And Widow Fatima, a close friend of Bibi and as bent and withered as she, had been making this walk every day for three weeks to find out the fate of her brother, her only support. Thus do men wreak their destruction and leave us women to pick up the few scraps they leave behind.

"Do the guards at the prison tell you anything?" I asked Widow Fatima as we tramped along the edge of the barren road, the sun's heat pressing onto our heads, the desert stretching out around us, flat, bare and hostile.

"They tell us nothing, daughter. We have no choice but to ask again and again, and then to wait again and again. It's all in the hands of Allah."

Our conversation was interrupted by the roar of an enormous military truck speeding past, followed by two more and then four Humvees, their wheels churning up dust, sand and exhaust. Coughing and clapping our hands over our mouths, we pushed on, squinting against the flying particles. Each hurtling truck whipped up such a vacuum that I could feel it sucking us under its wheels, so I clutched *Oum* Ibrahim to keep us both steady. In this way, holding one another tight, we and our companions pressed forwards along the side of the road, stumbling over rocks, bottles and burst tires, and skirting the carcasses of birds and dogs mowed down by those same barreling machines that had tried to catch us.

War has made a cemetery of the Iraq desert. I had not realized this in the car on the way to Bibi Maryam's house but on foot it was impossible to ignore. The skeletons of donkeys and camels, long stripped dry by vultures and maggots, rise up from the sand like ghosts. The rusting shells of military vehicles left over from the current war and the many wars before it lie scattered about like corpses. Shards of metal thrust up from their burial grounds like tombstones.

Crumbled houses, hidden landmines, pools of oil, plastic bags and bottles, tires, rags, tins, Styrofoam food containers—buried here is all the debris human beings invent and cast aside during the business of killing.

When we finally arrived at the gates of the prison, dozens of other families were already there, waiting beside the enormous nests of coiled razor wire that marked the entrance, their blades glinting in the sun like a thousand tiny knives. The prison itself looked nothing like a prison, but rather a sprawl of sagging, sun-bleached tents, surrounded by rows of yet more giant coils of wire and a wall of sand. Nonetheless, as makeshift and even decrepit as it looked, it was enough to entrap those we loved and render the rest of us afraid.

For more than four hours I stood with my companions that morning, waiting for some authority to come and offer us the information we were owed. I knew the rules of engagement, just as I knew that the Americans claimed they had come to rescue us from ourselves in exchange for our blood, our homes, our self-governance, our dignity and, of course, our oil. And what was our *diyah* to be, our compensation, for all this theft, murder and destruction? Why, the golden gift of Liberation, of course. How had Khalil fallen for this? Had we not heard this most chilling of euphemisms, "liberate," before? "Our armies do not come into your cities and lands as conquerors or enemies, but as liberators," oozed a British general as he dismembered Iraq in 1917. "We are coming not to occupy their country, not to oppress them, but to liberate their country," echoed that two-faced and considerably less poetic of men, Donald Rumsfeld, eighty-six years later.

Oh, Khalil.

Only when the sun had burnt its way to the uppermost point of the sky did I finally see a soldier approach, tramping through the sand to where I and my fellow supplicants stood. How puny he looked as he kicked up puffs of dust with his boots. He looked as though he could hardly hold up the helmet wobbling like a tub on his head, let alone the enormous sunglasses engulfing his face or the rifle clutched to his chest.

As he drew near, he began shouting at us in English and flapping a scrawny arm, igniting in me such anger I hardly recognized myself. How dare he and his compatriots rain ruin and lies upon us and then shout and wave at us as if we were no better than a pack of stray dogs? I stepped forward, about to shout at him myself, when I noticed something odd, something wrong.

He was a girl.

The minute my companions also realized this soldier was a girl, they turned bold. "What have you done with our children, bitch?" they screamed at her. "Is my Abbas in there? My Mahmood? Did you take my Hassan, my Ali, my one and only child? Tell us who you have in there, you useless murdering whore!"

"Stop," I begged them. "This shouting will get us nowhere. Have patience and I'll try to talk to her in English." The crowd murmured and shuffled, complained and coughed, but finally quieted. I stepped up to the soldier-girl, who backed away, as if she were more frightened of me than I of her.

"I can translate if you wish," I told her loudly and clearly enough for my companions to hear, although of course I had no intention of translating their insults.

She gaped at me. "You speak English?"

What did she think, that all Iraqis are uneducated peasants? "I do," I told her.

"Awesome." She sounded so young, her voice uncertain and scratchy. She looked young, too, as far as I could see, not much older than Zaki.

"We need to know who of our men you are holding here," I said then. "You have this information for us?"

"We're working on it. Tell these folks here that we're making a list of all the detainees and we'll get it to them ASAP. But right now, your buddies need to stop yelling and scoot."

"Asap?"

"I mean soon. Now tell them to leave."

"I will. But first, I must pose to you a question, Miss Soldier. We want to know when our innocent fathers and brothers and sons, they will be released."

The girl looked at me out of the side of her eyes. Or I surmise she did, as I could see almost nothing of her face under those engulfing sunglasses. "No idea. They never tell us shit like that. But not to worry, we treat the prisoners good in here. They get decent food, cigarettes, blankets, everything. Better'n we get. Now, like I said, you and your buds here gotta split."

I examined her. She was considerably shorter than I am and so thin that her uniform hung off her as if she were wearing her father's clothes. Orange freckles speckled what I could see of her pale skin. Her lips were painfully dry, cracked and bleeding at the edges.

The murmurs of the crowd were growing louder again. "What's the bitch saying?" a man behind me yelled.

I held up a hand to quiet him. "What you are telling me about this list, it is the truth?" I asked the girl then. "Because my father and brother, who you have locked in your prison here, they have done nothing wrong."

She glanced over her shoulder. "'Course it's true. Look, you gotta tell these people to quiet down and split. This is getting dangerous. For me and you both."

I looked at her a moment longer, trying to decipher her peculiar English, then turned to my companions and relayed her message. Not surprisingly, this only agitated them further. "Tell the whoring bitch to let our men out now!" they screamed. "Tell her I'll fuck her mother and father, too."

"We will go away as you wish," I told the girl then, "but first you must explain when you will have this list you promised. We came a long way to hear this and we stood here under the hot sun for even longer. We deserve an answer."

"The list'll come soon, like I said. Now, go!" And for no reason that I could see, she lifted her rifle and pointed it at my chest.

I ignored her. "Why have you put our children in your prison? You took my brother and he is only thirteen."

Glancing over her shoulder, she lowered her voice and her rifle. "Look, we keep the kids safe in a separate compound, OK? Your brother's fine, I'm sure. Now, for Christ's sake, leave!"

"You mean my brother, he is not with our father? He is all alone?" I was trying to retain my dignity but I could hear my voice quiver.

"Told you, I don't know. Listen, go, *please*!"

"My brother, his name is Zaki." I pulled out the photograph of him and Baba that I kept in my pocket. Zaki was sitting on our carpet in the picture, grinning up at Baba, who was standing beside him, one hand on his shoulder, his thick glasses reflecting the camera's flash. How innocent people look in photographs when they have no idea of what awaits them. How gullible. "This boy is my brother, and this man here, he is my father." I pointed. "Have you seen them?"

She glanced at it. "We got hundreds of detainees in here. Thanks for helping though." She held out a hand for me to shake, her dry lips stretching into a pained attempt at a smile. "I'm Kate, by the way. Kate Brady."

I ignored the hand but I did tell her my own name. "Please to keep the photograph," I said to her. "It will help you recognize them. I will come back every morning and translate for you, yes? These people here, they are losing patience. You need help to keep them calm, is this not so?"

"Cool, that'd be awesome."

"But I will not do this unless you make me a promise in return. You will search for my father and brother and tell me when you find them. And you will carry to them my messages." I touched the photograph. "My father, his name is Halim Mohanammad al-Jubur. And my brother, he is Zaki Jassim."

The girl pulled a pen from her jacket and handed it to me. "Can you write that down on the back? I'm no good at foreign names."

I complied. "You will search for them if I translate?" I asked again, handing the picture over.

"Yeah, sure. I'll try, anyways." She tucked the photo and pen into one of the many pockets on the bulky vest she wore over her uniform, glancing around again, as if afraid she had been seen.

I gave her a long look. "Keep your promise, Kate Brady," I said. "And if you do, I shall keep mine."

4

After Naema leaves, I go outside and almost trip over Pat, who's sprawled over the porch steps, elbows propped behind him, an unlit cigarette poking out of his mouth. "So, you finally decided to drag your ass over here, huh?" I drop down beside him.

He shrugs without answering. "I see your, uh, people arrived," is what he does say. "Was that the mom scooting around the corner just now?" He plucks the cigarette out of his mouth and sticks it behind an ear.

I look over at him. He's in his usual baggy black shirt and pants, flat brim pulled low over his eyes, along with a pair of oversized orange sneakers, laces dangling, tongues lapping his ankles. Kate always used to say Pat looks just like me, only prettier and shrunk down a size. Black hair, white skin, blue peepers. All over Irish, like our dad. Our baby brother, Rory, is the odd one out. Ginger-headed and copper-eyed. Like Mom.

"Yeah, that's her. So, you're here to meet them?" I ask.

"Uh, not yet. Maybe later." Pat hasn't looked at me once.

"What the hell is this then, a courtesy call?"

He shifts up to sitting, exuding a waft of gasoline and oil. Pat works as a grease monkey in our local garage and no matter how much he showers, and he showers a lot, he always stinks of it. "No, I got something to tell you." His voice wobbles. He's always had a high-pitched, not-sure-where-to-settle voice. Which pretty much reflects who he is.

"Oh yeah? What?"

He kicks at a spider web spanning the banister. "Yesterday, no, the day before . . . I don't know—"

"Fuck's sake, Pat, what?"

"Well . . ." He sucks in a breath. "It's about Kate."

I stiffen. "What about her?"

"She called Lisa."

Another flint in my chest. "So she calls your girlfriend but not me, huh? Did she say where she is?"

"'Fraid not." He pulls off his hat. Fiddles with it.

"She OK?"

"Seems to be. Lisa said she found some job."

"What kind? Teaching?"

"Don't know."

"She didn't say anything else? Like, why the hell she left, or how am I, or any tiny bit of human anything?"

"Nope. Lisa tried to weasel more out of her, but no go."

I count to five to calm myself. "Think she ran off with some dickface?"

Pat looks over at me at last, his blue eyes squinting against the sun. "You know she wouldn't do that, Jimmy."

"What makes you so sure? She left her job, didn't she? All her second-grade students stranded now with no teacher? I mean, who the fuck does that?"

"She must've had some reason for splitting"—by which he means what the hell did I do to make her run.

I rub my thumb over the scars on my hands, thinking back for the millionth time to the night she left, searching for clues. We'd spent the day fixing up the old pool room in the back of the house for Naema and her family, Kate hanging the posters of flowers and birds she'd found at a yard sale and scrubbing out the bathroom, while I tacked down a new rug and cleaned out the mouse turds from the chest of drawers I'd picked up at Salvation Army. After we were done, we rewarded ourselves with a couple beers in front of the kitchen fireplace, me in our big old rocking chair, Kate huddled cross-legged on the floor, feeding empty cereal boxes and junk mail into the fire. An April wind whipped around the house, rattling the shutters, tousling the flames. "I love this," I told her. "I love the fire and the wind and being here with you." She leaned against my knees, her curls glinting orange and gold in the firelight. She didn't say anything but she did climb into my lap and nestle her tight little body against mine.

Later that night, after we'd cleaned up dinner and left the fire to burn itself out, she came up to the bedroom where I was getting ready to meet up with some army buds. "How do I look?" I asked her. All those years in uniform had ruined my sense of how to dress. Left to myself, I would've worn nothing but brown.

"Like an executive, minus the tie. Why the jacket?" She kicked off her sneakers and flopped down on our bed.

"Should I change?"

"Nah, you look good. Handsome fucker." Her favorite name for me. "Who is it tonight, Bean?"

"Yeah. Him and Kalinski. They're assholes but they're my assholes." I sat on the bed and kissed her. "Wish I didn't have to go but I promised. Won't be late though."

She jumped up and followed me downstairs in her socks, leaning against the doorframe while I crossed the yard to the car. "Jimmy?"

I turned back. She looked so beautiful. So herself.

"Just remember you're driving. Don't talk about the fucked-up stuff and don't come home shit-faced. Promise?"

But when I did come home, very shit-faced indeed, she was gone.

This isn't the first time Kate's dumped me out of the blue like this. She did it back when we first got together during the war. We were both deployed to Camp Bucca then, a holding pen for POWs by the Kuwait border, where I was posted up on a guard tower a few yards back from the entrance. I remember the first time I noticed her there down on the sand, standing apart from the rest of her squad, tiny and alone in her uniform. A slip of a girl she was those days, nineteen years old and about as unlikely a soldier as anyone could be, with that bubbly red hair and those freckles, eyes the color of blue gin. A simple Catholic girl, fresh and soft as a button of butter. But then I wasn't much of a soldier myself yet, a boy of twenty-two, more focused on fretting over my brothers than on fighting. How we've both changed since then, Kate godless now, me in my lockbox. But that, of course, is what war does. You strap on the front of a soldier to hide the frightened kid underneath. And the next thing you know that front isn't a front anymore, it's you.

"Hey, Teach!" she yelled up at me that day, her voice thin and wispy in the desert air. Everybody called me Teach on account of my glasses. "Got any extra H_2O? I'm shriveling to a raisin down here." I tossed her a bottle, crushing on her already.

Like a lot of people at the start of the war, the two of us had managed to get there by mistake, having chosen to enlist in the Military Police Army Reserves, figuring all we'd have to do is show up for drill and a paycheck one weekend a month while we went on doing whatever we were doing. After all, when had the Reserves ever been sent anywhere, at least in our lifetimes? Kate had only joined up to please her sheriff dad and Jesus, and maybe win a little respect from her hometown buds, while all I'd wanted was to support Pat and Rory. But, like John Lennon said, life is what happens to you while you're busy making other plans. So, the next thing we knew, 9/11 hit, Bush dragooned us into first one war, then another, and soon we were attached to the 800th MP Brigade out of Uniondale, New York, and shipped off to Iraq before we could even find it on a map.

In the beginning, we only talked once in a while, trivial bull about our neighboring hometowns, the shitty food on base, the shittier command. But all that changed the day I saw our sergeant jump her. Staff Sergeant Kormick, one of those men who joined the army already angry, went to war and got even angrier—a man I can safely say nobody could stand. I saw the whole thing from my tower: Kormick's sidekick, Bonapart, commonly known as Boner, punching her out of the blue, the two of them dragging her into the guard shack while she struggled and fought. I scrambled down fast as I could to stop them, and me and our team leader, DJ, broke into the shack and pulled the fuckers off her just in time. Or I think it was just in time. She tried to suck it up. Refused to talk about it, admit it mattered. But I know it changed her, that moment. Maybe forever.

Command moved her to an interior compound then, either for protection or for punishment, we couldn't tell, and stuck her up on her own guard tower fourteen hours a day. She spent her entire shift alone up there, spotlighted under the desert sun, staring down at the detainees while they flung stones, scorpions and even their own turds at her. One perv in particular would jack off in front of her all the time, just to prove how much he and his buddies hated having a female guard.

I had it easier, posted at the compound entrance with a team of other MPs, bros to kid with, spell me when needed. So whenever I could get away, I'd grab a cup of desert dessert, a.k.a. ice chips, head over to her tower and climb up the ladder to join her. We'd sit together on the wooden platform not much bigger than an umbrella and hunker down under our Kevlars and shades, sucking ice and staring out at the sand, big as an ocean around us, watching it shift from one brown to another, and talking about trees and lakes, her little sister April, my brothers and everything else the desert and war neglected to offer. And all the time I wanted her so bad I had to sit on my hands to stop myself from touching her.

Wartime romance. It's never supposed to go anywhere and at first it didn't. We'd only just reached the point of kissing when she broke it off with no explanation, just like she's done now. But a few months later, while I was home for R&R, she showed up at my house—this house—unannounced, scared and homeless. She'd just run away from the VA hospital in Albany, where she was supposed to be recuperating from war trauma and a back injury she got from falling off her tower. "All they do is dope me up with meds in there, Jimmy," she told me. "I can't even feel who I am anymore. But if I go home, Dad'll make me go back." So even though I was messed up and mad, I took her in.

For a week, I made her stay in my old room upstairs while I slept in the master bedroom with Mandy, this girl I was seeing at the time, knowing I was probably hurting Kate, just like she'd hurt me. But finally, I came to my senses, asked Mandy to leave, took Kate's hands in mine and told her I loved her and always had.

"I love you, too, Jimmy, have from the start," she said, tears tumbling down those freckled cheeks. And then she told me that she'd only busted up with me at Camp Bucca because she felt so corrupted by war, she was afraid of corrupting me, too.

Bullcrap, I told her. Don't let the war define you like that. Peel it off like dead skin. We'll help each other find our way back to being the people we want to be. You'll see.

I undressed her slowly that first time, hands quivering. All those months of wanting her up on that tower, of yearning for her when we were apart. I laid her down on her back and looked at her, just looked for a long while, looked and touched. Ran my hands over every part of her, savoring, her nipples taut, my mouth eager. I spread her legs and touched her there as well, till I knew how bad she wanted me, too.

Seven years of love and trust. Seven years of riding the war machine, of navigating my returns home, of staying faithful during my deployments and being called a sucker for it, too. And now here I am, slumped, dumped and aching on my own doorstep, stunned as a fresh-shot deer.

"So she didn't even drop a hint to Lisa about where her new job is or anything?" I ask Pat.

"Not a word. Lisa tried asking why she left, too, but that only made Kate hang up."

"I bet. Know what her goodbye note said? *Don't look for me.* That's all I fucking got."

Pat slings his arm around my shoulders and gives the back of my neck a squeeze. "Listen, Jimmy, don't get all blue on me now, OK? I'll come around more often, help out. Mow the lawn, which is a disgrace. And I bet once Kate's got over whatever it is that's bugging her, she'll come home all sad and sorry, right?"

"Maybe."

"I'll bring Lisa over, too. She could be company for your . . . people. I caught a glimpse just now, the kid peeking around the corner. One leg? That is seriously fucked up."

"Yep." I rub my knees and stand. "We should go for a brew sometime."

Pat stands as well, easing his flat brim back on. "How about tonight? I'll get Rory to meet us at McGrath's."

"Can't. Promised the kid I'd play soccer with him. And it seems kind of soon to leave them here on their own, y'know?"

Pat thrusts his hands into his pockets, his narrow eyes squeezing up even narrower. "Saturday, then?"

"Sounds good." I watch him jump off the porch the way I can't anymore and cross the lawn to his pickup. "Pat?" He glances back. "If Kate gets in touch again, tell her to call . . ." I stop. Every time I call her, she won't pick up, so why the hell would she call me?

"I know, Jimmy." He climbs into his truck. "Already have."

Only after Pat has driven well out of sight does Naema show up again, joining me by my car, a black Honda CRV my brothers are always saying makes me look like a dealer or a hit man. She and Tariq are back in the clothes they wore when they arrived, she in a maroon tunic and loose pants, Tariq in a little blue track-suit, the left leg cut short and hemmed. The old lady looks the same, though, draped in her widow's black.

Tariq says something in Arabic, which must be a demand to sit in front because Naema helps him in beside me and then climbs into the rear with his grandma. I'd prefer him to stay in the back with them where it's safer, but it isn't my place to say. Most I can do is buckle his seatbelt, which stretches across his neck like a garrote, and drive carefully as I can to avoid throttling him, remembering too late that Kate told me to buy him a car seat. He settles in happily, leaning forward to twiddle the radio dial and chatting away to me in a jumble of Arabic and English I can't follow at all.

"Mama?" he calls after a few moments, twisting around and shouting something over the music.

I switch off the radio and look at Naema in the rearview mirror. "There a problem?"

"Tariq, he needs to get out of the car."

This, I've already learned, is code for a pit stop. We only just left the house and my VA medical appointment is at eleven-fifteen. If I miss that, who knows how many more months I'll have to wait. They've kept me warming my ass for eight as it is. Still, I batten down my impatience and turn into the first convenience store I see on Route 85, climb out and grab Tariq's crutches from the trunk.

When we walk inside, the nose-pierced teenager behind the cash register gapes. I can hardly blame him: me a clean-cut GI with Tiny Tim at my side. Naema with her scar and her tunic. Khalil's mom in her black sack.

The store is garishly lit and so covered in dust you can taste it. A rack of gardening gloves stands by the door, fleshless hands dangling from hooks. Six-packs of beer and rows of neon sodas fill the fridge along the wall: traffic cone orange, antifreeze green, stoplight red. Campbell's chunky soup, fossilized bread and single rolls of toilet paper line the grimy shelves. Stores like this always remind me of the Haji-Mart outside Camp Scania, where we grunts and Fobbits jostled to buy ramen noodles, knock-off watches, bootleg DVDs, souvenir Bush and Saddam lighters made in China, and all the other junk meant to keep us suckers happy. But Tariq gets excited.

Tariq's game is to point and make me name: potato chips, beef jerky, Slim Jims ("Jim-Jim sticks!"), Doritos, cheese popcorn, Tootsie Rolls. The crap we pass off as food in this country. When he tires of that, he finds a shelf of dust-caked toys and a grimy plastic bag full of tiny soldiers, a whole platoon's worth for three bucks. I look away quickly. Even a sack of inch-high grunts with faces the same olive drab as their uniforms and plastic tags sticking out of their heads can make my guts convulse. "Jim-Jim?" Tariq props a crutch against the shelf and picks up the bag.

"Put it back, buddy." I'm willing to buy the kid almost anything. Just not soldiers.

He isn't asking me to buy them, though. "Is bad GIs?" He stares up at me, big eyes serious.

"Bad? Nah, they're only toys." A burn of shame. "Go on, put them down. They don't mean nothing. Let's go, or we'll be late."

Back in the car, Tariq playing again with the radio, we head two towns over to a firehouse offering free chicken and doughnuts and whatever junk folks feel moved to donate. This was where Mom would bring me and my brothers for clothes when she was having one of her "slides," as she put it, avoiding our local firehouse so the neighbors wouldn't see. But how we hated wearing those castoffs. The reek of stale cigarette smoke and sweat. Urine-yellow of deodorant stains. Musk of old people's flesh.

Several cars are already parked outside by the time we arrive, CRVs like mine, pickup trucks, a decrepit old Ford. Most have some kind of sticker on them that I wish Naema didn't have to see. *United States of Americans. Jesus for President. My Girlfriend is a Combat Veteran. The USA: Love it or Leave it.* A big poster commemorating the firefighters lost on 9/11 hangs on the firehouse wall blaring the words, *Never Forget.*

Inside, I take a quick gander around the echoing concrete room and see what I've always seen. Muffin-shaped kids gobbling the doughnuts. Moms either veiny-nosed from drink or black-toothed from meth. A few shriveled granddads still pickled in last night's whiskey, skin the texture of dried apples. And a bunch of regular people picking through the heaps of old clothes and shoes. Like the teenager in the convenience store, they all turn to stare.

"How ya doin'?" I nod at each one of them, Naema and Hibah hanging back, and then bend down to Tariq, who's hiding behind his mom. "Go on." I point to a jumble of grubby toys in a corner. "Pick whatever you want."

He peeks out from behind her legs. A kid's bike is leaning against the wall, blue and silver with training wheels and red ribbons tied to its handles. He eases out from behind Naema, loops over to it on his crutches and touches it reverently.

"Take it," I tell him. "It's yours."

He looks at me. Little scrap of a face. "For Tariq?"

"Yeah, for Tariq."

Just as he reaches for it, a spiky-haired boy of about eight runs at him. "I want that!" And before any of us can react, he pushes Tariq hard enough to knock him off-balance.

Tariq doesn't fall, though. But what he does do, I do not expect. He swings a crutch through the air and whacks the boy on the hip with it.

The boy howls. His mother shrieks. Everyone else freezes. Tariq hurries back to Naema while the boy continues to yowl and the mom screams curses about foreigners and terrorists.

Naema says nothing. Only crouches to hold Tariq, who is sobbing now, while Hibah hovers protectively beside them. But I'm enraged.

"Ma'am, shut the fuck up!" I bellow at the woman in my fiercest sergeant voice.

She does.

I turn next to her son. "He had the bike first. Give it back. Now."

His face red and wet with tears, the boy wheels it over as promptly as any recruit. I grab it and plant it in front of Tariq. "There."

"Sergeant?" Naema straightens up. "What are you doing?"

"Giving Tariq back his bike. Why?"

"My son, he has only one leg. He cannot ride a bicycle."

Once we're all in the car again, it takes me at least ten minutes of driving before I can even speak. Tariq's crying silently beside me, Naema murmuring comfort from the back, while Hibah's mumbling something even I can tell is disapproving. Kate would never have made a mistake like that. Never.

"Listen, I'm sorry," I finally kick myself into saying, searching out Naema in the rearview mirror. "And I'm sorry that woman yelled those messed-up things at you. I never should have taken you to a place like that."

"It is of no importance. We are used to insults." She gazes back at me, her golden eyes steady. "Let us leave the clothes for today. I must meet my appointment at the Resettlement Center."

"But can't we get Tariq a prosthetic leg so he can ride any damn bike he wants? I'll buy it for him, that's what I'll do. I'll buy him a top-grade leg and a bike to go with it!"

Naema closes her eyes and when she next speaks, she sounds exhausted. "Sergeant, do you not know how much such a prosthesis, it costs in your country? Forty thousand dollars. Please, do not make such promises. It does nothing but break our hearts."

5

Only once the soldier drops us off and finally does us the favor of removing himself and his blunders from our presence, do I feel the tension drain from my bones. Yet my relief is short-lived because as we look up at the tall, factory-like building in front of us, that finger of ice once again runs down my spine. What if we meet other Iraqis here who have heard that we are living with an American soldier and not even his wife? Or who know that Khalil worked for the US military and despise us for it, as so many did at home? "*Ameel*," they would hiss at us in the streets. "Traitor!" And that wasn't our only warning. Telephone calls deep in the night. A bullet enclosed in an envelope taped to our door. A severed dog's head thrown over the wall into our garden.

Clasping my handbag full of precious documents to my chest, the identity papers, passports and visas that are all we have to protect us from arrest and deportation, I lead Hibah and Tariq across the crumbling, weed-clotted street to the entrance. Stepping over a soggy clump of litter, I push open the battered and creaky front door.

"Are you sure this is the right place?" Hibah asks, looking over the foyer, its walls the same grimy brown brick as the exterior. "You must have made a mistake."

"It's not a mistake, Mama." Tamping down my irritation, I usher her and Tariq into an enormous cage of an elevator that rattles and shakes all the way to the fourth floor, where, sure enough, we are confronted by a glass door with the words *United States Committee for Refugees and Immigrants* painted on it in gold. We pull it open.

A narrow white hallway stretches before us, empty of people but hung with large color photographs of refugees from all over the world. We stop to look. Women squatting outside cardboard shacks, eyes black with hunger. Men standing on dusty roads, clothes tattered, cheekbones jutting, hands empty. Babies as limp as dead birds, heads huge over twig-like limbs. All wear the same expression: mouths slack, eyes stunned. Much as we must have looked after the bomb.

Forcing myself away from the pictures, I lead Tariq and Hibah down the hall to the waiting room, which confirms my guess that this building was once a factory, for the wooden floor is splattered with black paint, the ceiling cavernously high and the room lit by an entire wall of latticed windows smeared with great quantities of soot. But here, at least, we do find people: a young Indian woman sitting behind a desk in a tailored gray suit, her hair wound into a perfect coronet, and a middle-aged couple on a stained orange sofa, who, given that the wife is in hijab, might indeed be my compatriots. Looking away quickly, I pull Tariq close.

"Your name, please?" the Indian woman calls to me, her voice as bright as her smile.

Sending Tariq to sit beside Hibah on another sofa across the room, I move to the woman's desk and tell her, but am so conscious of the couple's eyes on me that I speak too softly to be heard.

"Excuse me?" She smiles again. "I didn't catch that."

I lean closer and murmur my answer. A name, I have learned only too well, is not to be bandied about among strangers.

"OK, great. We're expecting you. Your caseworker will be out in a moment. Please, take a seat." The woman's tone is so gentle that my eyes prick. Even the smallest gesture of kindness can undo me these days.

We are kept waiting a long while, although this is no more than I have come to expect. During our two and a half years in Damascus, I spent every hour I wasn't working or caring for Tariq waiting in one room or another for this official or that to interrogate, examine, photograph or fingerprint me so that I could register with the UN refugee office, renew our visas or apply to come to America. This is life for a refugee.

Handing Tariq a picture book I find on the sofa, something in English about a fox and a rabbit, and leaving Hibah in one of her catatonic dazes, I leaf unseeingly through a magazine, my real interest in the couple on the couch. I glance at them whenever I sense they are not looking. The wife, who is in her early fifties and dressed in dark pink slacks and a matching blouse, is heavyset in the way of a woman who has borne several children, her plump face squeezed inside her black hijab, her eyebrows so thickly penciled they give her the lacquered appearance of a Russian nesting doll. Her husband, considerably older than she, silver-haired and handsome, wears the immaculate blue shirt and dark trousers of a businessman. But his brow is knitted and his eyes flit about the room with the same hunted look I used to see among my fellow displaced Iraqis in Damascus, and sometimes in my own mirror.

A tall, baby-faced African man appears in front of us, or I take him for African until he greets the couple in American English. The husband stands, replying in kind and asking about a form without bothering to translate for his wife, who clearly cannot follow. Thus are wives kept in the dark, just as Khalil tried to keep me.

Tariq hops up, recovered enough from his disappointment over the bicycle to swing around the room exploring, while everyone watches him with the pity I cannot bear. I regret that he hit that boy in the firehouse but it is only what he learned to do on the streets of Damascus. A child like him is always a target and a target must defend himself. Over by the soot-grimed window, he finds a plastic jug of water and a stack of paper cups. "Mama, can I have some? I'm hot."

"Shh, don't shout." I stand to help him.

"You're right, little heart, it is hot in here," the woman on the sofa says in Iraqi Arabic, smiling at him with true kindness. "We all need water." She joins us at the window, fills several paper cups and passes them around the room. Then, with a warmth that catches me entirely off guard, she introduces herself as *Oum* Ismail and wishes me the blessings of peace and Allah.

I return her greeting and give her my name, but before we can speak further, her husband announces that they are late and bids me a polite but hurried goodbye. As I watch them leave, such loneliness cracks open inside me, I almost run after them.

"*Oum* Tariq?" The baby-faced man is smiling at me now in that mechanical American way; not at all the same warm smile as *Oum* Ismail's. "Follow me, please." Draining my cup of water, I do, leaving Hibah to watch over Tariq. The young man leads me into a small, disorderly office, heaped with files, books and coffee-stained paper cups. "Make yourself comfortable." He gestures to a metal chair and sits behind his desk, pushing aside its mess. "I'm Derek. Would you prefer to speak Arabic?"

I sit and fold my hands on my lap, wondering where he learned my language. "There is no need, thank you."

He leans his elbows on the desk and smiles at me yet again, his round cheeks bunching with apparent sincerity. "First, I'd like to welcome you to the United States and congratulate you on getting here. I know it wasn't easy."

"It was not, no."

"And are you settling in OK?"

How to answer such an impossible question? "I believe so."

"Good. Forgive me now, please, but I do have to explain something to you that I'm afraid you might not have understood. We've seen arrangements like yours before, when military personnel sponsor SIVs and act as their anchors. We understand the impulse is generous but you need to know that it can get in the way of your benefits. If these soldiers you're living with are supporting you, it'll complicate your entitlement to government assistance."

I stiffen. "Mr. Derek, you are mistaken. We are not living with them. We reside in a separate apartment. Well, room. It is attached to the back of the house."

"Are you paying rent?"

"No. But—please understand—they give us no money." I fight down a blush. It's humiliating enough to have to admit to receiving the soldier's charity, but even more so to have to speak in the plural, as if Kate Brady were not missing. Yet I no more want this Derek to know the impropriety of my circumstances than I do the Iraqi couple I just met.

He looks unconvinced but keeps smiling. "I understand, *Oum* Tariq. But if a problem arises, you can always let me know, OK? Now, let's review your situation."

"My 'situation,' as you put it, Mr. Derek, is that I have been here for four days and yet I am still without any of the papers I was promised. The people at the refugee resettlement office, they told me that as soon as I arrived, I would be given a Green Card, a furnished apartment, something named Medicaid and one month's rent. I understand that I relinquished the apartment and rent when the soldier and his wife persuaded me that their place would be nicer and free, but none of the other paperwork has materialized. Why is this?"

"Well, I . . . "

"I have not finished, Mr. Derek. The papers I do have are the birth and marriage certificates it took my husband's old school friend months of hard work and bribes to salvage from the wreckage of Baghdad. And I have our Iraqi passports and the Special Immigrant Visas Sergeant Donnell helped us procure, for which we only qualified because my husband was so willing to sell his soul. But I have no driver's license, no credit or debit cards, no social number, no income, no proof of residence, and a work permit that will last a mere ninety days. I cannot open a bank account, enroll my son in school or even shop for our basic needs with such meager proof of my existence." I fling my braid over my shoulder for emphasis. "How long will this go on?"

Derek nods and I realize he must hear complaints like this all day. "I know it's frustrating, *Oum* Tariq, but the papers will come, don't worry, though it might take a month or two. Meanwhile, we can set you up with driving lessons or English classes for your mother-in-law. And find you a mosque, as well, if you want."

"A *month* or two? But what am I to do? How am I to find a job and feed my son? And already I know how to drive. As for my mother-in-law, I can teach her English. And I can find a mosque by myself. I have no need of your charity."

Derek leans over his desk, his round face earnest. "*Oum* Tariq, this is not charity, it's your right to receive these services. Your husband earned them."

I am taken aback that he has understood me so accurately and am touched by his words about Khalil. But then, of course, he deals with refugees all the time. "Thank you," I murmur, chastened.

He stands and hands me his card. "Call me or come by whenever you have a question, all right? And give yourself time, *Oum* Tariq. It's hard for everyone in the beginning. It'll get easier, you'll see."

I thank him again and leave the room. But the sourness on my tongue tells me that for all this young man's kindness, he has not, in fact, done anything for us at all.

When the soldier arrives to drive us home, I am too dispirited to speak. He, also, seems to be in no mood to talk, leaving Tariq to fiddle with the radio dial again. Even Hibah is quiet at first, huddled beside me in the back of the car and muttering prayers under her breath. Ever since the bomb, she has been unable to sit in a car without fearing that it might explode at any moment. But before long she resumes her usual complaints, her voice high-pitched and aggrieved. "I don't understand why you and the sergeant insist on dragging me around all day like this, leaving me to sit in a car here, a waiting room there, as if I'm no more sentient than a sack of beans."

"I'm sorry, Mama, but—"

"I don't care for this country, Naema. Everybody here stares at me as if I've risen from the dead. It's true what they say, every rooster crows on its own dunghill. I should have let you and Tariq come without me and gone back to Baghdad where I belong, even without my husband and son to greet me, may their souls rest in peace. *Ya Allah*, why didn't I go home to die amongst my own people?"

Turning a deaf ear to her laments, all of which I have heard countless times, I gaze out at the landscape around me, a curious mixture of the manicured and the savage. Most of the roads are cracked and potholed, flanked by fallow fields or forests. Yet when a house does appear, its garden is often as tidy and precise as an ink drawing. Many of the houses themselves are also unnaturally pristine, little yellow or white boxes that look as though they have been carried here whole and placed on the ground like toys. Some are so small they are dwarfed by the cars parked beside them, others surrounded by jumbles of trailers and rusting machines—those, I assume, belong to the poor. Yet, in Slingerlands, where the soldier lives, many of the streets are lined with enormous wooden houses as elaborate as wedding cakes, each skirted by its own field of shorn grass and flowerbeds, luxuries that surely only the rich can afford. But the soldier, whose own house is equally large, if dilapidated, is not rich, so this I cannot understand, either.

Everything about this country confounds me. Its derelict farms and tasteless food. Its shops the size of villages. Its crowds of whey-faced strangers. It makes me long so for home. Donkeys plodding through traffic, their hairy ears flicking away flies. Boys pulling bright, hand-painted carts heaped with tomatoes or oranges. Waiters dodging cars and people as they carry trays of tinkling tea glasses to workers. Women calling to one another across the sky while they hang laundry over their flat rooftops. Jasmine and palm trees, mosques and minarets, the ancient history rooted in the touch of a stone, the scent of cardamom, the language of a prayer.

I practice reading the road signs we pass as a way of honing my English. Some amuse me: the signs for Troy and Bethlehem, Cairo and Athens, tiny American towns trying to sound as illustrious as their namesakes. But others baffle me. *Watershed*—is that some sort of wooden house that stores water? *No Shoulder*—what could that mean? *Slow Children*—surely this doesn't refer to children who move slowly? And then those handwritten signs: *Garage Sale*, *Yard Sale*.

"Sergeant?" I lean forwards so he can hear me over the radio Tariq has turned up too loud again. My son is already showing an alarming predilection for the worst of American pop. I would prefer Hibah's oud music, tapes of which she packed to give us comfort in America but that are now wandering the world inside our lost suitcases. "Why are so many people here selling their garages and yards?"

"Sorry, what?" He lowers the volume.

"The signs everywhere. *Garage Sale.*"

"Oh. It doesn't mean that." He explains, and I suppose I should be grateful that he refrains from laughing at me.

Every hour I come across reminders that my English is not as advanced as I thought, phrases such as those the friendly young woman in the Resettlement Center used: "Take a seat." "I didn't catch that." The soldier, too, tosses out expressions I don't know: "What's up?" "He hit the ceiling." Expressions I must learn to understand if I am to survive in this country, let alone thrive.

I learned my English partly at school and from the few American films I managed to see, but mostly from listening to the BBC language tapes Baba bought on Al-Mutanabbi Street before it was bombed. He and I would practice together in the family room, hunched over the cassette player, repeating the words squawking out of the speaker, Mama teasing that we sounded like parrots with colds. I would run around the room pointing at objects, just as Tariq likes to do with the soldier here, challenging Baba to name them in English and crowing when he couldn't, for I was by far the quicker study. He would laugh his low chuckle, his sad eyes crinkling, never minding his defeat, so much did he, a poet, love the words of any language, and so proud was he of my talents. Who would have thought that this English, once a mere hobby, would end up being my only skill that mattered?

I am trying to train myself to think of Baba like this, to remember him and Zaki in casual, ordinary ways. For months after I heard of their deaths in that desert prison—and not even from Kate Brady but from another girl soldier who had no heart—I could only weep over how they must have suffered, my mind fevered by visions of torture and starvation, my dreams twisted by horror. Then, almost overnight, I could no longer think of them at all. Now I am attempting a compromise, a method of remembering them that will not leave me gasping for air, as do my memories of Khalil.

"Naema, call the airport," Hibah says abruptly. "Perhaps this time they will have our bags, *insh'Allah.*"

We have already called twice today but I ask to borrow the soldier's telephone again anyway. He hands it over and switches the radio all the way off this time. "I'm gonna play you some real music," he says to Tariq. "That singer sounds like a sick donkey."

After waiting through the ringing and usual convoluted menu of options, I finally reach a human being. "Our luggage, they have found it!" I cry out in English, startling Hibah. "Sergeant, we must go fetch it now."

"Sure. No prob." He turns around in a driveway and heads back.

All three suitcases are waiting for us at the airport, which makes me suspect that they were never misplaced at all, only kept by Homeland Security for inspection.

Once I hand in my claim form and our bags are released, the soldier piles them into a cart and wheels them out to his car. "Hope nothing's missing," he says.

I hope so, too, but I am not about to admit this or anything else to him. "When my parents, they took us to my grandmother's village to escape your war, another family moved into our Baghdad home and refused to give it back," I tell him pointedly. "And later, when the bomb drove Tariq and me out of our home in Al-Karrada, our house was looted. My mother went to pack our belongings and send them to us in Damascus. Everything was gone, down to the smallest button. So you see, Sergeant, we are inured to theft."

He has no reply to that, but I am focused on what we need, not on what we have lost, so back in the car I pick up the newspaper he bought for me and circle the few job advertisements from local hospitals. My plan is to use my medical degree and experience to find some sort of work in health care while I study for the American medical exams, and once I have passed, join a practice and earn enough to buy a house and support Tariq through school and beyond. Is this not every immigrant's dream? To survive, to work, to build security and a future for one's children? It does not seem so very much to ask from the country that destroyed my own.

When we arrive at the house, the soldier hefts our suitcases onto the planks of his shoulders and drops them at our doorstep in the back, after which I make it clear that he should leave. "Which one first, little moon?" I ask Tariq once the sergeant is gone, dragging the suitcases inside.

"This one, Mama!" He points to the biggest, so I heave it onto my bed while he balances on a crutch and spins around it like a whirligig, a trick he developed in Damascus to entice other children to play. I, too, am light of heart, not only at having recovered our possessions at last, but at being free of the soldier's presence. Every time he leaves my sight, I feel as though I have kicked off boots of lead.

With Tariq twirling beside me, I unbuckle the straps that hold the suitcase together. They are much looser than when I fastened them and clasped in a different order. Somebody has obviously rifled through the bag. But when I open it, a scent is released that makes my breath catch. It is the scent of Damascus, the tobacco and exhaust, jasmine and yearning that permeated the one-room apartment in which the three of us lived while awaiting our future.

Hibah lays a bony hand on her chest and looks at me, her dim eyes tearing. "You smell it, Naema?"

I nod. I never grew to love Damascus, my time there shadowed by all the bomb had done to us and the shock of finding myself a refugee. But there, in that unfamiliar American room, the scent curls around me like a rope, wringing from me a powerful longing: for Khalil, for the past, and yes, even for Syria, where at least I understood my surroundings and did not have to live with the man who killed my husband or the people who crushed my country.

I search quickly through the suitcase—nothing, to my surprise, appears to be missing—while Tariq leaves off spinning to plunge a hand in, too. He pulls out his favorite of my scarves, deep red and woven with golden threads. In Damascus, he liked to wear it as a cape, imitating a superhero he had seen in Syrian comic books. How it pained me to watch my little son pretending to fly and save people, as if he could swoop through the air with the grace of a swallow rather than hobble across the earth on wooden sticks.

"Look, Mama, remember this?" He waves the scarf in front of me as though we have not seen it for years. Dropping it to the floor, he reaches into the suitcase again, this time extracting Hibah's cherished prayer rug, a small, hand-woven kilim from her Kurdish grandmother. Laughing, he throws it over his shoulder. "Come, Bibi and Mama, you do it, too!" So all three of us pull out sheets, socks, scarves and shirts, the leftovers of our previous life, and toss them into the air, a whirl of bright, colorful shapes cascading over the room like tumbling rainbows.

Later that afternoon, with the sun dying the lawn a coppery gold, Hibah sets to cooking supper in our tiny kitchen, the oud music on her treasured cassette player singing to us of home and the wisdom of Allah. Tariq has gone outside for a game of football with the soldier, leaving me free to unpack and redecorate.

The soldier calls this place an apartment, but in fact it is more like a garage. I barely noticed this on our first night here, too exhausted to do anything but drop into sleep. But when the morning sun startled me awake by blazing through the upper window, an asymmetrical triangle placed too high to either wash or curtain, I gazed about in confusion. A dingy paint on the walls, neither gray nor white. A brown industrial carpet rough enough to graze our feet. A high, slanting ceiling from which a fan dangles so crookedly I'm afraid to turn it on in case it falls and lops off my head. And a pair of glass doors at the far end leading to a screened-in verandah cluttered with fraying deckchairs, old paint tins, cobwebbed birdhouses and chipped flowerpots.

There is another door, as well, at the back of the room, which leads to the rest of the house via the kitchen, but I have locked and bolted it. My way of keeping the soldier out.

The furniture in here is equally puzzling. Three single beds pushed against the walls. Two wobbly bamboo screens, their edges as ragged as broken teeth. A chest of drawers painted the pink of a tonsil. And a pale-green wardrobe that refuses to stay shut. I wonder if Kate Brady decorated this room before she disappeared or if it was the soldier's work alone. Either way, whoever it was clearly tried to make it welcoming, even going through the effort of hanging posters of birds and wildflowers. Yet it only reminds me of how dependent I have become; of how a refugee, the world's orphan, is so swiftly reduced to the status of beggar.

For the next hour or so, I do my best to make the room look like home. Hang some shawls on the walls, pull the screens around two of the beds, fill the drawers with our few clothes. Unroll Hibah's kilim in a corner, ready for her prayers.

"Naema," she says when I am done, "call Tariq in. Dinner is ready." She has made a simple meal, all we can afford at the moment and all we can cook on our two burners, but it is a meal from home: cumin and lentil soup, a salad of finely chopped cucumbers and tomatoes, and something called a tortilla, the closest we could find to our own bread, *samoon*.

I follow the noise of Tariq's squeals around to the front of the house, where I find him swinging over the grass on his crutches, kicking a football with great aplomb, the soldier chasing him. But to my dismay, the soldier is also on one leg, having tied up the other behind him and tucked an upside-down mop under his right arm. What is he doing, mocking my child?

I am about to shout at him when his mop catches in a hole and sends him flying to the ground with a yelp. Tariq takes one look and doubles over in laughter, while the soldier lies on his back, his glasses askew, clutching his neck with a wince, yet laughing, too. And before I quite know why, I am laughing with them. It may be the laugh of despair, of loss, of outrage and resentment; it may even be a laugh of anger. But it is a laugh.

6

"You know, Sergeant, it is not right the way Corporal Muller, he exposes his children. I would never do this with my Tariq." Khalil was standing beside me, both of us protected from the sun by our Kevlar helmets and goggles, peering over the edge of a bomb crater so massive that the civilians on the other side looked tiny as bowling pins.

I glanced over at him. "How d'you mean?"

"Those photographs, Sergeant. I think you should tell him to keep them away from the eyes of danger." Muller, our team driver, pig-pink and plump, was notorious in our platoon for having spawned five girls and three boys, and he was always pulling their pictures out of his pockets to show them off. Eight Texas blonds, faded and sandblasted from their year in the desert. "He is tempting . . . how you say?"

"Fate?"

"Yes. Fate. I have a dark feeling about it. Will you tell him?"

"I don't know, Ali. It's a hard thing to tell a man not to be proud of his kids. 'Specially a man stuck in this craphole." I knew that Khalil didn't much care for being called Ali, but it was his army alias intended to keep his identity secret and his body and family in one piece. It was also easier for me and the rest of our bumble-tongued team to say.

"Then maybe I will speak to him," Khalil said. "As a father myself."

We stopped talking then, silenced by the destruction nearby, the work of a powerful truck bomb that had flattened a Baghdad police station and destroyed dozens of buildings around it. Empty windows gaping like toothless mouths. The twisted shells of cars smoking in gutters. Gray rubble, gray dust, gray air, gray ground. The disembodied foot of a toddler lay nearby, still attached to its sandal, the bloodied toes tiny and round, as if to illustrate Khalil's point.

A crowd of locals had collected by then, mostly men in shirtsleeves or dishdashas, a few women among them. Some stared into the crater in silence. Others threw themselves to the ground, wailing and ululating. Yanking my scarf over my nose against the stench of charred flesh, I called over Muller and Bean, and we joined two other squads from our platoon to pull the bodies from the rubble. Five were already lined up on the ground: a woman and four small children, faces bubbled and black, arms clumps of charcoal.

"I used to come to the chai shop here all the time," Khalil told me through his own scarf as we eased a corpse onto a stretcher. "I think this man here, he was the owner, may Allah have mercy on him. I knew his children, little girls the same age as my Tariq."

"Can we not talk about that right now?" I tried to speak without tasting the air.

We spent the next hour retrieving the dead—twenty-eight in all—while their families gathered, some to help, others only able to shriek and sob. I could feel a steely numbness creeping over me as I worked. Burned skin sloughing off in my hands, faces peeling from skulls. I'm getting too used to this, I told myself—shoveling the shit of war.

When a relief platoon arrived, I ordered the squad to join me at what was left of the police station. The only part of it still standing was the right-hand corner, a single cell with its bars intact. Three men who'd been arrested earlier by Second Squad were huddled there on the floor, hands zip-cuffed behind their backs, heads bowed under hoods. "We picked these hajjis up across the road, Staff Sergeant," a triumphant female specialist told me. "Hiding on a roof. Armed. They put up quite a scuffle." She pulled off the hoods. Two bearded men and a boy, eyes darting, mouths bruised and crusted with blood.

"Twenty-eight innocent lives snuffed out, Ali," I said. "Go to it."

Khalil squatted in front of the prisoners and wasted no time in putting to use the interrogator's tools he'd learned during his two years with the US military. First, he played the friendly bro who could guarantee their safety if they wouldn't mind telling him who set off the bomb. Next, he claimed that we Americans had already caught one of their cronies, who'd been only too happy to squeal on his accomplices. Then came the threats: he knew where the men lived and if they didn't talk, we would raid their family homes and arrest every male over fifteen. And once all these inventions had sunk in, Khalil wielded the biggest stick of all: the promise that if the men stayed silent, the US of A would send them to Abu Ghraib, Saddam's old torture palace and Bush's new one.

The interrogation lasted twenty minutes, me shouting questions, Khalil translating, the beards choking out answers, the kid sobbing. Result: exactly zip.

"Screw this," I spat at the specialist. "Take these sons of bitches away." I strode off, fuming. Another day of meaningless war shit.

"Sergeant?" Khalil hurried up behind me. "I am sure the two men, they are guilty. But the boy, he was taken by mistake."

I climbed into the Humvee next to Muller, sending Khalil into the back with Jerome Green, aka Bean because he was small, dark and round, and of course because it rhymed. "Nothing's gonna happen to the kid, Ali. Intel will question him and if he's innocent, they'll let him go."

Khalil pushed his head between the front seats. "Do not treat me like a child, Sergeant. Tell them to set him free. The boy is no older than fourteen. He was crying for his mama, did you not hear? I am certain he has nothing to do with the bomb."

"Kids his age kill us all the time. You know that."

Khalil lowered his voice. "Sergeant, did we not agree to do no more harm than we must?"

We rattled along in silence after that, on our way with a chain of other Humvees and trucks to join the rest of our company at a new FOB north of Baghdad. I fastened my mind to the moment, eyes sweeping the streets. I had three men in my vehicle to keep alive. Two of those men were fathers. There was no time for that luxury called mercy.

We wound our way out of the city and along the highway for a couple of hours, the wind building up loud and strong, the view out of the windows pixilating into a swirl of brown splotches—another dust storm on its way. "Nothing out there but God's diarrhea," Bean shouted over the racket.

Muller leaned his pink face closer to the windshield. "Can't even see my own schnoz."

"You're doing fine, Corporal," I said. Muller could drive straight and true through just about anything, even a sandstorm thick as tar. I examined my M16. The condom I'd rolled over the tip of its barrel to keep out the sand was already covered in it, a little rubbery blimp of dust. "We're almost there, anyhow," I added to cheer us all up. I planned on Skyping Kate later that evening if this new base had enough computers, catch her just out of her morning shower, hair dripping, towel clinging, those summer-sky eyes of hers flashing mischief—

something to feed my dreams while I counted down the hours to home. That, along with my much-revisited memory of the night before I'd left, the two of us in bed, her lips teasing mine. "Come on, handsome fucker," she'd said in her gruff way, sliding a bare leg over my groin. "Let's do this good for you to remember me by."

The explosion hit the Humvee then, so strong and loud it kicked clear through my chest.

My eardrums snapped. Skull sucked in tight and tiny. Vision tunneled to a black dot. Muller's head a shattered stump beside me.

I couldn't breathe. Couldn't move. And all around me, flames.

The door flew open and somebody hauled me out, threw me to the ground, jumped on me. Rolled with me across the sand, face to face, away from the burning Humvee, away from Muller's corpse—rolled and rolled until every last flame was out.

Khalil.

Twenty minutes later, we sat on the side of the road, dazed, charred and coughing, waiting for ordnance to give the all-clear. Bean rocked and muttered in some kind of prayer. Khalil brushed the sand and charcoal off his uniform, pulling off his ruined gloves. I turned my eyes to the blackened skin on my hands, a scream ricocheting around in my skull.

"Sergeant, I think it best if you wipe." Khalil unwound the remains of his scarf and held it out to me.

I looked at him blankly, senses numb, hands useless, ears roaring. So Khalil wiped my face and mouth for me. The blood and jelly. The lumps.

7

"Mama! My leg! It hurts!"

"Shh, you'll wake Bibi." Slipping out of bed, Naema makes her way through the dark to sit beside Tariq, smoothing his brow. "Hold still, my love, let's see what's wrong." Turning on the small bedside lamp, she pulls back his sheets. Had her medical bag not been stolen during their travels, leaving her without so much as a stethoscope, she would take his temperature to check for infection and give him medicine to soothe the pain. As it is, she has to settle for unwrapping the Ace bandage around his residual limb and palpitating it to feel for swelling or lumps.

"Ow, stop!" His face, as slender as an almond against the white pillow, scrunches up in pain.

"All right, *ya amar*. But we better take you to the hospital in the morning. Your leg shouldn't be hurting like this."

"No! The hurt's gone now, I'm fine, I don't need to go."

She brushes a curl off his brow. "There's no need to be frightened, *habibi*. It won't be like the hospitals at home."

He searches her face for reassurance. He is so naturally full of light, her son, that when the war visits him like this, she can see it in the way his eyes skitter and his mouth compresses into a small, tight line. He does not believe her.

A few hours later, Jimmy gropes his way down to the kitchen, head heavy and mood blackened by a set of particularly cruel dreams, too much Ambien and the discovery of one of Kate's socks under his bed. Kate might have cleared out her belongings with brutal exactitude but she did miss some things. He is constantly being ambushed by the scraps she left lying around—a piece of rose soap, a blue wristband, that dusty white sock—and each time it tips him into another maelstrom of yearning.

"Oh," he says, taken aback to find Naema already there, making a pot of coffee. He adjusts his glasses, glad he thought to dress. Daylight hasn't yet penetrated the windows, so the room is hung with shadows. He wonders why she hasn't turned on a light.

"Tariq, he needs to go to the hospital," she announces, her back to him while she pours him a cup.

"Shit, why? What happened?"

"The suture, it is hurting him. He woke in the night crying. I fear it might be torn inside."

"Christ. Yeah, of course, I'll take you right away." Was it the soccer? Was this his fault, too?

Crossing her arms, she turns to look at him, whether in blame or contemplation he can't tell. Her hair is pulled into a taut ponytail rather than her usual loose braid, emphasizing the length of her neck and contours of her face—high sweep of cheekbones, thin nose, wing-shaped eyes. He can just see through the morning dimness that she's wearing fitted jeans and a long-sleeved green shirt; clothes that reveal, as Patrick's and her maroon tunic do not, the swell of her breasts and hips. With something between shock and shame, Jimmy realizes that Khalil's widow is beautiful.

"Your coffee you may have first," she says. "This is why I made it." She hands him the cup.

"Yes, ma'am." The phrase is only army habit but she frowns at him in puzzlement. He downs his coffee—can he do nothing right?—and runs upstairs to fetch the car keys.

Hibah declines to go with them, her terror of hospitals as acute as Tariq's, but although Naema is glad to be free of her dyspeptic company for once, she feels uneasy. Venturing into public with the soldier and no chaperone is compromising enough, but even more mortifying would be if people took him for her husband. Had she the confidence to negotiate the American medical system alone, she would ask him to drop them off before anyone saw him. As it is, all she can do is sit in the back of the car, her son in the front again, and wait for this latest humiliation to pass.

Once they find their way to the pediatric wing, which is crowded with beige furniture, scattered toys and wailing children, Tariq clutches her in fear, only letting go when she promises to stay close beside him. She rubs his back, so small that her hand can span its entire width. "Is it still hurting, *habibi*?"

He nods, then quickly shakes his head.

Settling him down at one of the children's video games in the room, she sits beside him with a clipboard and a thicket of forms to fill out. She brought along a fat envelope containing his medical records but the receptionist told her to fill out the forms anyway. The whole world, Naema reflects, is mad for forms.

Across the room, Jimmy squeezes himself into one of the beige chairs, arms folded, biceps bulging, ready to stare down any child who dares gape at Tariq. At times he's seen Tariq react to such attention by clowning, at other times by hiding, as he did in the firehouse, but this morning Tariq only ignores the other children, either too absorbed in his game, something to do with matching animals to the food they eat, or because he's afraid and in pain. His leg used to hurt all the time, Naema told Jimmy in the car, the nerves remembering their trauma. Now the pain only flares up occasionally. Still, she said, the suture remains more vulnerable than any other part of his body and always will.

After twenty minutes or so, a nurse appears and calls Tariq into an examining room, offering him a buoyant smile. Naema wonders where she was born, for her accent is not American, her eyes are black and her complexion dark. Several other members of the staff also look as though they might be immigrants: two Indian doctors, a Chinese nurse and a few brown-skinned secretaries. Perhaps this means that she, too, will be welcomed as a doctor at this hospital one day. With a flare of hope, she stands and, anticipating that she might need an interpreter, beckons Jimmy to come with her.

Surprised but grateful, he rises and reaches for Tariq's hand, only then remembering: you can't hold the hand of a child on crutches.

Inside the examining room, the nurse sends Jimmy to a chair in the corner and hoists Tariq onto a table, where he sits, his single leg dangling over its edge, his brow in an anxious knot. Naema squeezes one of his hands while she surveys the gleaming tray of sterilized instruments, the immaculate bed with its crackling sheet of fresh white paper, the floor as spotless as a newly scrubbed bath. She hasn't seen a hospital this clean for years, for although Iraq once boasted the best medical system in the Middle East, thirteen years of Western sanctions and two wars destroyed all that. She gave birth to Tariq in the Catholic hospital of Saint Raphael in 2004, a year after the US invasion, and already the hospital had descended into chaos and squalor. More than a thousand patients crowded in by the day, victims of bombs and landmines, bullets and disease, and yet the hospital had only thirty-five beds, virtually no medicines or anesthetics, and only two doctors, most having fled or been murdered. She was lucky to get herself and the newborn Tariq out of there alive.

The nurse, whose name tag Naema can now see—Flores—leans Tariq's battered wooden crutches against a wall, eyeing them with disapproval, and then returns to him with another ebullient smile. Tariq shrinks back. "Don't be scared, sweetie," the nurse says. "Just take off your shirt and shorts. Your bandage should come off, too."

He does not understand, so Naema translates. He pulls off his shirt himself, and Jimmy is struck by how skinny he is, torso ribby, shoulders little knobs. Nurse Flores eases down Tariq's shorts and unwinds the bandage wrapping his stump, the skin around the suture stitched and puckered above his missing knee, reminding Jimmy of the knotted end of a sausage. He looks away quickly. He has carried bleeding bodies, held severed heads, wiped Muller's flesh from his lips, but he cannot look at Tariq's cut-off thigh. This isn't because Tariq's a child. Jimmy has seen plenty of mutilated children. It's because Tariq is Khalil's son.

A woman comes in about ten minutes later and introduces herself as Doctor Feldman. She is surprisingly young, a tiny white person with auburn hair in a pixie cut, wire-framed spectacles and a little boy's face. Naema takes in her doctor's coat and stethoscope, her steady gaze and manifest confidence. Envy slaps her with a sting.

"Well, little man, what's the problem today?" the doctor says to Tariq, pushing her glasses up her nose and studying her clipboard. She raises her eyes to Naema. "You're Mrs. Jassim, his mom?"

"I am." Naema has already learned that Americans cannot or will not grasp that Iraqi women do not take their husband's surnames. Jassim is the family name of her grandfather. Khalil's was Pachachi.

"And you've been in this country how long?"

"It is five days, now."

Doctor Feldman lifts her eyebrows into two little arrows. "Why didn't you bring him in here right away?"

"It was not necessary. He felt no pain until last night."

The doctor purses her lips. "Sit, please." She waves Naema to a chair beside Jimmy. Naema sits with reluctance. She does not want the doctor looking down on her, literally or figuratively. "When did your son undergo his amputation?" the doctor asks then.

Naema explained all that in the forms on the clipboard but answers with what patience she can muster. "It has been two years and eight months. He was aged three. I am qualified, so I know how him to care."

Jimmy looks at her in surprise. Her English is never as scrambled as this.

Doctor Feldman regards her over her glasses. "You're a physician, is that what you mean?"

"Yes. A pediatrician. Like you."

"Oh." The doctor looks taken aback. "All right, good, so you'll understand. I'll examine his suture and order an x-ray to check the site for bone spur growth or a neuroma. You have any of his medical records with you?"

Naema hands them over. The doctor glances at them. "I can't read this, it's in Arabic."

"Oh, I . . . I am sorry." Naema rises to her feet. "If you tell me what you need to know, I can explain."

"Let's start with how he lost his leg."

"I wrote that there. In English." Naema points to the chart in the doctor's hands. Her own hands, Jimmy sees, are trembling.

"They were in a war, Doc," he interjects from his chair. "Shit happens."

The doctor takes in his bulk, his military haircut. "Oh. Yes. Of course."

But to Naema, the question has already done its harm. Tariq breaking from her arms to run into the street and say goodbye to Khalil. Naema tearing after him, calling, "Come back, it's not safe!" Khalil standing with his father by the car, blowing a kiss to Tariq, grasping the car door handle and pulling . . . The blast. The stretch of blackness. The rain of blood and bone. Tariq hurtling through the air like a doll.

"And the length of time in the hospital after the amputation?"

Silence.

"Mrs. Jassim?"

Naema gazes at her blankly.

The doctor repeats her question.

"Oh. I am sorry. Yes, it was two days we had in the hospital."

"They sent him home in *two* days? When he was only three years old? You should never have allowed that."

Naema rubs her forehead with a finger, a crease between her eyes. "I had no choice, Doctor. The hospital, it was not safe. But I was able to care for him myself, the wrapping and washing and exercise. I am, as I said, a physician."

"I see. And did the surgeons make any notes?"

"Notes?"

"Yes. Notes about the amputation, any complications . . ."

"There was no time for notes. The hospital, it had one surgeon for hundreds of people. We were lucky to even get anesthetic for my son."

Doctor Feldman's brow wrinkles. "But why doesn't he have a prosthesis? He should have been fitted with one at least a year ago." She eyes his crutches. "And he should be using much lighter crutches than those."

Naema pulls at her fingers. "In Damascus, we were strangers . . ." She stops. She no more wants to explain her isolation, her poverty, her second-class status as a refugee to this doctor than she wants to be scolded as an incompetent.

Jimmy jumps up. "Doctor, their circumstances weren't normal, for fuck's sake! Do you have to ask these questions?"

The doctor looks up at him. "Are you a veteran, sir?"

He hesitates. Nods.

"Thank you for your service," she says earnestly.

He glances at Naema and sits back down, staring at the scars on his hands.

"All right, let's take a look." The doctor pulls on a pair of latex gloves and bends over Tariq.

"Mama!"

Naema takes his hand again. "Don't be frightened, little one. If it hurts, squeeze my fingers as tightly as you can. Try to make them stick together."

Jimmy concentrates on inhaling, his eyes fixed on the doctor. If that woman hurts Tariq for even a second, it's going to take all his self-control not to punch her in the throat.

"Good," she finally says, letting go of Tariq at last. "I'm sure we can fix up this little guy with a prosthesis in no time." She sends Naema a smile. "There's no swelling. You've done the wrapping well. But he is a little bruised. He needs to be more careful when he plays."

Jimmy winces.

"His suture is irritated, too."

"Yes, I think this is because of the climate. My son, he is not used to the dampness in your air."

"Well, it's nothing serious. I'll give you some ointment." The doctor finishes examining Tariq and then winks at him. "You look like a strong little fellow. Just try to eat more so you can grow even stronger, all right? But I bet you'll be a whiz on your new leg in no time."

"Please do not tell him this," Naema says in distress. "We cannot afford it."

"But he has Medicaid. It's on your form."

"I do not understand."

The doctor peels off her gloves. "Medicaid will cover the cost of his prosthesis."

Naema stares at her. "You are saying that this Medicaid, it will pay for his leg, even though such a leg is so expensive?"

"Yup."

"You are able to give him a prosthesis now?"

"Well, not this second, no. But once the paperwork's cleared, sure. I'll send him in for his x-ray now, then we'll get the referral rolling and find him a clinic. Meanwhile, we'll give him a pair of aluminum crutches. Much easier than those heavy wooden things."

Naema lets out a sound unlike any Jimmy has ever heard her make. He looks over at her. Her face is alight with joy.

8

McGrath's Bar, where I'm meeting my brothers, has been standing in the same spot on Route 140 since Arty McGrath, father of baldheaded Mick the bartender, opened it in 1945. Its tin ceiling has long since turned nicotine-brown, its wooden floor black, while a row of ripped-up red vinyl booths lines the walls, foam rubber bulging out here and there like flesh from a fat lady's bra. Even better, the place reeks so powerfully of stale whiskey and unwashed urinals it blows new customers clear out the door. It was Dad's favorite watering hole before he took off the minute Rory was born, leaving Mom to drink and crack up alone. Now it's mine.

I'm just ordering a beer, knowing my brothers will be late because they always are, when I'm interrupted by a spray of gravel outside and a screech of brakes. "Some dipshit don't know how to drive," Mick grumbles, moving over to peer through the grime-smeared window. I peer out, too. It's Rory. He's teetering on top of a humungous red motorcycle I've never seen before, struggling to park it without tipping over. He normally drives a rust-splotched Hyundai that sputters down the street like an angry grandma.

"When the hell did you get a motorbike?" I ask when he lopes in, tall, spindle-shanked and long-necked as a goose, his head swallowed by a shiny black helmet I've never seen before, either. He takes a barstool one over from me and pulls the helmet off, which makes his ginger hair fly around his head in a fit of static.

"Sue's big bro lent it to me. It's a Ducati ST3. Hot as fresh shit, huh?"

"Who's Sue?"

"New girlfriend." He sets the helmet on the stool between us. "Hey, Mick, gimme a Bud. You can put it on my brother's tab."

"He's not having beer," I say. "He's eighteen. Give him a Coke."

Mick squirts a glassful and plunks it on the counter.

Rory pries his phone from his pocket, flips it open and stares into it. This is the first time I've seen him since Kate decamped but he doesn't say a thing about it, even though he's known her for near a third of his life. But then, I didn't expect him to.

Pat walks in then, carrying a greasy paper bag of pizza slices, the customary cancer stick drooping from his mouth, the smoke making him squint under his flat brim. "Hey, buttfaces." He sits on the far side of Rory, emitting his familiar perfume of oil and gas. He orders a Molson.

"Gimme," Rory says, reaching for the pizza.

"If you boys are gonna eat, go sit at a table," Mick growls. "And no smoking, for fuck's sake, like the sign says."

We move over to a booth of our choice—we're the only customers here—Pat and Rory sliding in across from me, Rory knocking his head against the battered brass lamp hanging over the table. Pat stubs out his cigarette on the pizza bag and eases out a slice, the smell of pepperoni twisting through my guts; those Iraqi bugs again. He shoves the bag over to Rory, who's so absorbed in his phone he eats without looking. "Want some?" Pat asks me.

I shake my head and lean back, folding my arms over my chest. I love my brothers but the pair of them look ridiculous. Rory in his wannabe rock star outfit: faded Metallica T-shirt, tight blue jeans ripped at the knees, motorcycle boots, his skinny face flushed with acne, that flyaway hair. Pat in his white-boy hip-hop gear, flat brim pulled so low I doubt he can even see. I was the kind of sergeant who insisted on keeping my soldiers immaculate, even in the desert: males clipped and shaven, females' hair smoothed tight, living quarters swept and tidied to the last grain of sand. Even their underwear had to be folded just so, left and right sides facing inward neat as a napkin. I tried not to be a pain about it. I just happen to believe that morale is boosted by self-respect and self-respect is boosted by neatness and order—a lesson I've clearly failed to impart to my brothers.

"So, how's life at I Scream Heaven?" I say to the top of Rory's head. I've never forgiven him for dropping out of tenth grade to do nothing better than work at a run-down ice cream shack. After all, one of my main reasons for enlisting was to send my brothers to college. I still have hopes for Pat, who at least graduated high school, 'specially now that he's with Lisa, his too-good-for-him girlfriend who's in college herself. But Rory's pissing his life away.

He shrugs, eyes still on his phone. "It's a job, which is more'n you got."

I have no answer to that, my lack of employment having become a sore point between us and an even sorer one for me. When I first got back from my last tour, I took a warehouse job at Home Depot. But then one of the lettuceheads I worked with ran his forklift into a twenty-foot stack of crates, knocking them over with such a crash that I hit the ground screaming, seeing nothing but flames and Muller's shattered skull. The supervisor called me a pussy for it. I punched him.

What I need is work that won't trigger me like that, though what that might be I haven't had a chance to find out. Every time I mention to employers that I'm a combat vet, they never call again. Maybe that's why Kate left. Not to run after some outside fuckhead, but because I'm such a deadbeat.

"How's the one-legged kid?" Pat asks then, still chewing his pizza. Rory is too deep in his phone again to listen.

"His name's Tariq." I'm already irritated enough by the both of them to bite their heads off. Leaning my elbows on the table, I stare down at the drawing on my beer mat—a cartoon leprechaun, nose bulbous with drink—trying to think what Kate would do. She was always good with my brothers, half mom, half big sister. Good at keeping me from losing my temper at them, too.

"Hey, you wouldn't believe this couple I saw at work this morning," Rory says, slapping down his phone at last. Unlike Pat, he has a low, booming voice, though how it makes its way out of that scraggly string of a throat beats me. "Dude must've weighed, like, four hundred pounds, with this little stamp of a face in the middle of a balloon of blubber. And the wife was all tiny and pointy, like a mosquito. I mean, you gotta wonder how they fuck, y'know?" His phone buzzes and he picks it back up. "You see the whole goddamn world from the window of I Scream Heaven, I tell you."

"Rory, how'd you get to be such a turnip?" Pat snaps. That surprises me. He and Rory are usually on the same side. Against me. "Jimmy, you OK? You look kinda wiped."

I take off my glasses and rub my face. "Yeah. No. Haven't been able to sleep much since Kate split." I don't confess all the hours I waste at night trying to find her online, combing through every second of our last night, dialing her number over and over.

"Yeah, what about that?" Rory looks up from his phone. "She didn't even say goodbye to me. What the hell made her run, anyhow?"

"Rory, he doesn't know, so shut it," Pat says.

"And why didn't you tell me something was wrong?" Rory goes on. "You guys never tell me shit. Kate matters just as much to me as she does to you."

There's nothing to say to that, so we fall into a long stretch of sticky silence, Rory back on his phone, Pat fiddling with his pizza crust. My brothers never know how to talk to me. Haven't since I shipped out to Iraq when Pat was fourteen and Rory only eleven, leaving them with our Aunt Maureen, who neither of them could stand. I know they resent me for that, but the army gave me no choice. And then I had no idea how else to support them at twenty-two, with an AWOL dad, Mom in the looney-bin and nothing in the bank.

The first time I came home for R&R, I'd been away eight months and my brothers were so happy to see me it hurt. "We got a present for you!" Pat announced the second I dumped my bag in the hall, his puffy teenage cheeks pink with pride. "We worked all kinds of jobs to earn the money to get it. Come see!" He and Rory led me out to Aunt Maureen's garage, the two of them so hopped up they were bouncing around like jumping beans. And there it was: a brand-new mountain bike with twenty-seven gears and a bright blue frame.

"Wow, that's so fucking cool," I told them, too choked up to say more. I knew it must have cost them a fortune. I gave them each a hug so hard it squeezed the breath out of their bony boy bodies.

"Can we go home with you now?" Rory asked then, his eyes scrunched up tight and pleading, orange freckles all over his little kid face. "Please? We can't stand it here. Aunt Maureen's so mean." But I was already too far gone, heart-crushed over Kate, soul-crushed by war, to look after anyone, even myself. So I patted him on the head, left the bike in the barn and them with our aunt, and ran back to Iraq.

"Hey, Jimmy, me and Lisa have some news," Pat says after our silence has stretched long enough to make us all itch in our seats. He sounds strangely shy.

I shove my glasses back on. Without them, he's fuzzed around the edges, like a felt puppet. With them, I can see a flush creeping up his neck like a stain. "What?"

He pulls off his hat, the long hair on top of his head flopping over his brow. "It's big."

"You didn't knock her up, did you?" Rory grins.

Pat scowls. "If you don't shut that hole in your face, I'm shutting it for you."

God, my brothers are young.

"So, what is it?" I ask Pat again.

His flush stains deeper. "Well. Um. We decided to get, uh, hitched."

"*What*?" Rory stares at him from under his electric hair. "You out of your mind? You're still a kid!"

For once I have to agree with him. Pat's only twenty-one; what the hell is he thinking? But a moment later, a true gladness spills through me. Lisa is smart and sensible, the most steadying influence he's ever had. She also happens to be Kate's best friend.

"Now that's worth a real drink," I say. "If it was anyone else, I'd tell you you're an idiot. But Lisa, she's special. I'm buying us a round."

I go to the bar to get a pitcher and a shot for each of us, even for Rory, knowing Mick'll turn a blind eye so long as I'm in charge. Back at the table, I lift my glass in a toast. "This is the second piece of good news this week. To the wedding. And Tariq's new leg."

Rory gulps his whiskey, shudders, then follows up with a long swill of beer, eyes back on his phone.

"Put that goddamn thing away!" Pat growls at him. "What's so important, anyway?"

"Business."

"What kind of business?"

"None of yours." Rory looks at me. "Did you say something about a leg?"

I tell them what we learned at the hospital and how happy it made Naema. I don't tell them what a garbagebrain I feel for not knowing about the Medicaid before.

"Wow, poor kid," Rory says. "How old is he again?" Rory has a soft spot for kids.

"Five. Six next month."

"Bet he gets bullied like hell at school. How'd he lose it? Was he born like that, or what?"

"They were in a war, powderhead," Pat tells him.

"Fuck, you're in a bad mood, Pat. Why don't you chill the hell out?"

"It was a VBED," I answer, ignoring them both.

"Speak English, for crap's sake," Rory snaps.

"Means a bomb in a car. We think the fuckwads who did it—"

"Jimmy, you don't have to—" Pat begins.

I hold up my hand. "No, Rory should hear this."

"Don't want to. Hate your gory war stories. Just tell me about the kid."

"I am. We think the fuckwads who did it planted the bomb in the tailpipe of his dad's car and wired the trigger to the door—"

"Which fuckwads?"

"Nobody knows for sure, most likely the Mahdi Army." Rory looks unenlightened. "Muqtada al-Sadr's militia of thugs—Shi'a fundamentalists who want to slaughter all Sunnis and Americans and anyone who works with us." Rory blinks. "Anyhow, that's the bomb that killed Khalil and his dad and tore up Tariq's leg. Scarred Naema's face, too."

"It blew off the kid's leg *and* killed his dad and granddad?" Rory raises his gingery eyebrows. "That's real-life tragedy, man. Is he super screwed up?"

"Not that I can tell. Come meet him. He's cute as a bug. Loves playing soccer."

"How's he do that with one leg?"

"You'll see."

"Were you there when the bomb went off?" Pat asks me then.

"No. Heard about it from a terp called Salim." I rub my eyes again. "Know what I can't stand? When Khalil told me he was getting death threats, I said not to worry. Promised we'd protect him and his family, move them into the Green Zone—I said that, me!"

Soon as I made that promise, I approached my lieutenant, my captain, even my colonel. "We need to move my interpreter's family someplace safe, sir, they're getting threats," I told each one of them. But Command only shook its collective head and said if we did that for one family, then all the terps would want it and the next thing we knew there'd be as many hajjis inside as out and the Green Zone would be so infiltrated we'd lose the war bad. I argued and argued, they stonewalled and stonewalled, till I couldn't even look Khalil in the face.

Pat reaches for my wrist. "Jimmy?"

I stare at his hand a second, shake it off and get up to buy me and Pat another shot. "Tell Lisa congrats," I say when I'm back, setting the glasses on the table. "Can't wait to have her as a sister. Fixed a date yet?"

"Nope. We haven't told her parents or anybody. We wanna keep it under wraps awhile."

"Then why the fuck you tell us?" Rory slurs. My lightweight brother is already well past three sheets to the wind. "And where's my shot?"

I ignore him. "Have the wedding while it's still warm," I say to Pat. "We'll find a tent somewhere. A band, too—maybe your old high school band, Rory." I look hard at Pat. "Did Lisa tell Kate about this?"

He slides his eyes away from me. "No. We hadn't decided yet when they talked." The silence swallows us again. Something makes me suspect that he and

Lisa are hearing more from Kate than he wants me to know. "Another shot?" he asks after a moment. "On me this time?"

"Sure. You can buy all you want now that you're about to become a man. Not for Rory though. He's had enough."

"The hell you think you are?" Rory retorts, the words sliding around in his mouth. "You're not my dad, you're not even a decent brother. Stuffing our house with refugees without even telling us. Fuck you."

"Hey!" Pat objects. "Jimmy worked his ass off to get those people here."

"So what? I wouldn't mind if he'd asked first. But he didn't. Bet he didn't even ask Kate. Probably chased her away so he could get into the mom's pants."

"Don't be disgusting," Pat says before I can.

"Oh yeah? You're the one who told me she's hot."

"I did not!"

"Oh yes you did." Rory snickers and then hiccups. "Said you caught a glimpse of her. Luscious little ass, you said. Big tits. I heard you."

"You lying shithole!" Pat is truly angry now.

"Me? You're the liar here, bro. You said what you said. And you know it."

9

Now that the soldier has finally left us alone in the house for an evening, freeing me at last from the pull of his guilt, I carry a tattered yellow lawn chair out to the stream beside his garden, set it under a willow tree and sit down to breathe.

I brought with me the brochure from Tariq's doctor explaining the types of prostheses and their accoutrements that are available these days, but it is impossible to understand. *Proximal femoral focal deficiency. Fluid swing and stance phase control. Polycentric hydraulic mechanical stance phase lock.* What could all this mean? Even my pocket dictionary cannot tell me; I shall have to ask the soldier if I can look it up on his computer. Still, I can draw hope from the pictures. Children with artificial limbs playing basketball, kicking footballs, running in a park. One is even riding a bicycle.

Leaning back, I gaze up at the willow branches dangling above me like the fringe of a giant parasol. In ancient days, weeping willows like this lined the streets of Babylon, having been imported from China, and before the war they were all over the parks of Baghdad, too, so to me, this tree speaks of my part of the world, of my home and history. How I would love to hear again the song of a nightingale on an evening like this, or watch a stork perched in her nest, clattering her long beak. Here, the only birdcalls I recognize are the chatter of sparrows and the rasping protest of a crow.

Zaki knew the calls of many birds, not only of his pigeons—he loved all animals so. During our holidays with Bibi Maryam, he was always trying to rescue her chickens from slaughter by smuggling them into the house under his shirt, until their kicks and squawks gave him away. He would do that with her baby goats, too. "It looks like you've eaten too much again, Zaki," Bibi would say with a chuckle, poking at the struggling lump beneath his shirt. The American soldiers at Camp Bucca claimed that Zaki had thrown weapons at them and tried to escape. They claimed they shot him because he was dangerous.

I shift in my chair. Better to remember the perfume released by the lemon trees in my Baghdad courtyard every evening, the scent so heavy it made my head reel. Or the call of the muezzins, their unearthly voices rising above the city. Khalil and I were never overtly devout, not like Hibah with her five prayers a day, her devotion to the mosque, but I have always been moved by the muezzin's call. To me, it is not only a call to prayer, but a call uniting all the people of our city, reminding us that there is more to life than commerce or ambition, rivalry or resentment. More to life even than war.

"Our little man is full of questions tonight," Hibah announces when I carry the chair back inside, driven to retreat by gluttonous mosquitos. "He wants a kiss."

I slip behind a bamboo screen to sit beside him; his bed, narrow as it is, still large enough to dwarf him. "Aren't you sleepy, *hayati*?" I stroke his forehead. "Is your leg still hurting?"

"No, that stopped. I'm thinking about my new one. I asked Bibi what it'll be made of but she didn't know. She doesn't know anything."

"Shh, don't talk that way, it's disrespectful. She knows much more than we do but this is a new country to her, as it is to us, and we're all learning. Your leg will be made of something especially strong and light. You'll see."

"Not wood?"

"No, better. I'll show you pictures soon. But no more talking now."

"Can I paint it, Mama? Like when you break your arm and people paint on that hard white bandage thing around it? Remember when Abid's arms were broken? We drew all over his bandages."

"Yes, I remember." Abid, one of Tariq's schoolmates in Baghdad, was walking with his mother to the souk when a mortar hit a building beside them. Abid's arms were crushed, his mother killed.

"Mama, that thing that happened to Abid . . . could that happen to us?"

"No, *habibi*. I told you, remember? We don't have to worry about bombs and mortars here."

He thinks for a moment. "Mama, why doesn't Jim-Jim sleep in this room with us?"

"Because this room is our home and the rest of the house is his."

"But why aren't we all together?"

"Shush. Close your eyes now."

"No, Mama, why?"

"Men and women only sleep in the same room together if they're married."

"Oh." His pointed face turns serious. "Mama, is Jim-Jim a GI?"

"He is. Was. Yes."

Tariq looks worried. "But is he a good GI or a bad GI?"

I hesitate. "A good GI, of course." But even I can hear the uncertainty in my voice. "Now, no more questions until tomorrow. Good night, little moon." I kiss his nose.

"'Night, Mama. I'm glad America doesn't have bombs."

When I step out from behind the screen, I'm surprised to see that Hibah, normally so fastidious, has fallen asleep on her bed in all her clothes. I peer down at her, struck by how sickly she looks lying there, her lips the color of clay, her cheeks sunken, her wrinkled complexion blending into the white of her hair, as though she is disappearing. Alarmed, I pick up her wrist, as frail as a bundle of straws, and feel for her pulse. How will I cope if she falls ill? I need her, just as she, however begrudgingly, needs me. But her heartbeat is regular, breathing steady. Perhaps she is only tired out from war and loss and traveling, for as hard as exile has been on me and Tariq, it is harder for her, the old having so much more to forget and so much less to anticipate. I place her stringy bundle of a hand on her chest and leave her in peace.

It's eight o'clock in the evening, many hours before I will be ready for sleep and the most difficult time of my day, when I am the only one awake, with nowhere to go and no defense against the past. Were I living in my own home, I could seek refuge in a book or television. But here I have no television or books, save for my medical texts, and sitting at the table for hours studying, as I have been doing most nights, is more than I can face right now. True, this room is better than the airless bedroom we shared in Damascus, its windows filthy, its ceiling greased with tobacco smoke, its corners echoing with the cries and quarrels of neighbors. But there, at least, I had friends—other Iraqi widows whom I understood and who understood me. Here, with the evening stretching before me empty and endless, I only feel a yearning for Khalil and a remorse that scrapes at my heart like a knife.

How I wish that we had spent our last hours together in peace rather than in squabbling and resentment—that we had not squandered that precious time. But I was so angry at him. I could not bear the way his work with the Americans had hung targets around all our necks, forcing him to move across town, change his name and live as though he did not know us. For months after my family had fled Baghdad in that first year of war, I had lost track of him, unable to find where he was or whether he was alive, and now he was forcing me to live through that all over again. So the minute I heard him come into the house that evening for one of his rare visits, I started in on him. "I can't live like this any longer," I told him for the umpteenth time, grasping his hands in mine, taking in the weariness that hollowed his cheeks, the pallor under his stubble. He looked as grizzled as a bandit. "I never know if you're alive or dead. I beg you, Khalil—leave this terrible job now!"

He shifted his soft brown eyes away from me, this man I had loved ever since we had been students together, since before the war and the deaths of Baba and Zaki at the hands of the very people he worked for now. "Please don't start this again, *rohi*," he said wearily, pulling his hands away. "You know Sergeant Donnell keeps me safe."

"*Safe*? Are you mad? He's our enemy!"

"Let me be. I need to rest."

"You can rest when you promise to stop working for those murderers."

Khalil grew angry then. "You want me to let you and Tariq starve, is that what you want? And our parents, too? Now I told you, enough!"

For the remainder of that night, we wasted our precious time together lying side by side in bed, refusing even to offer each other the caresses we had both craved for so long. Only when the time came for him to leave the next morning and I was standing in the door watching him go did regret drown my resentment. "Be careful, *habibi*, may Allah protect you," I called after him as he unlocked the outer gate and greeted his father, who was waiting by the car for a ride to the market. And that was the moment Tariq cried, "Baba, wait!" and hurtled into the street.

Feeling too stifled by these memories to stay inside any longer, I leave Hibah and Tariq asleep and walk back out to the garden, a shawl around my shoulders to fend off mosquitos. Dusk has given way to night by now, the swollen belly of a gibbous moon, ghostlike behind a veil of cloud, casting a metallic glow over the grass. A bat flutters its panicked path through the sky and I can just make out two early stars above the wild silhouette of the willow until they move, and I realize they are not stars but fireflies. We don't have fireflies at home—I must let Tariq stay up one night to see them. And then, again, I am overpowered by a longing for Khalil, for the family we once were, for his slow but promising smile, the shelter of his embrace. Three years have passed since his death and still I cannot shake my need to hold him, speak to him, hear his words and breathe his scent; to lie with this man I so loved and who so loved me.

To rescue myself from spiraling once again into this train of thought, I need to move and walk, yet I have little freedom to do even that, having already learned that venturing down the dark and empty roads here at night calls forth furious dogs and the fear of rape and kidnapping I have acquired thanks to war. But seeing no sign of the soldier's return, I can, at least, walk around to the front and look at the house without trepidation.

I am intrigued by this house. The soldier told me it was built as a tavern a century earlier and I can still see remnants of its former elegance beneath its peeling white paint. The forest-green shutters and old brick chimney, the six slender pillars holding up the porch roof, the latticework trimming its edge. I wonder why he and Kate have allowed their home to grow so shabby. The paint is not only peeling but stained. Wasps have woven a home inside the porch lamp, and three shutters are missing from the upstairs windows. Khalil and I would never have let our house decay like this. In Al-Karrada, we kept our rooms and courtyard swept clean, planted lemon and orange trees to perfume our roof, and bougainvillea to blanket our outer walls in a cascade of vermilion petals and feasting butterflies. It was our way of defying bombs.

A car swings up to the curb just then, catching me in its headlights. Realizing how foolish I would look if I ran away, I turn to face it. The lights switch off and the soldier climbs out, clearly as unhappy to see me as I am him, while another man emerges from the passenger seat, a cigarette protruding from the side of his mouth. He looks almost exactly like the soldier—black hair, narrow eyes, high-cheeked face—only smaller and thinner and without eyeglasses.

"Uh, hey, *Oum* T," the soldier calls with unnecessary volume. "This is the brother I told you about, remember? Pat."

"Hello, pleased to meet you," I say unwillingly, the memory of wearing his clothes disabling me from saying more.

"Hi," the brother replies with that American greeting we Arabic speakers find so abrupt. He glances at me with embarrassment before turning away.

The soldier opens the back door and helps a third person out, who, in spite of his height, appears less man than boy. "And this is our baby bro, Rory," the soldier says. "He's had kind of . . . an accident. Rory, meet *Oum* Tariq."

My professional curiosity aroused, I move closer and peer through the darkness at the boy's swollen face. "He has broken his nose?"

"Nope. Pat broke it for me," the boy replies, swaying on his feet. He is thin and gangly, and in opposition to his brothers, his hair is light and his eyes dark. His voice, also, is different, deeper yet more nasal, as if the higher voices of his brothers have migrated to the sinuses behind his now purpling nose.

I step back at the reek of his breath. "He is drunk?" I ask the soldier.

"Maybe. A little, yeah."

"Not my fault," the boy mumbles. "Bros did that, too."

"Put on his face an iced cloth. It will reduce the swelling. And make him drink many glasses of water."

"Will do. Thanks." The soldier pulls the boy's arm over his shoulders and after sending me an awkward smile, helps him across the grass and up the porch steps, the middle brother hurrying after them.

I watch them go a moment before turning back to my apartment. How foreign I am here. How profoundly I do not belong.

10

"Who you?"

The voice wakes Rory, who opens his eyes to find himself lying on Jimmy's couch, head pounding, mouth gluey, staring into the face of a small boy.

"Oh. Hey there." Rory sits up with a groan. "Fuck! Ow. Jesus." Slowly placing his legs on the floor one at a time, he squints at the boy, whose arms are inserted into a pair of elbow-high aluminum crutches and whose left pant leg is rolled up and empty. "You're that kid Jimmy brought over here, right?"

Tariq backs away.

"Listen, squirt, I don't bite, OK? Pass me that water over there, will you? Mouth tastes like a toilet." He points to the side table.

"My name Tariq. No Squirt." Swinging over, Tariq props a crutch against the couch, picks up the glass and hands it to Rory, watching him closely while he drinks. "You who?"

"Rory. Jimmy's brother."

"Why ugly?"

"Who, me?" Rory puts the glass on the floor with a wince. "Got whacked in the nose, that's why." He mimes a fist coming at his face.

Tariq looks scared. "You have bang-bang fight? You bad GI?"

Rory peers around for his boots, which don't seem to be on his feet or anywhere else. "No, not me. Jimmy's the GI around here."

"Uh?"

"My big brother Jimmy." Rory points to the hallway stairs. "Hey, uh, Tariq, go get him, would you? Get GI Jimmy." He mimes running with his fingers. "Can you do that?"

Tariq nods. "Jim-Jim good GI." Grabbing his second crutch, he moves over to the bare wooden staircase and hops up it in a rapid series of loops and swings, Rory gazing after him in no little astonishment.

While he's gone, Rory looks over the room to see if Kate's absence is visible in any way. Her framed prints are still hung all over the pale-yellow walls: flowers, mostly, and forest landscapes. Her computer is still on the desk by the window—he's surprised she left that behind—and her female heaps of red cushions are still smothering the chairs and scattered over the floor where he kicked them off the couch. But the room feels different, somehow. It feels wrong. He looks again . . . the photos are missing, that's it! The ones she kept on the side tables. Her little sister April messing around on a beach, all goofy grin and pigtails. The silver-framed one of the wedding, Kate looking stunned as a kidnapped bride under a bower of roses. The formal portraits of her and Jimmy in their army dress uniforms, staring young, earnest and innocent at the camera. Rory feels a plug lodge at the bottom of his throat.

Pulling out his phone, he dials Sue. He isn't sure what he thinks of Sue yet, having met her only a month earlier, but the evening with his brothers has left him feeling unusually hollowed out and in need of feminine sympathy.

"About frigging time," she answers. "Where the hell is Tom's bike?"

"Uh, I had a little problem last night."

"Shit. You didn't smash it up, did you?"

"No. Just my nose."

"Huh?"

"Got punched."

She laughs, which Rory considers less than kind. "Oh yeah? Who by?"

"Some asswipe. You should see his nose. Still, I look like a squished tomato." She giggles again. "It's true. That's why I couldn't bring the bike back, eyes too puffed up to see."

"Then who is gonna bring it? Tom's mad as a bear."

"I'll get one of my bros to do it." Rory pauses. He can hear her chomping gum. "What're you doing today?"

"Nothing. Chores for Mom. Boring as fuck. Wish I had a job like yours."

"My job's not so great. Listen, wanna get together tonight?"

"What, with a squished tomato?"

"It's not that bad. So?"

"Maybe." She yawns. "Call me later."

Rory hangs up feeling hollower than ever. Heaving himself to his feet with a wince, he hobbles to the downstairs toilet and peers in the mirror. Tariq has a point; his face is truly unnerving. Eyes swollen and ringed in black. Nose the colors of a baboon butt. Sue will never go for him looking like this. He feels a fresh surge of anger at Pat. Even Jimmy, with all his army bullshit, has never hit him.

After a long piss and a short wash, Rory removes a laptop charger from his back pocket and cracks it open along the seam to get at the stash of small round pills inside. Tossing one into his mouth, he grimaces at its bitter taste, snaps the charger closed and checks his phone. Plenty of time for the pill to mellow him out while he eats breakfast and waits for one of his brothers to trade the motorbike back for his car. Then, once his eyes have cleared, he'll return the charger to the box of other doctored chargers he has hidden behind the old VCR at home and then drive that box to Hudson, all of which will move him one step closer to getting as far away as he can from this loser town and his loser brothers. Forever.

He emerges from the bathroom just as Jimmy comes running down the stairs, barefoot and unshaven, Tariq hovering on the top step behind him. Rory tenses, expecting the boy to pitch forward at any moment and land in a heap of broken bones. But Tariq only places his crutches two steps below him and swoops, repeating the motion so fast he flies down with no trouble at all.

"How's the schnoz this morning?" Jimmy says. "Want some coffee?"

Rory lowers himself gingerly back onto the couch and tips his head up as if he's gargling. "Yeah. Percocet, too. Zoloft, Valium—whatever you got. Feels like a hippo stomped on it."

"I'll get you some Tylenol. You met Tariq here, I see."

"Yup. Told me I'm butt ugly."

"You are. It's a sight to see."

"I know. Looked in the mirror."

"Listen," Jimmy says then. "You were an asshole last night but Pat shouldn't have hit you like that."

"Well, he did. And you didn't stop him. Where is he anyway?" Rory's head is still tilted back.

"Up in his room."

"Why aren't I in my room?"

"'Cause you are too big to carry around like a baby. You going to work today? Won't be too appetizing for the customers."

"Have to."

"They cut your pay if you don't show?"

"'Course. Slave-fucking-labor."

Jimmy is tempted to embark on his that's-why-you-should-finish-high-school-and-go-to-college lecture, but for once he refrains. "Well, come get some breakfast. And watch the profanities, will you? There's a kid here."

Fifteen minutes later, the three brothers are sitting around the kitchen table, each disheveled and hungover in his own way, eating the eggs Jimmy fried up for them and drinking enough coffee to drown a cow. Tariq, perched on his own chair at one end of the table, is thrilled to find himself among men for a change, swaddled in their peppery scents of whiskers, tobacco and sweat. Although his memories of his father have fragmented to mere moments—the sound of a laugh, the brush of a bristled cheek, the occasional ache inside him like a hunger—the brothers' presence is awakening in him a long-forgotten sense of being cushioned by something large and reassuring and safe. It makes him, for the moment, deeply happy.

"Sue said if I don't get the bike back to her brother today, he's gonna slice off my balls and have 'em on toast," Rory says, chewing his own toast gingerly. He feels better now, thanks to the pill. "Can one of you do it and then take me to work? Can't see enough to drive."

"And I need to get my truck from McGrath's," Patrick adds.

"OK, I'll drive you both over there after breakfast and we can figure it out," Jimmy says. "Better not show our mugs inside for a while, though. Mick isn't too pleased with us."

Rory glowers at Patrick. "I can't believe you did this to me, dipshit. You owe me big."

"You asked for it. But yeah, maybe I shouldn't've jumped you."

Rory waits for Jimmy to order Pat to offer a better apology than that, but Jimmy only resumes eating. He never comes through. Look at all those times Rory and Pat were forced to visit their mother in the psych ward while Jimmy was away at war, Rory sad and scared in the waiting room, Aunt Maureen saying, "Now don't expect too much. Your mom's been having a rough spell lately." Their mother shuffling in, body swollen, hair lank, eyes rheumy, staring at them like she'd never seen them before.

Rory looks over at Tariq, his nose only just level with his plate of eggs. "Hey, squirt, don't you want the rest of your toast?"

"No. Nutpea!"

"What's the little bastard saying now?" Rory asks with a chuckle.

"Don't call him that." Jimmy stands to open the fridge. "It's how he says peanut butter. Eats it like candy. That and potato chips."

"Awesome." Rory helps himself to Tariq's toast. "You're turning into a regular American dude, aren't you, squirt?"

Tariq beams. "Me *Amareekye*." Jimmy hands him a spoon filled with Skippy's. He sucks on it eagerly.

"You're brainwashing him," Patrick remarks. "What about being sensitive to his culture and all that? Aren't you supposed to be, like, feeding him dates and bananas or whatever they eat over there?"

"Are you trying to make me puke?" Rory objects to bananas. He considers them stinky and obscene.

Jimmy collects the plates, which happen to be Kate's favorite, inherited from her Irish grandmother, white with a rim of tiny green shamrocks. He usually keeps them in the dining room for special occasions that never happen, so how they got into the kitchen cabinet he doesn't know. Hibah or Naema must have moved them in one of their frequent fits of tidying.

"Listen, doofuses, help me clear up this mess so we can get going," he says. Patrick stands. Rory stays put.

"I'd help but . . ." He gestures at his body and shrugs.

"You busted a nose, not a leg," Jimmy reminds him. "OK, whatever. Keep Tariq busy while I get washed." But he's pleased the boy seems to have taken to his brother. The fact that Rory is almost tolerable when he isn't drunk or showing off gives Jimmy hope.

He's halfway up the stairs when he hears a knock. Seeing Naema's small figure through the glass of the front door, he comes back down and opens it a crack, struck again by how graceful she looks in her own clothes, this time blue jeans and a simple white tunic. Her hair is in a different style, too, this morning, braided in a coil around her head. It makes him wish he'd at least taken the time to shave and put on a clean T-shirt. "Tariq's just finishing up breakfast," he tells her. "Want me to send him out?"

"Yes. Please."

"You need me to drive you anywhere today?" He steps onto the porch, closing the door behind him to shield her from Rory and Patrick. "I'm free if you do. Just have to shower and run my brothers somewhere first."

She considers a moment. "Very well. Perhaps, if *Oum* Khalil, she is feeling well enough, we could, I don't know . . ." She sweeps her hand vaguely over the distance.

"Do a little sightseeing?"

"My mother-in-law, she would like that, yes." Naema peers around Jimmy's bulk. "Hello, Mr. Donnell. Your nose, how is it this morning?"

Rory is standing in the door, which is wide open now, his hand on Tariq's head. To Naema, Rory looks more boyish and unkempt than ever, with his skinny legs, unruly hair and gruesome array of bruises. His eyes, now that she can see him in daylight, are the exact gingery copper of his hair.

"Nose good, thanks. Well, maybe not. Hurts like hell."

"Yes, it will hurt for some time. But this injury, it is not serious."

"*Oum* Tariq's a doctor," Jimmy explains.

"Oh yeah?" Rory appraises her. "So you think I'll be OK? Won't look like I got a smashed tomato in the middle of my face forever?"

She smiles, a surprising pair of dimples appearing on either side of her mouth. "You will be fine."

"You got a cool kid here," Rory says then, his mood improved, ushering Tariq through the door.

Tariq looks up at him, swaying between his crutches. "Uncle Ugly!"

"Enough of that now. See you soon, Nutpea."

"How soon?"

Rory glances at Jimmy. "Depends on GI Jim-Jim here. Ask him."

After restoring his brothers to their respective vehicles, Jimmy drives Naema and her family through the hardscrabble countryside for more than an hour, past tumbledown farms, collapsing barns and weed-blown fields, the collateral damage of a defeated local economy. He is taking them to North Lake, a forest reserve high in the Catskill Mountains that he and Kate have always loved, full of evergreens, bears, and soul-cleansing views. Only the previous summer, while the two of them were hiking deep in the woods there, no one around, she gave him a sultry look, pulled off her shorts and knelt on all fours among the pinecones, inviting him to her. He grows hard at the memory. *Please*, he pleads with her in his head, *please don't do that with anyone else.*

At the lake, he helps Tariq out of the car, while Naema does the same for Hibah, and then he leads them all to a small beach of gray sand and mud. They stand in a silent row to look, Jimmy relieved at being able to show them a side of his country that has nothing to do with economic wastelands or xenophobic bumper stickers. The water stretches out before them, glossy and black, its surface crimping in a breeze, the surrounding hills cupping it like a vast pair of hands. Buzzards circle above like choppers. Gulls swoop over the water with predatory grace. A family of Canada geese plods by on the sand, much to Tariq's delight, leaving a trail of fat green droppings.

"Sometimes you can see eagles here." Jimmy takes off his sunglasses and squints into the sky. "Bald eagles. You've probably seen pictures. Symbol of the USA."

He realizes he sounds like a Boy Scout but Naema seems interested, peering up at the sky with him. "We have eagles also in Iraq. Only ours, they are called Golden. We have storks, as well, and the hoopoe, King Solomon's messenger and the leader of all birds. Did you ever see the hoopoe while you were there, Sergeant? It is a wonderful creature, like a clown and an angel all in one."

"Huh, no. I hardly saw any birds when I was there. 'Cept for vultures. Kate used to wonder where they all went. She's crazy for birds."

"Your bombs, Sergeant, they killed many of our birds." Naema turns to look at him. "But speaking of your wife, where is she? You said you would explain. But you have not."

Jimmy slides his sunglasses back on. "There's a great view near here. I think Tariq and *Oum* Khalil can manage the walk—it's pretty flat." He's been dreading this question. But he knew it had to come. "I'll tell you on the way."

"Wait." She gestures at Tariq, who is trying to cross the beach to the water, struggling as his crutches sink into the muddy sand. Teetering, he lowers himself now and then to pick up a pebble or a shell. They watch him doing what children have done for millennia but having to labor so hard to do it. "If my Tariq, he can truly have the leg that doctor promised, this will not be so difficult for him." Naema presses her lips into a seam.

"*Oum* Khalil, would you like to sit?" he asks the old lady then. "There's a bench over there." He points to make his meaning clear. She frowns, muttering in Arabic.

"She does not wish to sit," Naema tells him. "She says she is content to stand and watch Allah give her grandson a moment's pleasure." Jimmy swallows. Reprimanded again.

Naema looks up at him. "So. Kate?"

Pulling off his sunglasses once more, he polishes them on his T-shirt. "There's not much I can say." He sucks in a breath. "She took off about three weeks before you came. Don't know why or where. Now I can't get hold of her." He pauses. "I'm sorry. I know you counted on her being here."

Naema folds her arms over her chest, her white tunic gleaming in the sun, her eyes fixed on him. "Tell me, Sergeant, why did you and your wife sponsor us to come here to America? And why did you bring us to your house? Are we—how to say—your path to make yourselves feel better? Your *atonement*?" She almost spits the word.

"Of course not!" He darts her a look of true shock. "We did it for Khalil. For you. Because I promised, because I owe . . ." He stops, silenced by the sorrow in her face. And then he says the only thing he knows to say. "Khalil was like a brother to me, *Oum* Tariq, and he made you feel like my sister. One day, I hope you'll feel that way, too."

She gazes at him with contempt. Then walks down the beach to join Tariq.

Hibah, who has been unable to follow the conversation but certainly feels its tension, decides to absent herself and succumb to the bench after all. Leaving Jimmy hovering uncertainly behind her, she hobbles over and settles down with a grunt. Ever since she landed in this brash, incomprehensible land, she has felt drained of strength, her limbs increasingly unwilling to do her bidding, just as her belly refuses to let her eat. For three years she forced herself to be stalwart, to put aside the devastation of having lost her husband and son in one blow for the sake of her grandson. But now that he is safe, far from bombs and starvation and terror, her will has drained away. Without Yasir, her husband of fifty years, who had grown to feel like part of her body; without her one and only child, whom she had loved with the strength of twenty mothers; without her home and her history, she can find no point to anything. Not even, may Allah forgive her, prayers.

Shifting on the hard wooden seat, her bones sharp and aching, she watches the sergeant pacing in front of her and wonders who his mother was, for a mother is the key to the truth of a man. She can tell that he is gentle, fighter though he might have been, and she knows her son loved him dearly, but she was singularly unimpressed by what she saw of his brothers that morning. Her guess is that their mother either left or died when those brothers were young, which is why they never learned better grooming or manners. Did Sergeant Donnell ever talk about such matters with Khalil? Was her son truly that close to him, this man for whom he died? Acid fills her mouth.

To distract herself from the strangling grief brought on by these thoughts, she moves her attention to the view: a dirty beach, a triangular lake and low, uninteresting hills fuzzed with trees. The sergeant said these are called the Catskill Mountains but mountains they certainly are not. Hibah knows mountains. In Damascus, she and Naema lived under the Qasioun Mountain—the very mountain that split in half to swallow Cain after he murdered his brother Abel. And as a child, Hibah often visited her mother's family village in the mountains of Kurdistan, craggy, snow-blanketed peaks that cut into the heavens with a majesty that puts these little lumps to shame. She closes her eyes, riding again up the steep and winding trails on the back of her donkey, the rhythmic sway of its step, the tinkle of its bridle bells, the gentle chafe of the blanket that served as a saddle, the murmur of her parents talking beside her . . .

Seeing that Hibah has fallen asleep, Jimmy forces himself to stop pacing in front of her and join Naema and Tariq, who are crouched on the damp beach together, building a sandcastle. Why he feels compelled to guard Hibah like a sentry he isn't sure, unless it's only that he doesn't know what else to do with himself.

"Look, Jim-Jim!" Tariq points proudly to the hump of sand by his knee. Jimmy squats beside it. It resembles no castle he has ever seen. It's more like a cake box with a ramp stuck to its front.

"This is supposed to be the Great Ziggurat of Ur," Naema says, seeing the ignorance on his face. She stands, brushing the sand off her jeans. "Ur was built more than two thousand years ago by the Sumerian Empire. The prophet Abraham, he was born there. You do not know of this from your Bible, Sergeant Donnell?"

Jimmy has never read the Bible. Kate went to church all her life, but the religious education of Jimmy and his brothers was entirely neglected by everyone except Aunt Maureen, who dragged them to her local church exactly twice before swearing she would never take such badly-behaved boys anywhere near a place of worship again. The name Ur does sound familiar, though, and even Jimmy has heard of Abraham.

"Is it near Nasiriyah?"

"It is. We used to take our holidays there when I was a child."

And then he remembers—it's next to Camp Adder, where some of his buddies were based. Some said the ziggurat resembled a fortress, others an alien spaceship from the time of dinosaurs and pyramids. Quite a few of his comrades possessed a pretty shaky sense of history. But the religious among them were awed.

"That's real cool, buddy," Jimmy says to Tariq. "Ready to come see the view now?"

"Ready!"

Naema helps Tariq up, dusting him off quickly. He looks dubiously at the sand.

"Want me to carry you?" Jimmy asks gently.

Tariq hesitates, then nods. Jimmy lifts him onto his back like a rucksack so he won't feel too much of a baby and carries him over to the parking lot, where he can put him on solid ground. Naema wakes Hibah, who has crumpled into a small black heap on the bench.

The view Jimmy plans to show them is only a few hundred yards away, across a grassy playground and down a trail through the woods, but before they've been walking for even five minutes, Hibah is clicking her tongue and panting.

"Sergeant," Naema says, "how much longer?"

"About fifteen minutes. There a problem?"

"I think *Oum* Khalil, she cannot walk so far. I will return her to the bench. She says she is willing to wait there."

"But you'll come back?"

She remains silent a moment, her eyes scanning the woods. "Yes," she says at last. "I shall."

While she's gone, Tariq catches sight of a chipmunk sitting upright on a log, its tiny body on high alert, glossy eyes fixed and wary. "Oooh, want!" he cries, just as it flashes away in a blur of stripes. Jimmy pretends to chase it, clowning at tripping over branches. It hurts his neck but at least it makes the kid laugh.

When Naema returns, they continue along the trail, Jimmy in front and Tariq between them, weaving through a scrubby landscape of pitch pine, spruce and laurel bushes, the mossy ground strewn with pale gray boulders, some as flat as stepping stones, others towering over their heads. The sun streams through the trees, dropping to the forest floor in a series of golden pools, gilding a leaf here, a fern there. When a wood thrush breaks into song, serenading them from its hiding place, its call echoing and melodic, Naema stops and raises her head. "What is that?"

Jimmy tells her. "It doesn't look like much, though. Just another little brown bird."

"Our nightingales, they also are drab but have a beautiful song." Naema runs her hand along a tree trunk, caressing the soft velvet of the moss clinging to its side. She will confess nothing to the soldier, but this is the first moment she has spent in nature since she fled Iraq, and she can feel her breath expanding, as if a band of steel has been loosened from around her chest.

Tariq takes the lead this time, picking his way carefully over roots and stones, his twiggy limbs and hopping motion reminding Jimmy of a cricket. Their progress is slow, not only because Tariq has to take such care with his crutches, but because he's fascinated by every twisted tree trunk and flower, insect, mushroom, squirrel and chipmunk, each of which he asks Jimmy to name.

Eventually, they reach a steep escarpment of angular brown rocks that Jimmy had forgotten about. Hibah never could have climbed this. "Can you make it up?" he asks Naema. "I'll help Tariq."

She waves the question away. So Jimmy swings the boy onto his back again, tucking his crutches under an arm, and leaps up the wall of rocks, while she, being smaller, has to use her hands and sometimes a knee. When he was Tariq's age, Jimmy thinks with a pang, he would have been able to scamper up these rocks like a mouse.

At the top, Naema emerges panting and flushed, her coil of braid disheveled, golden eyes bright. She's enjoying this, Jimmy realizes, and for the first time he sees that she's as pent-up as he, trapped in his house day after day, having to move at the pace of a one-legged child and a cranky old woman.

He carries Tariq for a few minutes more until they reach the clearing he's been aiming for, a narrow shelf of granite jutting out from the top of a dizzyingly high cliff. Far below, a nubby blanket of green forest, patched by fields and houses and ribboned by roads, stretches to the horizon. Vultures spiral beneath them, bare heads poking from their necks like skinned thumbs.

"*While the vultures of war feed upon the flesh of their young / prepare a pall and a funeral, Mother, for me / the dead man at your breast*," Naema murmurs. "My father, he wrote this. He wrote many poems about vultures."

Jimmy can't think how to respond. "You can see five states from here," is the best he can come up with, addressing Tariq, still clinging to his back. "And that river over there?" He points to the silvery line meandering across the middle distance. "That's the Hudson. Runs all the way down to the city and the ocean." Why the hell is he trying to sound like a tour guide?

"Jim-Jim, put down me," Tariq demands. Jimmy complies, handing him his crutches.

"Careful!" Naema grips Tariq's shoulders but he is too excited to listen. Jerking out of her hands, he swings forward much too fast and far, catapulting perilously near the edge.

"Watch out!" Jimmy yelps, grabbing him by the shirt and yanking him back. A sickening lurch of vertigo twists up his spine, a sensation he has never before felt in his life.

Naema gathers Tariq to her, shaken. "Thank you," she says after a moment, looking directly up at Jimmy, her eyes soft with relief. "Thank you so much, Sergeant. May Allah reward you."

For the first time since she arrived, he feels a skip of hope.

11

"So, tell me the truth, Ali. You think this'll make her feel better or worse?"

Jimmy handed his letter to Khalil, who pushed down the sand-encrusted *shemagh* hiding his face to take what breath he could through the hot dust in the air. He darted a cautious look around him. They were posted at a snap checkpoint west of the Tigris that morning, a tangled intersection of thread-thin streets and blind alleyways. Khalil had once thought this district of Baghdad quaint, even poetic, with its ancient yellow and pink houses, especially in contrast to the stark concrete apartment blocks that had taken over so much of the rest of the city. But now it only seemed sinister.

Wiping off the sweat pooling beneath his sun goggles, he squinted down at the letter, barely able to make it out under the flash and dazzle of the sun. He knew his friend had stayed up most of the night to write it, struggling to find the right words. If there were any right words.

"Dear Mrs. Muller, I am Staff Sergeant James Donnell, your husband's squad leader. I was in the Humvee with him when he was killed."

Khalil looked over at Jimmy, his pale face sun-scorched and glossed with sweat, his eyes hidden behind his own goggles. "That, Sergeant, is perhaps a little too blunt. Can you not find a more gentle word than 'killed'?"

Jimmy yanked at the collar of his body armor, which, in the 110-degree heat, pulled on him with the weight of a lead barrel. "It's not like she won't know. Ghoul Squad must've knocked on her door by now. Got a better suggestion?"

Khalil scanned the intersection once more, then read on.

"I can't say how sorry I am that this happened to Jack. He was a good man, a true friend and a great soldier. He talked all the time about you and the kids. Please let

me know if I can do anything for you or your family. I mean this from the bottom of my heart.

"Yours, SS Donnell."

"No, this letter, it is good." Khalil handed it back, touched. "But it will make her cry."

Jimmy folded it gingerly, his fingers still blistered and scabbed from the IED burns, and tucked it into his utility vest. "Hope not. I suck at this kind of thing, to be honest."

"Sergeant, it is fine. And it is good you write a real letter and not an email. What is not fine is that this man with eight children—a kind man—he is the one who dies."

"Yeah. Whose fucked-up idea was war anyhow?"

Both knew better than to mention Khalil's premonition about Muller's photographs.

Pulling out a pack of smokes, Jimmy offered one to Khalil and they each lit up, edging into the knife of shade offered by their blast wall, a towering concrete barrier blocking traffic from much of the intersection. Khalil pushed up his helmet and wiped his brow again, once more running his eyes over the stone buildings and elaborately carved wooden balconies hanging from their walls like baskets. Some leaned so far out over the street that they all but kissed in the middle, turning the passageways below into a network of long, dark tunnels. Ragged children spilled out of one, a group of loud young men in shirtsleeves from another.

"Sergeant, I do not have a good feeling about this place."

Jimmy glanced around. "Me neither. It's a fucking killbox."

Khalil peered into the shadows again, his eyes confused by the shimmering stripes of shade and sun. Catching something in the corner of his vision, he squinted intently into the darkness. A glint in a window, once, twice, three times, followed instantly by a glimmer across from it.

"Signal!" he barked, and the two men dropped to the ground, crushing out their cigarettes. Khalil grabbed his binoculars. Jimmy shouldered his rifle, gesturing at Bean and Kalinski, the lump of a kid who had replaced Muller, to take cover behind the team's Humvee. The children and young men scattered, leaving the street suddenly empty. Never a good sign.

A long stretch of silence, of held breath and fervent prayer, the air trembling and then falling still, while Khalil and the soldiers waited for the moment to resolve into either deadly pandemonium or nothing at all.

"Perhaps it was only the sun," Khalil murmured, raising himself to his elbows. "A reflection, I think . . ." But before he could finish his sentence, Jimmy flung himself on top of him, slamming him to the ground, bullets screaming around their ears.

12

"Mama," I say to Hibah, who is peering at me sourly from her bed, "what do you think I should wear?" I am standing at the door of our lopsided green wardrobe, surveying my paltry collection of clothes, for the day has finally come when I have my first job interviews in this country. Two of them, in fact, both at nearby hospitals. One is for a medical secretary. The other, the one I truly want, for a physician's assistant.

"How should I know?" Hibah snaps. "The women here look half-naked most of the time. Just make sure you are decent."

At home, I knew how to dress for interviews like this, just as I knew the signals of class and clan, whom to bribe, whom to ignore and whom to impress. But here I know none of these rules. Should I be in a feminine skirt or masculine trousers? Or should I wear the kind of professional suit worn by that young Indian woman in the Refugee Center, the likes of which I do not own? Hibah's opinion is useless, yet it would be much too immodest to ask the soldier for advice on such a personal matter. If Kate Brady were here, as she promised, I could have asked her.

I am worried about what I said to the soldier about himself and Kate. Khalil would have been deeply upset if he heard me speaking to his friend like that. He would have wanted me to see nothing but virtue in the man, to trust him as he had. "Why do you care for this soldier so much?" I asked him once. "Why do you keep insisting that you love him like a brother?"

Khalil set his glass down on the carpet—we were drinking tea during one of his rare visits home. "Trusting each other in battle forms a bond deeper than you can know, *ayuni*."

"Deeper than yours with me?" I knew I sounded jealous, and I was. The war had made my husband a fighter while keeping me a civilian. It had given him a brother while taking my own.

"Not deeper. Just different."

"Are you saying you love him because you saved each other's lives? That isn't love, it's gratitude."

Khalil pushed his hands through his curls, an old habit. He was dressed in a white dishdasha that day, which set off the shadows circling his eyes, the week-long beard hiding his face. He had taken this job only seven months earlier and it had already aged him a decade. Yet, to me, he was still beautiful.

"I can't expect you to understand what I feel, Naema. I only ask you to believe me when I say that Jimmy has a heart as white as a child's. He's trying to be as just as he can in the face of war. I've seen it."

I rested my head on Khalil's shoulder. He always saw kindness in others when it was only his own reflected back at him. "If your soldier's as noble as you say," I replied, "then why did he choose to become a killer?"

And yet in that same soldier's house these three years later, I do wish that I could feel as grateful to him for rescuing us as Hibah does. I know how hard he worked to win us visas, pleading with his general for support, writing to some thirty members of Congress, filling out forms, calling senators, saving and sending money, filling out more forms. But the anger inside me refuses to burn out. These Americans murdered half my family, and even though it was probably the Mahdi who killed Khalil and maimed Tariq, the Mahdi never would have held such power if it hadn't been for the American invasion. And they never would have targeted Khalil had he not been hired by his beloved Jimmy.

Stop, I tell myself. *You can't go to a job interview steeped in such thoughts. They will be able to tell.*

In Damascus, a doctor suggested that I take medications to blunt this anger of mine, as well as to help me sleep without dreams. I refused. Certainly, those dreams filled my nights with terror and awoke me with screams for months, as they often still do. Dreams of Zaki throwing himself at my feet, begging for his life. Of raptors swooping down to feast on my son's amputated leg. Of soldiers rising like corpses from graves to seize Khalil and drag him away. But I believe that one must endure these ordeals in order to master one's memories. Drugging oneself into oblivion surely only makes the horror fester until it bursts forth in even more destructive forms. No, I had wanted no medications then and I want none now.

The doctor offered drugs to Tariq as well. Antidepressants, sleeping pills, anxiety medication. All for a child of three. "My son has no need of your drugs," I told that doctor firmly. "All he needs is love, time, and my strength."

Love, time, and my strength. For the first two years of Tariq's life, I had little but these to give him, those being the years of almost no food and even less money, of war and suicide bombers, occupiers and resisters. After Khalil had finally found me at Bibi Maryam's house in Umm Qasr, having searched for many months, we moved back to Baghdad so he could practice as a doctor, for unlike me, he had been able to finish his degree while we were apart. But finding work that paid enough to live on had become impossible by then, so even though he spent days and nights tending to the wounded, he came home with little to show for it but exhaustion and despair. All of us were hungry those days, Khalil's father and mother, Mama, myself, but especially baby Tariq. And then, just as we were losing hope, Khalil's friend Salim appeared at our house and told us about Sergeant Donnell. "He wants to hire you as his interpreter," he said to Khalil. "He'll pay you twice as much as you earn now. That's what I get."

"Allah is great, but why me?" my husband asked, astonished. "I'm not an interpreter, I'm a doctor."

"I don't know why. But I told him you speak English. Also, he asked if I know your wife."

"Why did he ask that?" I interjected in alarm.

Salim was a small, slight man with long-lashed eyes, a nose as arched as a protractor and a heart as gentle as a kitten's. He was a good friend to us both. He turned to me. "Because, *Oum* Tariq, he says he's married to a woman you know."

"I don't know any American women. Your sergeant is spinning you lies, Salim."

"Forgive me, but he says you and his wife met at that American prison where your father and brother were held, may Allah have mercy on their souls. And that this wife asked the sergeant to find you and see if you or your family need help. Her name is . . ." Salim pulled a piece of paper from his pocket. "Kate Brady."

Kate Brady and Jimmy Donnell. Angels of deliverance. Harbingers of death.

I finally choose trousers, my black ones, with a matching jacket and a white shirt. None are new or elegant but they are the best I have. Wrapping my hair into a coil at the back of my neck, I fasten it with a clip of Turkish silver, a present from Khalil. I own no other jewelry but my wedding ring, having sold it all during our lean years in Damascus. I line my eyes in kohl but there is nothing

I can do about my scar. I only hope the interviewers won't be put off by it. To me, it doesn't matter—I have lost all interest in looking attractive. Yet I can't help but flinch when people stare at it, just as I cannot inure myself to the way they stare at Tariq.

Once I'm finished, I survey the results in the mirror screwed crookedly to the back of the bathroom door. I have no idea what I look like: A competent professional? A shabby immigrant? Or merely a disfigured refugee?

When I join the soldier by his car, I once more climb into the back. No doubt he thinks that I am treating him as a chauffeur, but I am not about to explain Iraqi propriety to him when he should have understood it long ago, just as I was not pleased at having to explain the history of Ur, which only happens to be one of the most famous landmarks in Iraq. How he remains so ignorant about my country after having spent seven long years waging war upon us is beyond my comprehension.

"So, you ready for the big moment?" he says as he pulls the car away.

I look at the expanse of his broad back, the thick neck, the shoulders like the haunches of a bull. "I am . . . what is it you say? Full of butterflies."

"You'll be fine. Wanna practice?"

I clasp my hands to stop myself pulling at my fingers, that nervous tic I picked up from Mama. "Very well."

"OK, here goes. 'Good morning, Mrs. Jassim.' That's probably what they'll call you. 'How are you today?'"

"Can you please get to the difficult part? We have not much time."

"Oh. OK, sure. How's this: 'Mrs. Jassim, can you tell me what experience you've had in this field?'"

"Yes, certainly, sir. I—"

"I wouldn't call them sir. We don't do that much outside the military and it sounds, well, kind of subservient for a job interview. Plus, you might get a female."

"Then how am I to address them?"

"Whatever they call themselves, I guess. Or just leave it out."

"I see. Is this more correct? 'Yes, certainly. I finished top of my class in medical college in Iraq—'"

"Uh, maybe it's better not to mention Iraq right up front, y'know?"

This is discouraging but I try again. "I am a pediatrician by profession but because of the emergencies of war, I have also brought many babies into life—"

"Um."

"Yes?"

"Never mind. Go on."

"And I have letters from American soldiers to prove that my husband, who is deceased . . ." My voice runs away for a moment. "Letters to prove that my husband worked for the US military. I also have here in my file the papers from the general in charge commending him . . . Sergeant, I need to stop."

"Don't worry, you did great. They'll hire you for sure."

After he drops me off at the hospital, an enormous cliff of a building striped with windows that flash in the sun, I walk in clinging, as always, to my handbag full of documents. In front of me stands a tall podium, behind which a thin, coffee-colored man with a gray mustache as skimpy as an eyebrow and small, circular glasses is reading a paperback. On his uniform is pinned a metal badge printed with the word *Security*. I wait in front of him for permission to talk.

He gazes at me without speaking for so long I become anxious. Finally, he says, "Hi there, sweetheart, something I can do for you?"

This mode of address takes me aback, especially coming from an official and an elderly one at that, but I press on. "I am looking please for the employment office. I am here to be interviewed."

"Sure. It's down the hallway there to the left." He jerks his thumb over his shoulder, scribbles something on a piece of paper and hands it to me. It is sticky on the back. "Put it on your lapel." He moves his hand towards my breasts. I jump back.

"Hey, I didn't mean to scare you." He peers at me over his glasses. "You speak English, sweetheart?"

"I do."

His face shows skepticism but he repeats himself slowly. "Put the sticker here." He pats his own shoulder. "Then go down the hall—"

"Yes, yes, I understand." I hurry away, flushing. I have never heard the word "lapel" before.

I pass many doors with words on them I know—Radiology, Financial Office, OBGYN—and two others I don't, TTY and Human Resources. But I see nothing that reads Employment Office. It's almost the time of my appointment, so I return reluctantly to the man who called me sweetheart.

"Can't get enough of me, huh?"

"I'm sorry, but I cannot find the employment door."

"You didn't see Human Resources? It's right there on the left, just around the corner, like I said. OK, sweets?"

I thank him, disconcerted. I thought resources were minerals, land and money, not humans.

The waiting room, a corporate cube painted a dull brownish yellow, is so crowded that people are leaning against the back wall. Asians, Africans, whites, even three women in hijab are here, two of whom look older than Hibah. I hope they are not all seeking the same job as I am. From both the news and the soldier, I gather that even though I arrived in America at a time when it has its first president of African descent and is supposedly full of new hope, it is also a time of economic depression and a severe shortage of jobs.

Disheartened, I find a chair hidden behind an enormous urn of water, only to notice yet more applicants coming in and stopping at a desk on the side. Realizing I must have to register in some way, I join them, but by the time I return, my chair has been taken, so I prop myself in a corner and study my résumé for courage. Surely my medical degree, my years of experience as a doctor, my letters from both the soldier and his general praising Khalil's service and confirming my status as a deserving immigrant—surely all this will raise me above this crowd.

Forty long minutes later, I am finally called, relieved to see that the interviewer who ushers me through the door is, indeed, a woman. Aged about forty-five, she is tall, thickly built and as white as an egg, with yellow hair gathered into a bun and small brown eyes heavily laden with makeup. She is wearing a beige skirt tight enough to embrace her entire behind, matching high heels, and a tailored pink blouse fastened at the neck by a large and floppy bow. I glance down at my own outfit. Trousers bagged out at my knees. Jacket bald at the elbows.

"I'm Mimi." Her voice is high and loud. "Please sit." She shakes my hand, her eyes tracing my scar. Pointing at a chair, she takes her own behind a wide metal desk, its surface bare but for one file, and plucks a packet of mint chewing gum from her purse, offering me a piece. I decline. Popping one into her mouth, she commences to chew on it with the squelching sound of a masticating goat. "Résumé?" She pats the empty desktop.

I lay my résumé in front of her, hoping she doesn't notice the trembling of my hand. She skims it quickly and then leans back in her swivel chair, chomping. "So, tell me about yourself."

I draw in a breath, trying again not to pull at my fingers, and launch into the speech I practiced in the car.

She interrupts. "This résumé says you're from Iraq." She pronounces it "eye-rack," as do most Americans I meet, even the soldier; a harsh quack of a sound that makes me feel more of an exile than ever. "Is that for real?"

"Pardon?"

"You really from Eye-rack?"

"I am, yes."

She stares at me. "But you've got no secretarial experience, right? No office experience?"

"No. I was a physician, not a secretary."

"Well, good for you. Can you do PowerPoint and Excel?"

I have no idea what she is saying. "I have the experience to work in pediatrics or obstetrics," I reply hurriedly. "I shall take the American exams when I can, so I can practice here, too, but meanwhile the doctors, I could help—"

"OK, thank you." She stands up. "Nice to meet you, Mrs. . . . um. I'll keep your résumé on file, just in case. Bye-bye."

At Saint Peter's hospital, a large and gloomy building that looks more like a prison for the criminally insane than a place of healing, my interview goes much the same. They are not interested in my medical qualifications, Khalil's service to the military or even the general's letter of support. They want only to see a physician's assistant degree from an accredited US college, which of course I do not have, and references from my Medical College professors, which I also cannot provide, as all my teachers have been murdered, imprisoned or exiled. Afterwards, the only words I can find to say to the soldier when he meets me in the parking lot are, "I have not the right skills. I shall have to aim lower."

"Damn, I'm sorry." He looks stricken. "Here, this might help." He hands me a box containing a new mobile phone. "Could make finding a job easier, y'know?"

"But I cannot afford this."

"Don't worry, I'll cover it. Got a cheap deal. Now you don't have to keep borrowing mine."

I climb into the rear of the car, battling my pride again. "I shall pay you back as soon as I am able. And I must learn more about computers, if you would teach me. I am badly out of date."

"Happy to." He slides into the driver's seat.

I hesitate. "This is kind of you, Sergeant." I can, at least, offer that.

"No problem." He twists around to face me. "But do me a favor, would you? Call me Jimmy. Please?"

PART II

13

On the morning of Tariq's sixth birthday, Hibah startles Naema by slamming her tea glass down on their tiny apartment table and announcing that she has made a decision. She intends, she explains in a tone that precludes all discussion, to honor her grandson with a special cross-cultural feast, by which she means her superior Iraqi dishes accessorized by Jimmy's inferior American ones. "Tell the sergeant we start cooking this afternoon and tell him to invite his brothers," she orders. "It is time for our families to unite."

Thus, a few hours later, while Jimmy is frying chicken and boiling frozen peas in the kitchen, Hibah is trying without much conviction to keep out of his way while she makes *laham b'ajeen*, four elaborate side dishes, and a defiantly square chocolate and coconut cake.

Naema, who would have preferred not to involve Jimmy or his brothers at all, is avoiding the two cooks altogether by setting the table in the dining room, where Hibah insisted they eat. Dark and rectangular, with oak-paneled walls and even a dusty chandelier, it is the room that most retains the house's past as a tavern—much too formal, she thinks, for the birthday party of a child. Hibah has also insisted they use a *sofra* from home as a tablecloth, a cream-colored cotton splashed with fleshy magenta flowers that Naema finds vaguely obscene. But it is her own idea to include the bright blue paper plates and cups she and Jimmy discovered that morning at a dollar store, along with seven matching helium balloons. She ties them to the backs of the chairs, where they float like neckless heads, emitting a pleasant, if pungent, scent of rubber.

Jimmy switches off the flame under his saucepan of peas and glances at her through the kitchen door. Not one of the jobs she's applied for these past two weeks has come through, and furthermore, she has just discovered that to practice here as a doctor, she not only has to pass the American Medical College Admissions Test, but also complete a twelve-month residency, as though her years of medical practice in wartime Iraq count for nothing. All this is eroding her resolve. He can see it in the way she moves, as if it were an effort to pull herself across the room.

Naema looks up, feeling his eyes on her, so he quickly turns away and heads to the sink to drain his peas just as Hibah cuts in front of him, almost knocking scalding water over them both. "Fuck!" he shouts. She freezes, blinking at him from within the frame of her black hijab.

"Sorry, sorry." He clatters the pan into the sink, his few Arabic words deserting him.

"Mama, watch where you're going," Naema tells her, coming into the kitchen to gather up some spoons.

"*I* watch? That clumsy donkey almost poured boiling water on me! Son of an ass!" Clamping her wrinkled mouth shut, Hibah turns back to the stove.

Tariq is out of harm's way, at least, sitting on the living room rug in front of the television, watching the old *Iron Man* cartoon series Jimmy gave him that morning as a birthday present. Tariq has been obsessed with Iron Man ever since Jimmy found a box of his boyhood comic books in the attic. He likes other superheroes, too, especially Superman, whom he recognizes from his Syrian comics and whose red cape still appeals. But the bionic quality of Iron Man has a special resonance for him, as Naema is only too aware. It worries her. Now that the Medicaid approval has come through and his suture has healed, the soreness having turned out to be nothing but a few bruises and a cluster of mosquito bites he scratched too hard, the fitting for his prosthesis is only a week away. She doesn't want him fantasizing that his artificial leg will be supernaturally strong, make him fly or turn him into a hero. She wants him to be ready for the reality of it, the hard work of learning to walk and sit, climb and fall.

The front door flies open, startling her badly, and Patrick and Rory catapult in. They are always bursting in unannounced like this, and each time it seizes her heart with fear. "Hey, Naema, where's the birthday boy?" Patrick says cheerily, handing her a plastic bag stuffed with gaudily wrapped presents. All the brothers call her Naema now, even Jimmy.

"He is watching the television." She notices the brothers are more dressed up than usual: Patrick in an oversized black T-shirt covered in words she doesn't understand, sagging black trousers and a thick gold chain, although without his usual cap; Rory in faded jeans and an orange band shirt that clashes with his hair but is, at least, clean. They have clearly made an effort for her son. This touches her.

"Hey, Nutpea!" Rory calls, his voice a tad too loud. He pokes his head into the living room.

"Uncle Ugly!" Tariq levers himself to his feet and swings over, beaming.

"Happy Birthday, squirt." Rory lifts him high. "Oof, you're heavy. What're you now, fourteen?" Tariq giggles, his crutches dangling, his stump waggling oddly.

"Put him down!" Naema snaps.

Rory glances at her in surprise but obeys. The whites of his eyes, she notices, are shot through with pink.

"I see your nose, it is better," she remarks, trying to make up for her tone. His nose has improved, its rainbow of bruises faded to a faint bile yellow.

"Yeah. Doc says it's not even broken, just smooshed." He turns to Tariq. "Got any presents yet, big boy?"

"Yes. Come." Tariq scoots back to the TV, Rory following.

A bright-faced young woman appears at the door then and introduces herself as Patrick's girlfriend, Lisa. "Can I help you with anything?" she asks after she and Naema shake hands. She sounds American but Naema wonders where she is from, with her cinnamon skin and hair as glossy and dark as her own.

"No, it is not necessary. Please, Lisa, Patrick, come to sit." She gestures to the living room, even though it is dominated by the TV turned up painfully loud. Patrick scowls. He doesn't appreciate a stranger inviting him to sit in his own goddamn house.

"Hey, guys." Jimmy emerges from the kitchen, rubbing the steam off his glasses with his shirt, something his optometrist has begged him many a time not to do. He puts them on, takes one look at Patrick and knows he's been drinking, which means that Rory has, too. Jimmy warned his brothers there'd be no booze at the party, given the presence of teetotaling Muslims, trusting them to have the respect not to tank up before they came. More fool him.

"Lisa, my future sister-in-law!" He gathers her in a hug, the first woman he's touched in weeks, the yield and spring of her making him ache. "Nice dress."

"Thanks, it's new." The dress is a shiny red wraparound, cut low enough to show off quite a bit of bosom and high enough to reveal a long stretch of thigh. Naema wonders if it passes for good taste in this country or the opposite.

"I got OJ, 7UP, Coke," Jimmy announces with forced cheer, still smiling at Lisa. "What's everyone want?"

"Coke," Patrick replies glumly.

"Nothing for me, thanks." Lisa turns to Naema. "You're sure I can't help with something, Mrs. . . . um . . .?"

"Please to call me Naema. But yes, perhaps you can help me with the cake." She leads her into the kitchen.

Patrick pulls a flask from his pocket and hands it to Jimmy. "Here, bro, brought this in the event of a worst-case scenario. Which it clearly is." He hopes Jimmy will drink it all. He has some news he knows will be a shock.

Jimmy is tempted, his anxiety about the evening already squeezing his injured neck into a cramp. "What is it, whiskey?" It would mortify him if Naema smelled it on his breath.

"Vodka."

Jimmy takes a slug and hands it back. Their mother's old trick, odorless vodka disguised in orange juice or, much too often, her coffee.

"Keep it," Patrick says.

"Nah, that's enough."

"Maybe later then." Patrick jams it into his back pocket.

"How wasted is Rory?"

"Quite a bit. Know what this is?" Patrick pries a white pill out of his wallet. "I found three of these on the floor behind our old VCR. Pretty sure he popped one before we came."

Jimmy turns the pill over in his fingers. "Shit, it's an OC 10. He probably stole it from me. How long you think he's been taking these?"

"No idea. I thought you were off that poison now."

"I am. Gave it up years ago."

"Then maybe you should hide your meds better, know what I mean?"

"Fuck. Why's Rory such a pain in the ass? Listen, keep him in line tonight, will you? And see if you can find out how deep into this shit he is."

"I'll try." Patrick notices Hibah peering out of the kitchen doorway. "The old bat's after you. I'm going outside for a smoke."

Rory himself is happily nestled into a heap of Kate's red velvet cushions on the living room floor, Tariq in his lap, the two of them watching *Iron Man*. Tariq seems to be enjoying the story, whooping every time the hero suits up in his robotic uniform, but as soon as the action turns to fighting, he twists around to hide his face in Rory's chest.

"What's wrong, Nutpea, you don't like it?"

Tariq shakes his head.

"You're quite the movie critic. What is it, the acting or the story?" In Rory's opinion, they both suck.

"No like bang-bang fight." Tariq's face is still buried in Rory's shirt.

"OK, I get it." Rory picks up the remote. "I'll fast-forward. Watch, it's funny." Tariq peeks out at the cartoon figures whizzing by and laughs. "See?" Rory wraps his arms around him. "Nothing to be scared of. It's only pretend."

Patrick wanders back in from his smoke to find Tariq and his brother so close to the TV they're almost underneath it, just the way he and Rory used to watch as boys. Patrick shoves his hands into his pockets. He's self-conscious around children. As a kid, he hated it when grown-ups talked down to him and wants so badly not to talk like that himself that he can't figure out how to speak to children at all. "What're you watching, *Iron Man*?" he finally blurts.

"No, *Bugs Bunny*. Asshole." Rory has not fully recovered from his umbrage over that night in McGrath's.

"Well, happy birthday, Tariq."

"Thank you, asshole."

Patrick scowls at him. "Hey, don't repeat every word my brother says. You'll get yourself whacked in the nose like him if you go around calling people those names."

Tariq squints up at him. "You hit Tariq?"

"No, no, I didn't mean that." But Tariq is edging away from him now, his stump dragging across the carpet. Damn, Patrick thinks, I *am* an asshole.

During all this, Lisa and Naema are decorating Hibah's cake in what was once the pantry but is now a no-man's land piled with desert boots, camouflage uniforms, Jimmy's Combat Lifesaver bag, boxes of army patches and medals, and everything else he's been meaning to stash in the attic for months. Having cleared a space on a cluttered side table, Naema is writing *Happy Birthday Tariq* in loopy red icing. Lisa wonders why the words aren't in Arabic.

"Lisa, do you think we should make a flower there in the middle, beside the candles?" Naema tilts her head to survey the cake.

"I think it's great like it is. Simple, y'know?" Lisa glances at her. Naema's oval face is so smooth that the shrapnel scar etched into her right cheek is truly disconcerting.

"No, I think a flower." Naema leans over and squeezes a curly line around the edges of the cake and a pile of frosting in the middle, which she manipulates into a perfect red rose, her mind drifting to another birthday, Tariq's first. He in his highchair, kicking his baby legs; her mother, Khalil and his parents clustered around him, snapping pictures, kissing him, vying for his smiles. How is it possible for an entire family in all its human tangles of anguish and joy, rivalry and devotion to be so thoroughly erased?

"Wow, you're good at this," Lisa says, admiring the rose. She refrains from asking why the cake is square.

"Thank you." Naema bends to place six candles on the cake, close enough to one another for him to blow out in one puff.

"Where do you want me to put the seventh candle?" Lisa asks.

Naema looks at her. "But he is six only."

"It's for good luck . . . You don't do that?"

"We do not, no. But it is a nice idea. Although perhaps it will confuse him when he counts the candles?"

"Sure, no problem." Lisa pushes the extra candle back into its box. Too bad, she thinks. If anyone needs luck around here, it's that mangled kid.

"There," Naema says, stepping back in satisfaction.

"It's so pretty." Lisa smiles at her. "I like your shirt, by the way. Is it from your country?"

Naema is only wearing her old green shirt and the loose black trousers she wore to her job interviews. She possesses no party outfits, never having needed them in Damascus. Nor does she have any of her clothes from Iraq, having been forced to flee the hospital with no more than the single bag Hibah packed in a rush, along with the jewels she had sewn into the seams of Naema's sanitary pads and the wads of Khalil's dollars she had tucked inside the soles of their shoes.

"Thank you." Naema is unsure of how else to respond to Lisa's compliment, especially as she can find nothing nice to say about her loud red dress.

"Food's up!" Jimmy calls. Naema turns to leave but Lisa is disappointed. She'd hoped for more time alone with Naema, to offer herself as a friend. Jimmy told her that, aside from him and his brothers, Naema doesn't know a single soul in this country, and Lisa can see it. For all the woman's reserve, she radiates loneliness.

The dinner is elaborate, long, and heavy. It's really two dinners because Hibah took one look at Jimmy's contribution and decided to renounce her plans for a cross-cultural meal after all, reasoning that if she cannot talk to these Americans or take any joy in the texture of her days, she can at least fend off their horrible food and give Tariq a true Iraqi feast. After all, he is her grandson, is he not, the son of her son? Even Naema lacks the blood tie to him that Hibah has, the line from father to father stretching back generations. So who else but she is left to protect Tariq from forgetting the traditions of his people? As the saying goes, *I went to the House of Allah and returned / Yet I found nothing like my home.* Which is why, as well as her platter of *laham b'ajeen*, she made a dish of beef and bulgur *kubbe*, another of spinach spiced with coconut and cumin, a tub of rice mixed with almonds, and enough spring rolls for everyone to have three.

Lisa looks over the heaped table in dismay. She is trying to lose weight—she's always trying to lose weight—but especially now that she's thinking wedding dresses. How's she supposed to eat Jimmy's chicken *and* those little pizza things, not to mention all those dumplings and side dishes swimming in spices and oil? She glances around the table to see how the others are coping. Gobbling it all with relish, as far as she can see, but then men can eat anything. Only Hibah and Naema are picking, but they're so skinny they probably pick all the time. On second glance, Jimmy, who is sitting at the head of the table between the old lady and Rory, isn't eating much either. His face is so blank and sad. He must be missing Kate.

Lisa feels Kate's absence herself, especially once the conversation, stilted to begin with, sputters into silence. If Kate were here, she would be joking with the brothers in that easy way of hers and no doubt charming Tariq, too, being accustomed to children from her years as a second-grade teacher. But instead, that tiny old granny is in her place, draped in black and glowering at them from under her headscarf, while Naema looks drawn and mournful, even with that blue balloon bobbing above her head. No wonder we're all afraid to talk, Lisa thinks. She glances at Patrick beside her. Is he going to tell Jimmy the news about Kate? He promised he would.

Rory is the first to break the silence. "You make this, Naema?" he calls down the table to where she's sitting beside Tariq, who has been given the place of honor at the foot. "The ravioli's yummy." He waves a dumpling around on his fork.

"Thank you. It is called *kubbe*. My mother-in-law made it, not I."

"Well, good for Mom-in-Law then." Rory raises his paper cup of orange juice, secretly spiked with a fair bit of Patrick's vodka. He has already parachuted an OC—he's learned to wrap the pills in toilet paper to mitigate their taste—and between that and the booze is feeling more pleasantly buzzed by the second. "To Mom-in-Law and her kubble or whatever."

Hibah can't comprehend the words but she catches the gist. Her crinkled face breaks into a smile, revealing her missing tooth. "I'm glad you like it, loud person," she says in Arabic.

"She is saying thank you," Naema tells him. "The name to call her is *Oum* Khalil."

"*Yum* Khalil, more like."

"You are a funny boy." And to Jimmy's amazement, Naema tosses her braid behind her shoulder and laughs.

Rory shrugs. "Hey, Nutpea," he calls down the table to Tariq, "how's it feel to be six years old and ready for kindergarten, huh?"

"I fly in my school and kick ass!" Tariq flings his arms up, his paper birthday crown slipping over one eye.

"Did you teach him to say that?" Jimmy glowers at Rory. "I told you to watch your language. You'll get him in trouble."

"Screw you. You're such a—"

"Rory, could you get Tariq's presents?" Lisa interjects, sending him an appeasing smile.

Rory scowls for a second, forgets why and relaxes. "Sure." He lopes unsteadily out of the room. Patrick squeezes her thigh in gratitude. Jimmy picks up Rory's spiked juice and downs it himself.

Naema, meanwhile, is deep in the dream that has occupied her during most of the meal, a dream not of the past this time but of the future. She is in a house of her own, a doctor again, and instead of this loud and battling family, she is dining with *Oum* Ismail and her husband, the couple she met in the Resettlement Office. They are speaking their own language, choosing their own topics, and nobody is pretending to be sober when they are obviously and disrespectfully drunk. They are talking of Iraq, of the latest elections, of whether their homeland will emerge from its years of occupation and war intact and whether they will ever want or be able to go home. In short, they are talking about what matters.

She is jolted out of her reverie by the sound of Rory singing "Happy Birthday" as he parades back in carrying a pile of presents. Shoving Tariq's nearly full plate aside, he plunks them in front of him. "All for you, Nutpea."

"All me?" Tariq beams.

Not wanting to be outshone, Patrick jumps up and darts into the pantry for the cake. Lighting the candles, he marches back in with it, singing the song again. Lisa joins in to show support and so Jimmy feels he should, too, and then

Rory, while Naema and Hibah sit there, confused. Patrick puts the cake next to Tariq's presents with a flourish. "Make a wish, Birthday Boy!"

Lisa and Naema both notice that a seventh candle is there after all, a thick blue one shoved right into the middle of Naema's carefully constructed rose.

Hibah gazes about in bewilderment. All her dishes are still on the table, only half eaten—it is not yet time for cake. Why are these Americans ruining her meal?

"Know what it means to make a wish?" Rory asks Tariq.

Tariq looks up at him expectantly.

"Close your eyes and think about what you want more than anything in the world. Then blow out all the candles in one go and it'll come true." Rory mimics blowing, swaying on his feet, his hair straggling over his face.

Naema is about to object—she cannot bear the idea of Tariq believing anything that might lead to more heartbreak. But he has already squeezed his eyes shut, his little face screwed up with the effort. "I wish . . ." he says. "I wish . . ."

Resigning herself, Naema closes her eyes, too. *Please wish for something you can really have,* habibi. *Please don't choose something impossible.*

"Don't say it out loud, else it won't come true," Patrick says quickly. But Tariq either doesn't understand or is concentrating too hard to pay attention.

"I wish . . ." he finally says after a long pause, opening his eyes. "I wish Jim-Jim be my Baba!" And taking a deep breath, he blows out all seven candles at once.

After the cake has been consumed, the presents opened, and everyone has pretended not to have heard what Tariq said, Naema murmurs a hurried good night and ushers him and Hibah to their back apartment, leaving the brothers and Lisa to sprawl around the living room in relief. The vodka is out in the open now and Patrick and Rory have made themselves screwdrivers. Lisa is curled up on the couch, her head on Patrick's shoulder, inhaling his familiar smells of gasoline, cigarettes and deodorant, which somehow turn her on. Patrick is stretched out with his boots on the coffee table, hair dangling over one eye like a raccoon tail, his hand caressing Lisa's thigh.

"That was one hell of a flop," Jimmy mutters from an armchair.

"No, it wasn't!" Lisa objects. "Tariq had a great time. That's what counts, isn't it?"

"Don't know how you do it, myself," Patrick says. "The old lady gives me the creeps, hobbling around in that black body bag and sending everyone the Stare."

"Naema's worse," Rory remarks from the floor. Propped on an elbow, his drink beside him, he is flipping through one of Tariq's Syrian comic books.

"I think she's nice," Lisa says. "Just sad, which is natural enough. Anyhow, she obviously likes you, so what's the problem?"

"She called me a boy, for fuck's sake . . ."

"Hah." Jimmy kicks his feet up on the coffee table with Patrick's.

"'Hah' yourself, Baba Jim-Jim." Rory cackles.

"Leave it, Rory." Patrick glances at Jimmy.

Rory shrugs and returns to Tariq's comic. "This is so whacked. It's a total rip-off of Superman. Know what Nutpea told me he's called in Arabic? Nabil Fawzi. *Nabil*? What kind of a wussy name is that?"

"Gimme," Patrick says, holding out a hand.

Rory tosses it over and flips onto his back, resting his head on one of Kate's cushions. "Hey, Jimmy, when's Tariq getting his leg?" His brother only stares at his hands. "Jimmy, you got potatoes for ears or what?"

"Huh?" Jimmy puts his feet back on the floor and rubs his temples.

Rory rolls his eyes but repeats the question.

"Oh. Soon. Maybe next week." Jimmy moves his hand down to massage his neck, the skin around his skull so tight it feels like drying leather. At his last VA appointment, he learned that he has two compacted vertebrae near the top of his spine and that the Iraqi bugs in his guts are a flourishing colony of parasites from the water on base, which was not as purified as either the army or its sidekick Halliburton claimed. He's supposed to be killing those parasites with pills but the pills mean he has to stay off booze, so they are still sitting on his bedside table with all the rest of his meds, waiting.

"What about the fact that I can't think straight half the time?" he asked the doctor, a washed-out army medic in his fifties with stubbly gray hair and a face like a collapsed cake. "And those things I keep seeing?" Jimmy didn't say what, having no wish to be clapped in a nuthouse like his mother.

"PTSD." The doctor sounded as depleted as he looked. "But you need to go to a different department to get that confirmed. You filled out the questionnaire, right?"

"You mean the one where they asked if I saw any dead bodies?" Jimmy didn't even try to keep the sarcasm out of his voice.

"Yes, that one. I'll order a brain scan, too, check for TBI."

"Great, so my brain's a mush. Does this mean I get my disability upped, at least? 'Cause what's the point of getting fucked up in a war if you're not even paid for it?"

"I know." The doctor emitted a weary sigh. "I'll try."

"I mean, maybe I'm too much of a mess to hold a job, so I need ninety percent, right?" If Jimmy can get his disability rating raised from its current sixty, that would bring in another six hundred bucks a month, which he badly needs, given that his luck finding work continues to be no better than Naema's.

"You need to take more tests to determine that. It's tough getting rated that high."

"So, what the fuck am I supposed to do, keep popping all these goddamn pills and getting turned down for jobs?" Jimmy realized he was shouting.

"Calm down, soldier," the doctor said in the wrung-out tone of one who says this many times a day. "I'll give you a prescription for your refills, but I'd be happier if you got off the Ativan."

Jimmy would be happy to get off the Ativan, too. His army doctor prescribed it after Khalil was killed and Jimmy was too gutted to eat or sleep, let alone soldier. But once he came home and tried to kick it, afraid of turning into a pillhead like half the vets he knew, he stayed awake three nights in a row, the drumbeat of his heart so violent it seemed about to break through his ribs, his stomach convulsing into one agonizing spasm after another, phantom scorpions crawling over his skin. Anything seemed better than that, even addiction.

Maybe that's why Kate left, he thinks there in the living room. Not because of some wife-stealing fuckface, not even 'cause he can't hold down a job. But because he's a pillhead after all.

"How's Sue?" Patrick asks Rory to take the spotlight off Jimmy, who's slumped over his knees now, deep in whatever world he falls into when he's like this. Patrick pulls Lisa closer. He wants to go home and have wild sex with her tonight—doggie, missionary, sixty-nine. Perhaps it's the vodka putting a horn on him like this. Or all the goddamn sadness in this house.

Rory sits up with a yawn. "Don't know. Been too busy to see her much."

"What've you got to be busy at?" Patrick narrows his eyes. "Scooping butter pecan?"

Ignoring this, Rory looks back at Jimmy, still slumped over his knees. "Hey, soldier boy, has Naema decided where Nutpea's going to school in the fall?"

Jimmy gazes at him blankly. Then he sits up, pulls off his glasses and rubs his eyes. "Depends on where they're living."

"They're not staying here?"

"Nope. Naema wants to move. She needs a bigger place."

"Or maybe she isn't comfortable here without Kate," Lisa interjects.

Silence.

Jimmy jams his glasses back on and gets to his feet. "Head's killing me. Clean up, will you?" He leaves the room and soon they hear him climbing the stairs.

"Damn, Lisa," Patrick mutters.

"I know." Her face is burning. "I'm sorry."

"Don't be," Rory says, standing up, too. "He's such a dickwipe. No wonder Kate split."

"I don't think that's fair," Lisa says.

"Why?" Rory looks at her. "You heard from her?"

Lisa shakes her head. "Nope. I just know it couldn't have been easy for her to leave. She loves you guys."

"Fuck her. Some love, skipping out on us like that. Listen, I wanna get outta here. Let's get this shit over with and head to a bar."

"Don't want to go to a bar, want to go to bed," Patrick says. "You two get started. I'll be back in a minute." And with a significant look at Lisa, he mounts the stairs after Jimmy.

When he reaches the landing, he pauses, glancing down the hall to his brother's room. He so dreads this conversation that he's tempted to avoid it altogether, go back down and lie to Lisa. Instead, he turns into his old bedroom around the corner, the one he left for Aunt Maureen's place the first time Jimmy deserted him and Rory for war. He sits on the boy-sized bed, still covered with his Batman quilt, and tries to work up his courage. Kate redecorated the house not long after she and Jimmy married, scraping the painted floors down to their original wood, painting the walls cream or shell pink, stuffing the rooms with too many chairs and all those cushions. She and Jimmy were saving up to get the outside fixed and painted, too, but with Jimmy out of work, their dwindling military payments and her meager teacher's salary, they hadn't been able to save much. Meanwhile, she'd left his and Rory's rooms alone to do with what they wanted because she'd always hoped they would all live together as one big family. Instead, he and Rory chose to get out from under Jimmy's thumb by renting a cheerless basement apartment in Cairo, a pokey little town about an hour south of Slingerlands with nothing much to offer aside from a supermarket, a few bars and a strip joint tucked away in the woods. As a result, Patrick's room is exactly as he had left it at age fourteen. Posters of Derek Jeter and Stone Cold Steve Austin on the walls. A lime-green pump-action water pistol propped in a corner. A secondhand orange rug decorated with a giant football helmet. And a shelf lined with comic books, Pokémon cards and Star Wars action figures, most of them headless, thanks to Rory's homemade guillotine. Patrick gazes at it all dolefully, less because it's frozen in time than because it reminds him of how little he's moved on. He needs to make himself go to college and expand his brain, just like Jimmy is always saying. He wants to, in fact, to keep up with Lisa if nothing else. The obstacle is that he can't stand giving in to his big brother in any way, certain that he will lose his Patrickness if he does, turn into nothing but a Jimmy-shadow. He's almost one already.

If only to get away from this thought, he rises to his feet, pulls in a deep breath and propels himself down the hall to the master bedroom. The door is open, his brother lying on his back in bed, shoes off but clothes on, hands held up in front of his face, staring at his scars again. Bottles of pills crowd the bedside table next to an empty water glass, along with the OxyContin Rory's been pilfering. Jimmy hasn't drawn the curtains or turned on the lights, so the moon's as bright as a headlight in the window, sending a steely cast over the bed. Jimmy's face and arms look steely, too. His glasses are off, and Patrick can see even from the doorway that he has that look again—the one that takes over when his head is back in the war. It makes Patrick's skin crawl.

"Jimmy?"

His brother sits up and looks at him. His eyes seem to have separated into two layers, one that sees Patrick, the other as flat and blind as a wall. He lies back down without a word.

Patrick walks over and sits on the foot of the bed, facing him. "Jimmy, you OK?"

"What d'you want, Pat?"

"There's something I need to tell you."

"If it's about Kate, I don't want to fucking hear it."

"I know." Patrick looks down at his lap and picks at his fingernails. "I'm sorry, bro." He squints back up at him. "But I think you have to."

PART III

14

When I first fled my homeland with Hibah and Tariq, I knew, of course, that like all refugees, I would be plagued by loss, homesickness and sorrow. But I did not foresee the eviscerating guilt that would also eat away at me—over those I left behind, those who died, those I may have stepped on to survive and those who are still suffering the persecution and violence I managed to escape. Yet by far the most painful source of my guilt is Mama, for I cannot overcome the shame of having left her behind. True, I was given no choice. The visas granted to interpreters only include their immediate families, not their in-laws, which is why, in essence, I was forced to flee with the wrong mother. Yet I violated the most basic tenet of daughterhood by abandoning Mama to live and die alone. It is something an Iraqi woman does not do. So, when the soldier goes out again tonight, leaving us alone in his house for only the second time, I take advantage of his absence to creep into his darkened living room so I can call her on his computer in privacy. Having no money to send her and no ability to visit, it is the only way I have left to show her my love.

I turn on the desk lamp for company, attracting a cloud of moths to the nearby window, where they bat softly against the glass as if calling me out to play. For a moment I am tempted to join them because, as eager as I am to speak to Mama, I know our conversation will only bring us sorrow, reminding us both of the impossible distance between us, of the past that cleaves to us like a skin, and of a future in which we shall probably never see each other again.

Smoothing back my hair in the monitor's glass—what daughter ever grows out of wanting to impress her mother?—I type in her Skype address, hoping her electricity is working. In southern Iraq at the moment, households are lucky if they receive two hours of current a day.

The screen takes a long and quivering breath, and then, after a series of popping bubbles and beeps, there Mama is, peering in confusion from its frame, as though she is on the other side of a dark and murky mirror.

"Naema, *habibti*, is it you?"

"Of course it is, Mama. Can't you see me?"

She pushes her face closer. "There you are! I still can't believe a machine can bring you to me like this." And then, as always, she begins to weep. "*Ya Allah*, it hurts to see you and not be able to hold you, *habawi*. It's been so long since we last talked. I miss you with every breath in my body!"

"I know. It's the same for me, Mama." I struggle to hold back my own tears. Each time I see her this way, diminished by the camera, always looking in the wrong place, I am newly pained by how much war has stolen from her. Forty-seven years old, yet her hair is white and her face sunken. Before the American invasion, she was still strong and youthful, hair as black as mine, green eyes bright with vigor, an ophthalmologist living in a good neighborhood in Baghdad with Baba, her poet-professor husband, and me and Zaki, who, if sometimes difficult, were at least studious. Now, these seven years later—is it really so short a time?—she is without a job, a husband, a son or even me, living alone instead with an old uncle just outside of Basra, as dependent upon him as a spinster. It's as if her life has wound backwards and she has never escaped her peasant village or its constricted fates at all.

"Are you and Uncle well, Mama?"

"Yes, but things have gone from bad to worse here, have you heard? So many bombings since the elections, so much corruption! And these suicide bombers and ISIS fanatics, Naema! They are hurting our people even more than the enemy is, pushing us back in history like this, as if they want to erase every shred of joy we have left. I do believe, *habibti*, that they want to stamp out even laughter." Mama sighs and plucks at her fingers. "Everybody has war in his heart now and lust for power. With leaders like these, how are we ever to find peace?"

"I don't know, Mama. The greedy have kicked our country around for so long it's in shreds. I fear it's beyond repair now. But are you really all right?"

"Yes, yes, I'm fine, *habibti*. Now, tell me, how are you adjusting to life in America? Is it as free and rich as they say?"

How to reply to such questions? "We're doing the best we can. It's very different here."

"Are you working in a hospital yet?"

"It's too soon. I have to pass exams first."

"Exams? But that's ridiculous! You've already passed exams and you're such a good doctor. With all your experience, they should beg you to work for them."

The experience Mama means, of course, is everything I had to endure in the war. By the time Tariq was a year old and I ready to resume my studies, Baghdad had grown so dangerous that I had to hire a neighbor to drive me to the medical college in his taxi and home again every day, while I hid on the floor in the back to avoid being kidnapped or shot. And later, when Khalil was off helping the sergeant and his platoon persecute our people, I was working in understaffed hospitals at constant risk from one militia or another, the Sunni not wanting me to treat the Shi'a, the Shi'a likewise the Sunni. Before the war, nobody I knew had cared which we were, let alone that I was half-and-half, but now one's religious inheritance was enough to get one killed. Each time I was stopped by some officious thug on the road demanding to see the sect stamped on my identity card, my fate hung by the most fragile of gossamer threads, as subject to the man's religious affiliations as it was to whether he had liked his breakfast that morning or fought with his wife. How many American doctors have had to undergo all this just to be able to study and treat the sick?

"They want qualifications from here, not from Iraq," I tell Mama, too ashamed to mention that I take food stamps now, as well as public assistance from the government. Derek of the Refugee Center, to whom I have been forced to return for help, having had no success these past three weeks in securing a job, keeps reminding me that I am entitled to these benefits. But the food stamps and checks do not feel like entitlements; they feel like pity. "I'm sure I'll find something."

"Of course you will. And how is my darling grandson?"

"Excited about starting school. And, Mama, in a few days, his new leg will be fitted. He'll be able to walk free at last!" My voice quavers. Merely speaking these words aloud brings all my grief for Tariq out of its hiding place.

"*Alhamdulillah!* Does this mean he'll be able to walk like a normal child?"

"Mama, he *is* normal. I wish you wouldn't . . ." I stop myself. "But yes, *insh'Allah*, he will be able to walk without crutches. We'll Skype you together so you can see. Now what about you? Are you truly well?" My guilt is laid bare by these questions, as I am certain she can hear.

"Yes, we're safe enough here, *habibti*. Please don't worry. You know how I've been passing the time? I've been rereading your father's poetry. I must confess, when I was younger, I always thought it foolish. He exposed himself with every word, your father, *rahimahullah*. But now I see it as brave. Alas, it's too late to tell him." She smiles sadly.

"Are you sure it's wise to dwell on Baba like this?"

"Wise or no, I don't care. Listen to this one—he wrote it not long after we fled Baghdad." And in the same singsong chant with which Baba used to recite in his poets' cafés, she chants,

I walked down the road and met a lone refugee.
She lifted her head and cried,
"To survive is to live in a prison of solitude."
I walked further down the road and met a wounded soldier.
He raised his voice and said, "To love is to lose—"

"Stop. I can't stand it." I know this poem: one long dirge of despair.

She hesitates. "Very well. You haven't the same needs as I. Now, tell me about Hibah. How does she like America?"

"Not much, but you know how she complains." What does Mama mean by our having different needs? Is this a reproach? "But are you sure you aren't too isolated down there with Uncle?"

"Well, it's no Baghdad. But Uncle is kind and Nour is keeping me company. We do everything together."

"Oh?" I cannot keep the jealousy from my voice, this cousin who has replaced me. "How old is she now?"

"Sixteen and—"

The living room door bangs open just then, shocking me to my feet, and the soldier stumbles in. He straightens up at the sight of me, grasping the back of the sofa. His glasses are crooked, mouth loose. Patrick shuffles in after him, the brim of his cap pulled low over his eyes.

I look back at the computer. "Mama, I'm sorry but I have to go."

"Already? Why, what's happening?" She pushes her face up to the monitor.

I move to block her view. "Nothing. The sergeant's come home, that's all. I have to turn this off now."

"But we've barely talked!"

"I know. I'll call again soon. Go back to bed. Next time we should speak later so I don't have to wake you before dawn." I send my love and switch off the connection, watching her ghostly face vanish.

"Sorry, interrupted, don't hang up," the soldier mumbles. He collapses onto the sofa, his glasses falling off. Patrick picks them up and puts them on the coffee table.

"He is drunk?" I ask Patrick, aware that this is the second time I have posed this question to the brothers.

"A little on the pixilated side, maybe."

I put my hands on my hips. I abhor drinking, less because of my religion than because I cannot fathom why anyone would willingly poison his body, blunt his brain and turn himself into a fool. "I shall make him some tea to clear his head. Perhaps you could take him upstairs to his bed?"

"No!" The soldier's voice is so fierce I back away. Pitching to his feet, he staggers to the bathroom.

"Maybe coffee would work better?" Patrick lifts off his cap and runs his fingers through his hair, his brow puckered. He has always struck me as a kind young man, only scattered in the mind, his attention flitting about like a sparrow's. Now, however, he seems altogether present.

"You will take some coffee as well?"

"You bet." He follows me into the kitchen. "I was watching TV at home when he called. Had to drive up to East Durham to get him. Cops were everywhere. Seems he caused some kind of ruckus, so I had to talk them out of cuffing him, tell them he's a veteran and all that shit... stuff. Then he wouldn't get in the car. Said he was such a bonehead he wanted to make himself walk home as punishment or something. Yelled about army discipline."

"But what is it he did?"

"Wouldn't say. All I know is he was boozing with some war buds and they got into a brawl..." He glances at me. "Damn, sorry."

"It is all right." I turn to take two mugs out of the chipped red cabinet above the sink. "Perhaps it is best I do not know." But as I put the mugs down, I see my hands are shaking.

"Thing is, it's not like him to get into fights. He's just been so fucked up since Kate left. Anyhow, think you can handle him OK? 'Cause I can't really stay. Lisa's waiting for me and I'm already late."

"Do not worry, we shall be fine. Have your coffee and go. And please, give Lisa my best." I'm proud of having learned to say that, although I can't help but wonder, best of what?

After Patrick leaves, the soldier stumbles back from the bathroom and falls into a chair, his hands palms up on his knees, his head hanging, the reek of vomit emanating from his mouth. His white skin is even whiter than usual and glossed with sweat.

"Here." I put a glass of water and a mug of coffee on the table beside him. "Drink." Retreating to the other side of the kitchen, I stand in front of the fireplace and fold my arms. He picks up the water and drains it.

"Now the coffee."

He shakes his head.

"Why did you do this?" I ask him. "Why did you make yourself drunk like your silly brother?"

He mutters.

"Pardon?" I pull out a chair and sit in front of him. "What is the matter, Sergeant? Is it your wife?"

He raises his face to me, his squinty blue eyes, naked without their glasses, glazed and reddened. "Yeah." The words are sliding around in his mouth, his tongue chasing them. "She left the US and nobody knows where she is. Pat told me the night of Tariq's birthday party. It's screwing me up, Naema. Can't handle it. Why's she need to get so far away from me that she skipped the whole fucking *country*?"

I fold my arms again.

"How do you do it without Khalil?" he says then. "How do you keep going?"

I stand. This is none of his business. "Wait here. I shall find you some aspirin." I leave the room to search the bathroom medicine cabinet, but when I return and see him slumped in his chair, my umbrage melts. True, he has suffered little compared to the suffering he has inflicted upon others. But what is the point in measuring sorrows? A broken heart, no matter whose heart it is, is still broken.

"Here." I hand him the tablets.

"You're a kind person, Naema, know that?" His voice is almost a sob. He drops his head into his hands, his muscled back hunched. "Khalil was, too. He was such a good man. He and Muller both."

I say nothing.

"Why's everything suck so bad, can you tell me that? Why's it always the good people get slammed the worst?"

"Sergeant," I say quietly, "I think it best if you swallow the aspirin and go to bed."

"Not Sergeant—Jimmy! I told you. Can't you just be my friend?"

"All right—Jimmy. Now, go to bed."

He sways to his feet. But rather than turning to leave, as I expect, he suddenly lurches towards me, throws his arms around my shoulders and pulls me hard against his chest.

"Leave me alone!" I cry in shock, struggling against him, his weight and height bearing down on me. "Let me go!"

But he only moans and holds me tighter, burrowing his mouth into my neck.

"Stop!" This seems to startle him because he loosens his grip. Wrenching free, I rush out of the house.

15

The tea shop Khalil had chosen was as narrow as an alleyway and so dense with narghile smoke that he could barely make out the faces inside. Threading his way through the clutter of people seated at the low, inlaid tables, he had to peer about for quite a while before he could spot Naema. She was sitting far in the back, holding Tariq close on her lap, her face drawn with anxiety, Tariq's open and curious as he gazed around the room.

Khalil's chest tightened. He hadn't seen them for weeks, not since the kill-box ambush, and the sight of them pierced him with love. Looking over his shoulder to make sure he wasn't being followed, he slipped onto a stool beside them, not daring to touch even Naema's arm, as much as he longed to, for fear of attracting attention.

"Baba!" Tariq cried, wriggling to break free of his mother.

"Come, *habibi*." Khalil lifted him off her lap onto his. "I can only stay a short while," he whispered to Naema, taking in the shadowy strain around her eyes, the pinched set of her mouth. She was dressed in loose black trousers and a tunic of dark blue, her matching hijab emphasizing the golden-green of her irises. He found himself wanting her fiercely. "I'm sorry to be so hurried." She nodded and glanced away.

Tariq twisted around and knelt upright to see his father's face. "You look funny, Baba." He tugged at the stubble of Khalil's normally thick hair, cut like a soldier's now to reduce the heat under his helmet, and ran his hands over Khalil's cheeks with a giggle, rubbing the bristle of his whiskers. Khalil smiled at the soft tickle of his son's little palms. At three, Tariq was round-cheeked and chubby from all the treats his grandmothers Hibah and Zaynab were stuffing him with, now that Khalil was earning enough to feed them all. "Baba scratchy," Tariq announced, nestling down into his father's lap with the ease of a drowsy kitten. "I made a drawing for you. Mama has it."

Khalil nuzzled his hair, inhaling his little-boy scents of scalp and innocence and home. "That's wonderful, *habibi*. May I see?"

Naema took a square of paper from her bag and passed it over without comment, her face closed against him. Unfolding the paper, Khalil held it up to the shaded lamp on the wall. A stick figure of a boy clasping the hands of two enormous women. One was clearly Naema, yellow-eyed and in a blue abaya; the other, her face scored with lines, no doubt one of Tariq's grandmothers, who had taken to battling each other for his attention at every opportunity. In the space above them, five red tubes were flying at their heads.

"What are these red things, little love?"

"Bombs."

Khalil lowered his face into Tariq's hair, the bitter line of a poem forcing itself into his mind: *Pity the Iraqi infant, for his caul is his shroud and his future his coffin.* "And where is your Baba in this picture?"

"Baba will be in my picture when he comes home." Tariq's lower lip quivered. He buried his head in his father's chest.

Khalil had been working with Jimmy for eight months by then, during which he had only seen his son and wife four times. He knew they were trying to make the best of it, show him a brave front, but on each of his rare visits, he saw afresh how much he was missing of Tariq's development and how deep Naema's resentment had grown. Already, they had fallen into three quarrels about his job. "Why can't you just support me?" he had shouted at her the last time. "Why can't you stand with me the way you always used to?"

"Because," she had replied coldly, "you and I promised each other that we would devote our lives to curing people. Not killing them."

Now she was sitting across the café table, gazing at him with a look of fresh accusation. "What's going to happen to us?" she whispered and then quickly sat back and put on a bright face. The waiter, lean and dour, his upper lip obscured by a thick Saddam mustache, had appeared bearing a tray of tea glasses, a bowl of sugar cubes and a yogurt drink for Tariq.

While they waited in silence for the man to serve them and move on, Khalil ran his eyes over the tea shop, in the habit of checking for his safety at every second. The room was as dark as a cave back here, between its low ceiling, the smoke and crush of customers. He had chosen to meet in this place precisely because he thought its crowds and dimness would provide cover. Now it only seemed more dangerous than ever.

Naema leaned forward, her eyes fixed on his. "Khalil, did you tell you-know-who about . . ." she lowered her voice even more, "the thing on the house?" A week earlier, she had telephoned him in terror after finding a bullet in an envelope fastened to their door.

"Shh." Khalil scanned the room once again. He didn't like the look of the lone man at a nearby table huddled unconvincingly over a book, his head wrapped in a red and white *shemagh*. "Yes," he whispered. "He'll move us to a safe place as soon as he can. But I can't tell you more here. Try not to worry."

"Not worry?" She leaned closer to him, her gaze even fiercer. "This is our third warning, Khalil! Are you sure you can trust him, truly sure?"

"Yes. I trust him. Just as you, *qalbi*, must trust me."

"'A drowning man will grab even onto a snake,'" she quoted, not for the first time, and sat back, her mouth grim.

Khalil felt the anger rise in him yet again. Why could she not understand how punishing his work was, and that her lack of faith in him and Jimmy only made it more so? He tried to steady his hand as he held the cup of yogurt to Tariq's lips. "Don't talk like that," he finally said. "You're allowing this war to turn your heart black."

"And you aren't?" Naema dropped her gaze to her lap a moment, pulling at her long fingers in exactly the manner of her mother. When she raised her eyes again, he could see her own anger flickering in them. "Do you truly believe that it's worth leaving us alone at home and risking all our lives just to sell yourself to the Americans?"

"I'm not selling myself!" Leaning forward, Khalil glanced again at the man in the *shemagh* and lowered his voice to an urgent whisper. "You know I don't do this work only for the money, *ayuni*. I do it to win freedom for our country, to take back our honor and hope. And to save as many innocents from death as I can. Please, if you have no faith in me, how am I to have faith in myself?"

She reached over to wipe the yogurt from Tariq's chin and chest—the child could never eat without making a mess. "My love," she murmured finally, gazing back at Khalil, her eyes no longer angry but tender, "of course I have faith in you. You are the heart of my life. It's the war in which I lack faith. I am afraid of what it will force you to become."

16

The Resettlement Center is beginning to seem like a second home to us, for here I am yet again with Tariq. To avoid asking the soldier to drive us here, we had to walk for thirty minutes to a bus stop, wait for nearly an hour, take a long and circuitous drive and then walk again, which used up most of the morning and too much of my monthly allowance. It is a refugee's lot to suffer ignominy, of course, for the world does love to punish the unwanted, yet I cannot help but feel demoralized by the constant effort of fighting for my dignity and time.

Tariq is exhausted by the time we arrive, long walks never being easy for him, so we sink into one of the orange sofas with relief. I've brought a book to ease our wait until Derek is free, a fanciful English alphabet book I found in the Slingerlands library, its letters dancing in little hats and boots. "You say the letters, *habibi*, and I'll read the words," I tell Tariq. "And remember, books in English start from the back."

Spreading the book over his lap, I flip the pages in a random order to force him to read rather than recite by memory, as he is wont to do. It reminds me again of the days when Baba and I studied English together. How proud my father would have been of his little grandson. How he would have loved this resilient child he never knew.

"S for sugar," Tariq announces in English.

"Yes, good, but I don't see the word sugar here, my heart. It only says, "Sausage, Saucepan, Saddle and Sassafras.'"

"What's sassafras?"

I have to use the dictionary on my new portable phone to answer him. I turn to the letter F.

"F for fuck," Tariq declares.

"No! I mean, F is correct, but you mustn't say that word."

"Jim-Jim says it all the time. Uncle Ugly, too."

"I know, but they don't speak a very fine English. It's a bad word, rude."

Tariq looks up at me, his large eyes indignant. "Jim-Jim isn't rude! He speaks good English. He's teaching me. He speaks the best of anybody!"

I pull my son close. What am I to do about his adoration of Sergeant Donnell? How am I to explain to my openhearted boy that we were wrong to trust this two-faced soldier? That Khalil was mistaken about him, just as I had always thought. That Tariq must lose this man he has come to love, as he has lost so many.

"F is for Fudge, Fiddle, Ferret and Flapjack," I read.

Tariq pouts. "I don't know those words."

I'm surprised by how difficult the book is. Fudge and Fiddle I know, but Ferret and Flapjack defeat me. This is humiliating; a book meant for a kindergartener and I cannot understand it myself.

I glance up, hoping the other two refugees in the waiting room are not secretly laughing at us. Neither look as though they speak Arabic, however, both being Asian: Burmese, perhaps, or Tibetan. But I am disappointed not to see *Oum* Ismail and her husband again. After what happened last night with the soldier, I yearn more than ever for the company of my own people.

Derek appears at last and leads us to his cluttered office. Smiling in his ready way, he hands Tariq a jar of lollipops to choose from and invites us to sit.

"Mr. Derek, it has become urgent that I take a job as soon as I can," I tell him right away. "I must be able to pay for our own apartment." I lift Tariq onto my lap, where he nestles in, sucking on his sweet. "It is no longer possible to stay where we are."

Derek asks no questions, no doubt assuming that I, like so many refugees, have worn out my welcome. "Well, a new job list did come in this week," he says. "There isn't much, I'm afraid, but they're hiring cashiers at Price Chopper—seven-fifty an hour. And there's a job at Soft-Tex over in Waterford, about thirty minutes from here. They make mattresses. That pays a little more. You'd be a seamstress. They hire a lot of Iraqis, so you'd have a good chance there."

"A lot of Iraqis? I did not know there were a lot of us here." From what I have read, most of us fled to Jordan, Syria or Iran.

"Yes. Four hundred or so just around Albany."

"Oh? Are they from this war or Saddam?"

"Mostly a mix from this and the first Gulf War."

"I see." I am about to ask why four hundred of us have been sent to an area of failed farms and so few jobs that not even an American soldier can find work when Derek adds, "I know these positions aren't great, *Oum* Tariq, 'specially for someone of your qualifications, but they're all I have at the moment. Oh, and a couple hospitals are looking for cleaners."

"Thank you, but no. I will try for those first two only." I could not bear to take such a menial position in the place of my chosen profession, to become a hospital janitor instead of a doctor, although I know foreign physicians are sometimes driven to do just that. "But I have also come about something else. Is it possible for you to find a woman to drive us to New Jersey? The prosthetics clinic, it is in a place called Edgetown there and Monday is our appointment."

"Aren't there any clinics nearer than that? Why go so far?"

"Because it is the best and I must have the best for my son."

Derek takes this in. "OK. I'll ask around among our volunteers. But *Oum* Tariq, you're going to need a car. You can't get to any of these jobs without one."

I look at him. How am I to buy a car when I have no job? No job without a car, no car without a job—what does this Derek expect me to do?

Back in the waiting room, disheartened yet again, I am about to leave when *Oum* Ismail arrives with her elegant husband after all. I dare not approach, however, because she is chatting in Iraqi Arabic with another family I have not seen before, two elderly parents and three adult children. The familiar finger of ice slips down to my belly.

"*Yalla*, let's go," I whisper to Tariq. But just then she spots us.

"*Oum* Tariq, *as-salaam aleikum*! I'm so glad to see you again! And your little boy. Come, meet the Rasheed family. We knew one another at home—our mothers are cousins."

Returning her greeting, I bring Tariq over, hoping she cannot read the wariness in my face. She introduces me to *Oum* and *Abu* Mustapha, the wife small and stout, the husband short and thin, and their three children. Two are handsome sisters in their early twenties, Zahara and Yasmin, both in hijab. The third, the aforementioned Mustapha, is a short, thick-shouldered man of about my age, with abundant black hair swept back from a square, expressionless face. Neither he nor his sisters are with spouses, and I wonder whether they are widowed. Virtually every Iraqi has lost someone.

They greet me and Tariq with warmth, their eyes skipping discreetly over our wounds. "It's such a pleasure to meet somebody from home," Mustapha says, his voice low and weary. "We've been here for two years, yet we know almost no one else from our country, aside from *Oum* and *Abu* Ismail here." I am taken aback. Two years in a place with four hundred Iraqis and yet his family is almost as isolated as I am? "Please excuse me," he says then, and after a polite nod to me, approaches the young woman behind the desk and speaks to her in English. Was he an interpreter like Khalil, I wonder? And if so, did he, too, believe that what he was doing was honorable?

"We would love to have you all to our house for supper," *Oum* Ismail is saying, addressing both me and the Rasheed family. "May I telephone you, *Oum* Tariq?"

In a spill of gratitude, I accept, giving her my new telephone number. But as I lead Tariq out of the office, the finger of ice runs again through my belly. If these people grow suspicious because of my widowhood, my scar and Tariq's leg—if they think we were targeted because I or my husband were traitors, how would I defend myself? After all, Khalil did work for the occupier and that could well be seen as treasonous, even if one believes the occupier has come to overthrow a monster. Anti-Americans and Saddam's henchmen weren't the only people who saw Khalil this way, so did our resistance fighters, who believed that we should arrange our own revolution without American interference, a point of view to which I have always been more sympathetic than Khalil liked. Furthermore, there is the complicated matter of who the Rasheed family might be. Their names could be Sunni or Shi'a, so that tells me nothing. For all I know, they were spies for Saddam and that's why they have so few friends.

The truth is, however, that even if we are able to lay aside all these suspicions, the legacy of living under dictatorship and war, I can never befriend these people or any other Iraqis while I live where I do. Should they find out that I share a roof with a single man, and even worse a man who is a US soldier, they would consider me—as, apparently, does he—no better than a whore.

17

The minute I wake up the morning after my brawl in the bar, head burning with last night's alcohol and today's remorse, I know what I have to do. So, skipping my morning workout, I wash, dress and jump into my CRV to race down Route 32 to Kate's family house in Willowglen. My plan is to confront her parents once and for all and find out if they can tell me why the hell she left the country and where the fuck she went. And then make myself deal with Naema.

I know why I drank so much last night; I always do when I meet up with army buds who carry me down a rabbit hole of war memories and horseshit. But how did I manage to mess up so bad with Naema, of all people? Especially given the fact that the fight I had with Bean and Kalinski was about Khalil. They insisted that the army should never have hired Iraqi terps like him but only trustworthy Americans who can speak Arabic. I pointed out that such Americans are far and few between and that Khalil lost his life for us all, so they should show some damned respect. The discussion turned into a debate, the debate to an argument, the argument to a fist fight, and then there I was throwing myself at her with no more control than a horny teenager. Khalil's *wife*.

Shooting past a prim white church and its crumbling graveyard, tombstones stretching all the way back to the Revolutionary War, I roll into Willowglen, a hamlet so small I can drive through it between one shudder of shame and the next. The house sits up on a wooded hill just behind a collapsed barn and a sign printed with the words *The Brady Compound* in bright, belligerent purple. In all the years I've spent with Kate, I've only met her parents four times, each a worse debacle than the last, which is why I'm here in person on a Sunday instead of giving them a chance to shut me down over the phone. I pull up and park.

There's nothing about the house that looks like a compound at all—it's only a white prefab in the shape of a brick with a giant US flag flapping out front. But Kate's mom has turned the front yard into quite a display of her horticultural skills. Flowerbeds laid out in perfect diamonds of yellow tulips and purple iris. A row of trimmed boxwoods hemming the porch. Lawn shaved short as a rug.

As I approach the door, a Doberman I've never seen before barks and lunges at me from the end of a chain, the racket doing nothing to help my hangover. Suppressing the urge to kick the beast in the jaw, I ring the bell. Soon enough, heavy footsteps approach, the door swings open, and there he is: tall, stern and stiff as a shovel, face a crisp rectangle, eyes two hostile pebbles of whitish-blue, hair a metallic bristle. County Sheriff Daniel Brady. Kate's dad.

"Donnell." The man looks less than pleased to see me. "What are you doing here? Tyson, shut up!" The dog whimpers and does.

"Good evening, sir." I pull myself up to my full sergeant height. The sheriff might be tall, but I'm taller. "Sorry for intruding."

"Answer my question."

I clear my throat. "I don't know if April told you, but Kate's left the country. I was wondering if you know where she went."

"April did tell me, yes. And no, I don't." The sheriff studies me a moment, his jaw muscles flexing. "Sally!" he yells without moving.

Kate's mom bustles up from the foyer, round-bellied and doughy, one of those vague, soft women whose sweetness is like a candy bar full of razor blades. She blinks at me. "Oh. It's you."

To my relief, April runs up behind her. Fifteen years old, all leg and dangling blond hair, full of affectionate kisses for her sister and sarcastic remarks for their dad. She was the flower girl at our wedding, cute as a bug in a little pink dress. She, at least, looks happy to see me. "Jimmy!" She flings her skinny arms around me. "You find out anything about where Katie is?"

I hug her back. Sweet kid. "No. I was hoping you have."

"We'll discuss this inside," the sheriff says. "Though we were just about to have lunch." He marches me into the living room and points to an armchair. "Sit."

I'd forgotten how glitzy this house is, how unlike my down-to-earth Kate. Polished side tables wobbling under fat porcelain lamps, their gold shades fringed with tassels. An ivory wall-to-wall carpet so clean it looks like nobody's ever dared step on it. Oatmeal-colored curtains that remind me of the hospice hotel where my mom died. A waxed mahogany sideboard in which, I know from Kate, the sheriff keeps his guns.

I lower myself gingerly into one of the pristine white armchairs, looking up at the family arrayed around me. "So none of you have heard anything from her at all?"

"No, and I'm worried." Sally Brady folds her arms across her belly, kneading her elbows. "She doesn't get in touch with us very often, as you know. Still, it's not like her to leave the country without telling us." She squints at me with the same suspicion her husband did. Back when Kate was about to graduate high school, her mom told her that she would be doing God's work if she joined the army and that it was all in the Lord's plan when Kate would die, whether she went to war or not. And now Sally and her husband blame me for their strained relations with their daughter when, in truth, Kate has never forgiven them for pushing her to enlist and so, as she sees it, sending her to get screwed over and up by the army, Iraq, and especially by Kormick.

Kate refused to do anything for a long time after that maniac attacked her, too busy blaming herself to see straight. But finally, her best friend, a specialist named Yvette Sanchez, persuaded Kate to go with her to the one and only female officer on base and report him. That female officer acted all sympathetic and shocked, giving Kate back some faith in the military after all. But only a few days later, she and Yvette were put on shooter mission, which meant Yvette riding in the front truck of a convoy, Kate bringing up the rear, both of them right in the line of fire. Known as a suicide mission, it was what the army did with the grunts it wanted to punish. Or silence.

Kate and Yvette survived anyhow—that is, until they got to Camp Warhorse at the end of the day. The two of them were in the MWR building with a bunch of other soldiers, some checking their email, others playing Ping-Pong or watching TV, when it was hit by a mortar. The whole building lifted right off the ground, shook and smashed down again. Kate was knocked over. Yvette and three others were killed.

I went to see Kate soon as I could after that. She was up on her tower, hunched in her chair, hot wind and sand blasting at her like dragon breath. She had her rifle pointed right at the prisoners milling around in the compound below.

"Can I come up?" I called over the racket.

She didn't answer. I climbed the ladder anyway and squatted beside her. She glanced behind me. "You alone?"

"'Course I am."

"I keep hearing things." She shook her head as if a fly was caught under her helmet. "You hear that buzzing sound?"

I listened. Wind. Yells. The usual clamor of panic and yearning inside my brain. "Nope."

She pressed a finger into her ear. "It's like I got cicadas trapped in my head. I think that mortar screwed up my hearing."

I touched her knee. "Listen, Kate, I'm real sorry about Yvette. I know how much—"

"Yeah." She stared out at the sand. "It's my fault, you know."

"That's not true!"

"It is. They never would've sent her out on that mission if she hadn't helped me report Kormick. It was me they were trying to punish, not her. She was just collateral damage."

I pulled Kate close then, the prisoners' leers be damned. "You gotta stop blaming yourself for everything. You didn't do anything wrong."

"Yvette was gonna be my roomie when we got home," she said into my chest. "We were gonna help each other get through everything."

I hugged her tighter. I had something else to tell her, too, something I wished I didn't have to say at all. Fumbling in my utility vest, I eased out the photo of Naema's father and little brother that Kate had given me in the hopes I would find them among the detainees I was guarding. The photo was torn and crumpled now, the father missing. Only the kid's goofy face was left, creased right across his forehead. I handed it to her.

"What's this?"

"Read the back."

She turned it over. The original name Naema had written, Zaki Jassim, was there. But next to it, in different writing, were the words: *July 9, 2003, shot in attempted escape. Deceased July 10.*

Kate crushed the photo and threw it off the tower.

"What are you doing?"

"I don't give a fuck," she said through her teeth. "Those hajjis killed Yvette. They tried to kill us all. They're stinking shits and I hope they all die."

I was shocked. Even in the middle of all the bullcrap of war, I was shocked. "It doesn't bother you that we killed a thirteen-year-old kid?"

"I almost killed a kid myself out there on the convoy, Jimmy. Little boy same age as April. Shot his donkey instead." She glanced at me, her mouth tight. "I wanted to kill him, *really* wanted him to die." She spat over the side of the tower. "That's who I am now."

"Come on, Kate, don't talk like that."

"It's true. I've hurt so many people. You don't even know."

I longed to shake her, rid her of whoever she was impersonating. "Stop," I said. "You're a good person, Kate. Don't let this place make you forget that. I know things are fucked up here, 'course they are. But I love you, and I want us to help each other when we get home."

"No." She pushed me away. "We aren't gonna work, Jimmy."

"What do you mean?"

"I mean what you and me have here isn't real. It's got nothing to do with life at home. With who we really are. And if we stay together, we'll just screw each other up even worse."

"That's not true! We can get through this together, don't you see? Who else will understand us like we can?"

"But I don't want to go home and be the person I am with you, Jimmy. I don't want to bring the war home with me. Or the army, either. I hate who I am here. I hate who I am even with you."

I jump up from the Brady's white armchair—nobody else is sitting anyway—and look at Kate's family one by one, each holding a trace of Kate herself: her dad's pale eyes, her mom's strawberry curls, her sister's smattering of freckles. I can see they're telling the truth about not hearing from Kate, 'though this only worries me more than ever. "Well, if she calls, let me know," I tell them. "And if I hear from her, I'll let you know, too."

But the sheriff is glaring at me now. "Donnell, I've got something to say to you, and you need to listen."

"Sir?" I tense.

"If Kate's run this far to get away from you, then obviously something's very wrong."

"Yes, I—"

"I said *listen*. I don't know what you did to scare her off like this, but I do know it couldn't have been good. You'll get her back over my dead body. Understand? Now get out of here!"

"But . . ."

"I said leave!"

I'm sorely tempted to knock the man's head clear across the room but force myself to walk out of the house instead, slamming the front door so hard it sets off the dog again.

Back in the car, I'm just about to drive away with a furious screech when I hear a tap on the window. I roll down the glass. It's April peering in, her brow rumpled. "Jimmy, I know you wouldn't hurt Katie for anything," she whispers. "Dad's being a dick. I'll call you if we hear from her. Promise."

I look at her young face a moment, a face I've known since she was eight, its worried expression so like Kate's it hurts. "You're a good kid, April. Kate must be missing you like hell."

Soon as I get home, I kick the couch a few times, curse a few more, and then throw myself into the desk chair to search through Kate's email and Facebook pages on her computer yet again. I've long since given up expecting her to write to me but I can't help doing this several times each day and night anyway, like I have for weeks, even though it makes me feel like a perv and a stalker. We share a password—that's how much we trusted each other—so I've been able to comb the ten pages of messages and posts that have come in from her friends and the principal of her school demanding to know where she is. "Kate, see my email now!" "Kate, I HAVE to talk to you today." "Ms. Brady, we're holding an emergency staff meeting tomorrow at 8:00 a.m. *All faculty required to attend.*" "Ms. Brady, your students need you."

Not one has been answered. Or, far as I can see, even read.

I pry my phone out of my pocket and dial Pat.

"How's the noggin?" is his greeting. "You were boiled as an owl last night."

"Not too good. Listen, you doing anything after work?"

"Nope. Want some company?"

"Yeah. It's feeling a little too quiet around here. Naema isn't speaking to me."

"What? Why? 'Cause you were plastered?"

"No. Something happened she . . . misunderstood."

"Uh-oh. You didn't make a move on her, did you, bro?"

"'Course not! Well, thing is, she thinks I did. But I didn't. I don't think. Don't tell Lisa, OK? I mean it."

"Woo boy. OK, I won't. Want us to bring a movie over?"

"Yeah, that'd be good. Advil, too. I've run out."

"Got any booze?"

"Nope, and I don't want any. I'm on the wagon right now. But Pat? You know I don't watch movies about war, right? And don't bring one about love, either. I'm not in the fucking mood."

"That cuts out just about every movie ever made, but I'll see what we got. And I'll pick up some beer, wagon or no wagon."

I spend the rest of the day trying to purge my system of last night's booze, the memory of Naema in my arms and the battery-acid taste of guilt in my mouth, along with an ever-deepening spin of hurt over Kate. I tidy up the house until everything is either in a straight row or perfectly squared. Hunt down every dust mouse and suck it up with the vacuum. Wash and dry the laundry, folding it into immaculate piles. Sprint my twelve klicks around the sleepy streets of Slingerlands. Pound weights in the basement till every muscle screams and force myself through my usual marathon of push-ups. Then I shower, my eye falling on the mangled clot of Kate's rose soap dissolving in the corner, which I still can't bring myself to throw out. I even bury my face in one of her empty drawers, hoping to catch a remnant of her scent. Nothing helps.

My phone rings just as I'm getting dressed. "Hey, Jimmy?" It's April, sounding small and wistful. "I still feel bad about Dad being such an asshole."

"That's OK, kid. Not your fault."

"But I don't understand, Jimmy. Why hasn't Katie even sent me a text saying where she is? Or sent you one? It's been, like, six weeks already. Why's she being so mean?"

"Good question." I pace the bedroom, my head revving up into a new bout of vicious thudding. "What about you, April, you OK?"

"Guess so." She hesitates. "I just, like, miss her, y'know?"

Of course I know. "I'm sure she'll get in touch with you soon. She loves you too much not to. You will call me when you hear from her, right?"

"You know I will, I already promised. I'm on your side, Jimmy, don't worry, no matter what Dad says. Gotta go now. Mom's calling me."

The phone clicks off and I stand gazing down at it. A little slab of misery in my hand.

"You do look like a boiled owl," is the first thing Lisa says the minute she and Pat walk in that evening, Pat with a six-pack, Lisa with a sack of potato chips. "I hear you got seriously trashed last night."

I shrug, sending my blabbermouth brother a scowl, and we all pry off our shoes and squeeze onto the couch, kicking our feet up on the coffee table alongside the chips and beer. Lisa takes the middle, her warm body pressed up just close enough to make me ache all over again for Kate, while Pat starts up the DVD and nestles in beside her. I gaze at our row of feet. My toes long and wax-white. Pat's hairy. Lisa's round and smooth, the nails painted neon pink. I look away quickly. That severed baby foot in its sandal.

The movie turns out to be one of Pat's picks, a comedy about a gaggle of teenage boys trying to get laid, which might have amused me at fifteen but certainly doesn't at thirty. I close my eyes, memories of last night burning through me yet again. *Remorse* and *regret,* I tell myself. *Reparation, atonement, amends. Restitution* and *recompense, conciliation* and *compensation.* So many words for saying, *I fucked up.* For saying, *I'm sorry.*

About twenty minutes into the film, Lisa stands, stretches and yawns. "This movie's sucking my brain. I'm going to see Naema." And before I can react, she's out the front door.

I reach for a beer after all.

18

Pushing open the screen to the back porch, Lisa ducks under a line of drying underpants and bras, knocks on the glass door to Naema's apartment and turns away, embarrassed. The room is so exposed and, well, *unprivate* from here. She can see all the way inside as clearly as if it were lit up by a spotlight.

Naema looks up from her medical books, startled. No one ever visits her here, not even Rory, who has been coming to the house almost every day to play with Tariq. Seeing Lisa through the glass, she gets up from her rickety desk and opens the door warily, suspecting that Jimmy has sent her as an emissary. "Hello, Lisa. How nice to see you," she says anyway. "Please to come in."

Smiling shyly, Lisa steps inside and takes a quick look around. This used to be Jimmy and Kate's rec room, but now the pool table and barbells are gone, a woven rug lies in a corner and, instead of their Modest Mouse and Foo Fighters posters, the walls are hung with a scarlet tapestry and an array of embroidered shawls. "Wow, you've made it amazing in here," she exclaims. "It doesn't even look American."

Naema laughs.

"Oh, I didn't mean—"

"No, it is funny what you said." Naema turns to Tariq, who is sitting in the middle of the floor, absorbed in a book. "*Habibi*, aren't you going to say hello to Aunty Lisa?"

He raises his eyes to her, his narrow face preoccupied. "Hi, Aunty Lisa," he says in a perfect American accent.

"Hey there." She crouches beside him. "What're you reading?"

"*Ali Baba*. Look—bad guys in pots." He shows her a picture of the forty thieves cowering in their urns. "Morgiana, she trick them bad!"

"You're reading that in English?"

"He is beginning, yes," Naema replies for him. "But mostly he guesses the words because he knows the story so well. It is from our part of the world, after all."

Lisa nods. She has no idea who Morgiana is, so decides to keep mum on the subject. "Where's *Oum* Khalil?" she asks.

"She is sleeping. Please, sit. I will make tea."

Lisa follows her across the room, catching a glimpse of the old lady behind one of the bamboo screens. She's lying on her back, her white hair spread over the pillow, her body barely making a bump under the sheets. "She's gotten so skinny," Lisa whispers. "Is she alright?"

Naema gazes at Hibah a moment. "I am not sure. These last few days, she has refused to leave her bed or eat. I can only make her take soup and tea. If I had my medical equipment, I would be able to check her. But her pulse and temperature, they are normal. I think it is only that she is sad, and that our move here has made her tired."

"You don't think she should go to a hospital?"

"She is afraid of hospitals. But if she continues like this, yes, I shall make her go."

Moving to the tiny alcove that serves as their kitchen, Naema places a kettle on the countertop burner and tells Lisa to sit at the small, black disk of a metal table beside her, the kind normally seen at outdoor cafés. Lisa obeys, watching Naema curiously. The weather has turned unusually steamy for June and the room is stifling, yet Naema is encased in jeans and a long-sleeved red shirt, her braid draped over one shoulder. In comparison, Lisa, in a bright orange sundress, feels naked. She glances up at the ceiling fan, wondering why Naema hasn't turned it on.

"So, Lisa, you are enjoying the classes in your college?" Naema flicks her braid behind her and opens a packet of tea.

"They're over for the summer. The semester doesn't start up again till September."

"Oh? Then what is it you do during the summers?"

"Work." Lisa smiles up at her. "I waitress at this place in Albany on weekends. Pays pretty good, 'least with tips. And I'm helping one of my professors research her book."

Naema spoons the tealeaves into a little saucepan, douses them with boiling water from the kettle and sets the saucepan inside a larger one of hot water to brew. This girl, so young and not even out of college, has two jobs, whereas she, a mother and a doctor, cannot find even one. "The book by your professor, what is it about?"

"How small businesses affect the economy. I'm majoring in business admin. So I can, like, run an office one day?"

"You must be a good student for your professor to have hired you like this." When the tea is ready, Naema pours it into two tulip-shaped glasses she bought in Damascus. "Sugar?"

"No thanks. Trying to slim down for the wedding dress, y'know?"

Naema sits opposite her, sending the table into a fit of wobbling. She hands Lisa a glass. "The tea, you might find a little strong without sugar." She pushes over a bowl of sugar cubes and a saucer of gingersnaps. "In Iraq, we do not expect our women to be thin like a boy. You will be beautiful in your wedding dress. Have you chosen the day yet?"

Lisa shakes her head, understanding that she will have to take a cookie out of politeness and probably the sugar, too. "We're talking a year from now, maybe?"

"That is far away. Why do you wait so long? My husband and I, we were forced apart early in the war but when we found each other again, we married immediately and, *wallah*, I was pregnant within a month." Naema tosses a sugar cube into her mouth and drains a sip of tea through it.

Lisa blinks. "Um, well I want to graduate before I get married. And—this is supposed to be a secret—but Pat's decided to apply to community college this fall. Don't tell Jimmy, though. Pat wants it to be a surprise."

Naema wonders why anything about education would be a secret, but then she is not planning to speak to the soldier again, anyway. She braces herself for a plea from Lisa on his behalf, but after several minutes of conversation have passed with no further mention of him, she relaxes. "Lisa, may I ask of you a question?" she asks eventually, cupping her hands around her tea as though the room were cold, not creeping up to ninety degrees.

"Sure." Lisa takes a bite of cookie, its gingery spice fizzing pleasantly on her tongue.

"This restaurant where you are a waitress, do you think I could get work there? For weeks I have looked for a job but the only one I can find is in a town far away and I have no car. It is a seamstress job in a factory. I was a seamstress in Damascus. I would wish not to do that again."

Naema still has nightmares about the mounds of headscarves she had to trim every night in Damascus, one of the only two ways she had found to earn a living, Syria having banned refugees from legal employment. The problem with piecework, though, she discovered too late, is that it only makes money if you are fast and skilled. She had to buy the undecorated scarves from a supplier, trim their edges with lace or beads, and then sell them back to him for a profit. If she sewed the trimmings crookedly, as her unpracticed fingers tended to do, or failed to produce the required fifty scarves a day, the supplier would dock her pay and she would end up earning less than she had spent in the first place.

"I don't know if they need anyone right now," Lisa replies carefully. "I'll ask when I go in this weekend." She knows the restaurant will never hire Naema. They want fresh-faced young girls like her, not war-scarred widows. "And if that doesn't work out, I'll see what else I can find for you." But her eyes flick away just enough to quash Naema's hopes.

Lisa takes a second cookie. "Any news about Tariq's leg?" she asks to ease the silence.

Naema gathers herself. "Yes, it is good. We go to the clinic tomorrow to have it fitted, *insh'Allah*. The clinic, it is in New Jersey and we must stay there for three days. The Resettlement Center has promised to find us a driver."

"Jimmy isn't taking you?"

"No."

Lisa senses not to ask why. "What time is your appointment?"

"In the morning. Nine o'clock."

"Then I'll take you. Where're you staying?"

"We shall find a cheap hotel. I have saved the money for this."

"Cool. I'll drive you there and then come pick you up when you're done."

"But what about your job, Lisa? This drive, it will take much of the day."

"Not a problem. Long as I put in enough hours, my prof doesn't care when I work. And I only waitress nights."

"You could truly do this?" Naema's mood lifts. She would so much prefer to drive with this friendly girl than a stranger.

"Yeah, it'll be fun! And hey, maybe we could swing into the city on our way back. You haven't seen it yet, have you?"

Naema breaks into a smile, her face lighting up in a way Lisa has never yet seen. "No, we have not. This is very good of you, Lisa." She turns to Tariq, who is building an elaborate tower with the wooden blocks Rory gave him for his birthday. "*Habibi*, Aunty Lisa, she is taking us to see the big city!" she says in English.

He looks up. "New York City?"

"Yes, my love."

Seizing his crutches, he wrenches himself upright and swings over to Lisa. "Aunty Lisa, you're the best!" And with a grin, he snatches a cookie and crams it into his mouth.

By the time Lisa returns to Jimmy's living room, the brothers have given up on the movie, too, and are watching a game instead. "Wanna beer?" Patrick asks when she comes in.

"No thanks." Squeezing between them again, she leans her head on his shoulder. "Naema stuffed me with tea. My head's spinning, it's so strong. Hey, know what?" She sits up and turns to Jimmy, who looks about as funereal as she's ever seen him. "I'm driving her and Tariq to New Jersey tomorrow. Then we're gonna do the big city!"

"New Jersey? Why?"

"You don't know? Tariq's getting his leg!"

Jimmy's jaw tightens. "She didn't tell me."

Lisa takes in the hurt in his eyes. What could have happened between him and Naema? Lisa has long noticed that Naema feels uncomfortable around the brothers, which doesn't surprise her, given their bulk and swagger, the masculine restlessness they exude like a sweat and the powerful miasma of love and resentment that swirls between them. Lisa had needed a while to get used to the Donnell brothers herself, coming, as she does, from a family of girls. But clearly something more than that has gone wrong. Could it be because of their histories in the war? Or is it something to do with Kate?

"Jimmy," she says gently, "I don't think this arrangement you've got going here is working out. Have you seen how they're living back there, all cramped together like that, no room to move and no privacy? They need a real home. They need a place of their own." She puts a hand on his knee. "I know it's hard, I know how much it means to you to have them here. But it's time you let go."

19

An old dream of mine returned to haunt me last night, tearing me out of sleep with familiar cruelty. Perhaps it was Derek's offer of the seamstress job that brought it back, or my conversation with Lisa, but there I was again, sewing Tariq's severed leg back onto his body as if it were a stocking, not flesh and bone, holding his torso across my knees while he screamed and writhed. Over and over I plunged the needle in, but either it refused to penetrate or it pierced my own leg, causing spurts of blood to leap from the wounds until I shouted myself awake.

Too disturbed to fall back asleep, I lay there helplessly, the dream spinning me back to memories of those first days after Tariq's amputation, when I was too numbed by shock to push my mind beyond what had to be done from one moment to the next. Khalil's friend Salim found us there in the hospital, I sitting by Tariq's cot, staring at the space where his leg had been and at a future without Khalil; Tariq himself still asleep, sedated from the operation, his residual thigh wrapped in bandages.

"*Oum* Tariq, I'm sorry, but you have to leave now," Salim whispered urgently, leaning close so as not to be heard by the people crowded around us. "The militias are searching for you. Quick, pick up Tariq and come!"

"Now?" I looked up at him, too stupefied to grasp what he was saying.

"Yes, now." He glanced about nervously. The hospital room was crammed with the wounded and their families, with cries and screams and blood. "Take your son and come! *Oum* Khalil is waiting in my taxi. We have your passports and visas, but all our efforts will be for nothing if you don't come this instant."

I stood as if in a trance and gathered up Tariq, his bandages already stained with seeping blood, his little face and arms pocked with shrapnel wounds. "Whose efforts?" I just managed to ask. "And visas to where?"

"Sergeant Donnell's and mine. You're going to Syria." Salim darted another look about the room. "Follow me. Speak to nobody, look at nobody. Hurry!"

In the taxi, I held Tariq tight as Salim careened from one side of the road to the other to avoid hurtling cars and military vehicles, roadblocks and soldiers, muttering prayers all the way and checking his rearview mirror to see if we were being followed. Tariq was awake now, his little face pulled tight with pain, his cries tearing at my chest. Hibah sat beside us, in too much shock to speak. *Allah,* I prayed without even knowing what I was saying, *please make all this a dream, please make it not real, please save my child from death.*

The minute we reached the airport, Salim hurried us inside and handed me our documents, along with a wallet of cash. "Telephone me whenever you wish," he said, his eyes full of tears. "And don't be afraid, *Oum* Tariq. I loved Khalil, *rahimahullah,* as did Sergeant Donnell. We will do all we can for you." And with that he left, taking with him our last ties to home.

On the airplane, the first I had ever ridden, I sat gazing through the glassy rectangle of window beside me, watching the lights from the runway blur and smear the glass, a jet of cold air tattooing the back of my neck, my mind reeling somewhere between the earth and the underworld. *See what this job of yours has done to us?* I whispered to Khalil. *How many times did I beg you to stop*? Tariq lay across my lap, just as he does in my dream, moaning in his sleep. Hibah stared at the seatback in front of her, still mute and unmoving. I shut my eyes, my body a tangle of fear, anger and despair.

The flight to Damascus took only ninety minutes. Once we landed, each one of us still in a daze, we cleared passport control and customs without trouble, for Syria had not yet begun to close its doors to us, and my ignorance of the treasures Hibah had hidden in my shoes and sanitary napkins perhaps also helped us avoid suspicion. We then joined a string of other passengers outside to wait for a taxi, although to where we did not know. Hibah gripped the handle of our lone little suitcase, still not speaking a word. I clutched the whimpering Tariq in my arms, praying that he wouldn't start screaming again, while the sweat rolled down my face, stinging the fresh stitches in my cheek. The other passengers eyed us and edged away.

No taxis would take us. Driver after driver approached, took one look at my mutilated son and his bloody bandages, at the fresh stitches in my face, and refused to let us into his car. For more than an hour we stood there, Tariq weeping in my arms, my back aching under his weight, Hibah swaying until she had to sit on our suitcase. Only after I agreed to pay three times the price of the trip, enough to live on for a fortnight, did one man deign to take us. "I'll bring you to a cheap hotel in Qudsiya," he said. "That area is full of fugitives from Iraq like you. But please, lady, keep that blood off my seats."

The hotel, of course, was not cheap, as was evident the minute we passed under a stone archway into its chic scarlet lobby, although it did probably belong to a friend of that driver. Had Tariq not been wounded, my poor child, he would have been enchanted by the sweeping staircase, gleaming mosaic floor and multicolored lanterns, whereas I could only think of the cost. But we were much too distraught and exhausted to even consider venturing out to seek a cheaper hotel, so I beckoned Hibah, whose eyes seemed to have sunken into their sockets, and approached the man behind the reception desk to ask for a room.

A stiff little grandfather with a bristling white mustache and almost no hair, he wasted no time in demanding that we pay for two nights on the spot or leave. "I've had too many people like you disappear without paying, daughter," he told me in a hollow attempt at an apology. How the fortunate like to suck from the unfortunate, I thought. But I drew Salim's wallet from my bag.

Our room, tucked down a corridor behind the hotel courtyard, was, unsurprisingly, nowhere as glamorous as the lobby: an iron bedstead holding a mattress just wide enough for two, a bare concrete floor, a naked lightbulb swinging from a wire in the ceiling, a slit of window above the door. It mattered not to me. I only wanted to climb into bed and sleep all the horror away.

"It looks like a prison cell in here," Hibah grumbled, speaking for the first time all day. She peeled back the sheets to inspect for bedbugs and fleas. "Have they nothing in their chests but stones that they make us pay for a palace and give us a hovel?"

I laid Tariq down on the bed and slid a clean towel beneath him, preparing to unwrap his bandages and wash his wounds. "This is not a hovel, Mama, it's fine. But thousands of us Iraqis are arriving here every day, so perhaps you are right. The hearts of our hosts must have long since drained dry. Please, fetch me some water and whatever you can find that's clean enough to wash him with."

My little Tariq. His tiny round legs. Carefree eyes. Joyous smile. All gone. I looked over at Hibah and longed for my own mother. I looked into space and longed for Khalil. I looked at Tariq, who was weeping again with fear, pain and exhaustion, and longed for him to be whole.

"Hush, *habibi*, it will stop hurting soon," I told him when I finished my ministrations, wiping away his tears and kissing each cheek. "I'm going out now to find some food for us and medicine and fresh bandages for you."

"No, Mama, stay here!"

"I'll be back very soon, little heart, don't worry. Bibi will stay with you."

"I want Baba!"

I closed my eyes.

"Don't be long," Hibah said then, and I could hear a new fear in her voice. She, like I, was only just beginning to understand the depth of our isolation, exiled as we were now from our country, our home, our friends and our family.

Wrapping myself in one of her black abayas, I ventured down the hall to find the proprietor again and ask him for guidance. He was still behind the reception counter, perched on a high stool, watching the state news on a tiny black-and-white television mounted on a shelf. Syria was trembling to its roots then, a cruel drought, its own murderous dictator and the revolutions in Tunisia and Egypt stirring discontent throughout the land. But it was not yet at war, as we were, and so was still a haven for us.

"Grandfather," I asked, "would you please tell me where I can find something to eat for my child and medicine to help him with his pain?"

The little man switched off the television, jumped down from his stool and leaned on the counter to face me, his white mustache tickling his nostrils. "My daughter, your misfortunes are our misfortunes, your wounds our wounds," he said to my surprise. "May Allah punish all who had a hand in your war. Go to your room. My wife will bring you everything you need, do not fear. Go rest now, and peace be with you and your little boy."

So he did have a heart, not a stone, after all.

That night, after we had eaten the simple but good meal the proprietor's wife had brought us, washed and redressed Tariq's limb, all three of us climbed into the narrow bed to try to sleep. Only Tariq succeeded. I was still too shocked to even close my eyes, and I could sense the equally wide eyes of Hibah beside me, her silent tears soaking the pillow, her breath quavering. Looking back now, it is astonishing to me that we were able to breathe at all, let alone sit on an airplane, walk, bathe, eat and talk. I only know that my mind kept rejecting all that had happened, accepting, rejecting, accepting, memories of those last moments with Khalil wrenching through me over and over until the pain was so great, all I could do was reject them again.

The next morning, I pulled on Hibah's abaya once more, left her to look after Tariq and went out in search of our future.

The minute I stepped into the street, I found myself caught in a whirlwind of color and noise. A market had sprung up overnight, pulling in crowds of people and dozens of stalls, the vendors calling out their wares in a chorus of chants and shouts while shoppers wheedled and bargained. All around me were carts heaped with potatoes, onions and cucumbers gleaming in the sun; tomatoes nestled like rubies against bright yellow napkins; piles of oranges and dates, olives and melons; sacks of rice, lentils, tea . . . After all our years of deprivation and hunger at home, of stale crusts and watery soups, this abundance so disoriented me that I had to lean my back against a wall, close my eyes and wait for my body to remember that this was not the Baghdad of my youth but the Damascus of my present.

For the next five hours, I walked down one busy street after another, accosting anyone I overheard speaking Iraqi Arabic to ask where I might find a home and a job. All I met with were shakes of the head or improper suggestions. I did not know yet that this was not the ill luck of one day but the way my luck would go for months. Sometimes ignorance truly is a blessing.

As the weeks passed like this, our money dwindling away on hotel bills and food, Hibah lost patience with me and we fell to quarreling. "Why can't you find work?" she would scold, deaf to all my explanations. "Aren't you a doctor? Or is it that you are too proud to take the menial work of an immigrant?"

"Mama, I'd take anything, I keep telling you!" I would snap back. "But no one will hire an Iraqi refugee." I did not mention that the only jobs offered to me were by pimps and brothel madams, or how many Iraqi widows like me I had seen succumb to their offers.

One day, after two months of this fruitless searching, I was sent by the baker from whom I bought our daily *samoon* to ask advice of the proprietor of an Iraqi hair salon across the road. Her eyes were painted the same purple as her hijab, and her lipstick so bright I suspected that hairdressing was not all she did, but she was kind enough to me. She had moved from Mosul to Damascus many years earlier, she told me, and thus had learned how to negotiate the city. "I know a building you could move into, sister, but you must put your name on a long waiting list to get an apartment there and then wait many months to crawl up it." She smiled slyly. "There is one way to speed your ascent, however."

I paid her my bribe.

Not long after that, my luck turned again. I was in the bakery once more when someone behind me called my name. I looked up, and there was my childhood neighbor and playmate, Nassar, smiling at me. "Naema, my sister, peace be with you, how wonderful to see you!" he cried in delight. "Are you, too, an escapee now?" I said I was, and shrugging the shrug of a fatalist, he invited me to a nearby chai shop for tea. Like us, Nassar had only just left Iraq with his family, although in a more orderly manner than we had and with more money. "I can help," he said when I revealed our predicament. "My mother, Allah bring her rest, is dying. Would you come to sit with her in the night while we sleep? We would be honored to have a doctor like you look after her, and we will, forgive me for mentioning this, be able to pay."

I accepted, trying to hide my humiliation under a smile.

A week later, I also took on the piecework that later gave me those nightmares, spending my nights trimming hijabs beside the old woman's bed until she needed a spoonful of soup, a bedpan, her clothes changed, her aching body massaged or her bedsores medicated. Once Nassar's wife rose in the morning to take over, I would creep back to the hotel, my fingers sore from needle pricks, eyes watering with yawns, where I would sleep for a few hours, play with Tariq for a few more, and then leave again to buy food, run errands, or take him to a doctor.

We stayed in that hotel for three months before my name finally reached the top of the housing list, my bribe only stretching so far. The room we were given was small and dark, the ceiling yellowed by nicotine, our window filled with the concrete wall of the building next door and the squabbles and lovemaking of our neighbors. And, just as in the hotel, we had only one bed. But at least, between the occasional sums of money Sergeant Donnell sent us and the pittance I was earning, we could eat and pay the rent.

For two and a half years, we lived in that room. Tariq learned to use his crutches, fend off bullies and work hard at clowning to win even one friend. Hibah looked after him with devotion, while perfecting the arts of complaining and scolding me. I nursed Nassar's dying mother and sewed, gathered documents, filled out forms and spent hours waiting in queues.

And now, here we are, in the land of golden promises, riches and rights, of glistening opportunity and whitened smiles, still without status or respect, and still living, cooking and sleeping in one room, our futures no more visible now than they were the instant the bomb exiled us from home.

20

Tariq sits in the back of Lisa's red Fiesta, his head clamped between a pair of enormous black earphones, his mind awhirl with pictures of bionic limbs and futuristic cities. Lisa's promise to take him and Mama to New York City, which he assumes from cartoons will be spiky, glittering and abuzz with flying cars, warms his stomach like a swallow of hot chocolate, but even more intoxicating is the thought of having two whole legs. He will be able to run and jump now, play football without crutches, climb gigantic rocks like the ones Jim-Jim carried him over on that mountain. He will be able to do all the things other children do, and nobody will even notice he's different.

The music filtering through the iPod and earphones Jimmy lent him is a mix of the Coldplay and U2 he wants Tariq to like, the high-pitched women singers Tariq favors and Hibah's oud music. Naema wanted Tariq to listen to children's songs in English, but he met this suggestion with scorn. He doesn't care for all of Jimmy's music, either, the aggressive guitars and growling male singers stirring his old, frightening dreams. Nor does he like the yearning notes of the oud, which put an ache behind his eyes. But he does enjoy the perky voices of Beyoncé and Taylor Swift, and a beat that makes him bounce in his seat.

Naema twists around from the front to watch him, his eager face tiny between the earphones, his head bobbing to the music as he hums along. For so many years she feared that the war and loss of his father and leg would drain the happiness from him forever. But look at him now.

"Hey, Naema?" Lisa says, smiling at his tuneless warble as she hurtles downstate to the thruway. She drives almost as fast as the soldier, to Naema's alarm.

"You figured out a school yet? Jimmy said you don't want Tariq to go to one near him."

"No, I am still looking." Naema turns back to her, struck by how fresh Lisa looks for six-thirty in the morning, her yellow sundress crisp and bright; her broad, capable hands guiding the steering wheel. She, on the other hand, feels anything but fresh. She should have had more coffee. "Derek at the Resettlement Center, he recommended that I choose a school where Tariq can be with other children who are immigrants. I do not wish my Tariq to be, uh, how you say...?"

"Bullied?"

"Yes, bullied. But I am worried, Lisa, that in any American school, he will forget his Arabic."

"He won't if you keep it up at home. That's what my gramma did for us." Lisa changes lanes to pass a black pickup festooned with the American flags that had become so ubiquitous since 9/11, its bumper sticker blaring the words, *Support Our Troops*.

"You did not grow up speaking English?"

"No, Spanish. We're from the DR originally—Dominican Republic? Though we're Americans now."

"Ah, I see." Naema plucks again at her fingers. Will she and Tariq ever reach a time when they can say they are Americans? She looks back at the truck. Will they even want to?

Lisa glances over at her. Despite the heat, Naema is dressed in formal office attire, a black jacket and pants, white office shirt, heavy black shoes. Her hair is pinned up, her eyes lined with kohl. Once again, Lisa feels underdressed.

"Lisa, may I ask of you another favor?"

"Ask away." Naema's formality tickles her.

"Thank you. Could you please visit *Oum* Khalil while I am gone? She refuses to eat even her soup now without encouragement. Also, I fear she might grow afraid at being alone."

"Happy to. But isn't Jimmy keeping an eye on her?"

Naema gazes out the passenger window, the landscape unreeling before her. Blond fields. Lavender mountains. Sunlight flickering through leaf-heavy trees. The carcass of a deer rotting by the roadside, mouth gaping, eyes glazed. "I would not know," she says and not a word more.

When Lisa drops them off at the prosthetics clinic, a squat gray building in the middle of a squat gray street, Naema checks her customary folder of forms to make certain she hasn't forgotten anything, trying not to succumb to her usual conviction that something will go wrong. The officials inside will tell her that she lacks the correct papers or that Medicaid will not pay after all or that Tariq is too old or too young—something will make them send her poor son away with nothing, as they so often have before. Pulling him close, she sends a silent plea to Allah while they wait for Lisa to park and join them.

Inside the clinic's cramped waiting room, which is small, square and brown, more like a car rental office than a medical facility, Tariq takes one look at the other three people sitting against the wall, each missing a body part—something he hasn't seen since Baghdad—and breaks into terrified cries. "Mama," he screams, "take me away! Take me now!"

Startled, she drops to a crouch and wraps her arms around him. "Shh, my love, it's all right. Try to be brave like Iron Man. They're going to make you a new leg, remember? Then you'll be able to play football all the time."

But he refuses to be comforted. "I want Jim-Jim! Mama, take me home!"

Lisa glances at the other patients, wondering what they think of this child wailing in Arabic. Two of them, an elderly woman and man, each without a foot, are watching him with open, if wary, curiosity. But the third, a youth of about twenty with a shorn head, bulked-up shoulders and a gaunt, tense face, is darting agonized looks at Tariq. He is missing both legs below the knee. Oh, Lisa realizes—a veteran.

Tariq takes some time to calm down, but at last he stops crying and consents to sit on his mother's lap, although he is still shuddering and sniffing back tears. She holds him close, the plastic chair wobbling beneath them. "I won't let anyone hurt you, *habibi*, I promise. But no more crying, all right?" He sniffs and nods.

A heavyset young woman with an unusually long neck and cropped blond hair emerges from behind a glass window then, as though she's been waiting for the storm to clear. "Hi, cutie, you all right now?" She pulls up a chair and sits facing him, her white shirt and pants bagging around her. "I'm Marilyn, the nurse. There's no need to be scared. We got a whole bin of toys waiting for you inside. And you know what we're gonna do? Measure you to see how tall and strong you are!"

Tariq hides his face in Naema's chest.

The nurse glances at Lisa, who is still on her feet. "Do they understand me?"

"Yes!" Lisa flushes on Naema's behalf. "Don't talk to me, talk to them." She looks around nervously. The place is making her queasy. All those prosthetic legs propped against the walls. They don't even look like legs; they look like vases on metal stalks stuck into a fake foot, the vase parts decorated in an array of bizarre patterns: musical notes, diamond checks, psychedelic swirls, Stars and Stripes. Who would want a leg like that? An entire tower of them stands in a far corner, stacked like paper cups, the bottom one planted into a large red sneaker, the top one touching the ceiling. But most unsettling of all is the pair of disembodied women's legs sitting on the counter in front of the nurse's station, crossed at the knee as coquettishly as if they're at a cocktail party, the feet inserted into sexy black stilettos.

"Okey-dokey," Marilyn is saying to Naema. "What about your son, does he understand English, too?"

"Some, yes." Naema is still shaken by his outburst. "Talk to him directly and I will translate if he does not." She rests her hand protectively on his head, his face still pressed against her.

"No problem." And then Marilyn, pink-cheeked and eager, more like a child in Naema's eyes than any nurse she has ever seen, explains that once the prosthetist has evaluated Tariq, the technicians will make his leg right there in the building. "You wanna see the lab where we make our legs and arms? It's pretty awesome."

This being beyond Tariq's English, Naema explains, but all he can imagine is a room full of severed arms reaching out to grab and drag him away. He presses his head deeper into her chest.

Shrugging, Marilyn stands, picks up one of the cocktail party legs and brings it over, leaving its partner alone on the counter. Taking off its shoe, she opens it like a book and shows them how the inside is constructed out of carbon fiber, titanium and aluminum, all resilient and hard, while the outside is made to feel almost as soft as real skin. "It's foam covered with a special plastic. Touch it, go on." She closes the leg and holds it out to them.

Naema runs her hand along it, struck by how cold it feels without the pulse of life. The surface prickles slightly and she realizes that it's been implanted with tiny hairs. "This technology, it is very good," she says. "Lisa, you want to feel it?"

Lisa battles her queasiness and reaches out to touch it, too. "Wow." She sits down hard on a chair.

"How about you, hon?" Marilyn proffers the leg to Tariq.

He shrinks back. Why is this woman trying to make him touch a dead person's leg?

"All right, you don't have to." She returns it to its mate. "But you want pretty pictures like those, right?" She points to the tower in the corner.

"I would rather his leg, it appears natural," Naema says firmly.

"We recommend pictures. They help kids feel comfy with their prostheses.

But they're only for the inside, don't worry. When we put the skin on, it'll look just like his normal leg."

"I want pictures," Tariq suddenly declares in English, surprising them all.

"But the skin, it will not be that pink color, I hope?" Naema gestures at the leg she has just touched. "My son, he is not pink."

"No, no, we'll match him. You'll see." Marilyn stands up again. "Alrighty, follow me, folks. Time to meet Mr. Montini."

"Go ahead," Lisa says, not wishing to risk any more quease-inducing sights. "I'll wait here."

Handing Tariq his crutches, Marilyn leads him and Naema into another room, this one long, rectangular and blue, lined with parallel bars and a wall of shelves. One is crowded with wooden feet, a second with plaster arms, a third with hands, a fourth with legs. It looks like a doll factory, only for dolls the size of humans.

A short barrel of a man with slicked-back hair, a smoothly shaven chin and aviator glasses walks up to greet them, smiling with a mouthful of bleached teeth. Rather than wearing the white clinician's coat Naema expects, he is dressed in casual navy slacks and a short-sleeved shirt in lemon yellow, revealing freckled arms sinewed with muscles. Introducing himself, he offers a hairy hand for Naema to shake, which makes her uneasy. At home, a woman extends her hand to a strange man first, and then only if she chooses. She shakes it anyway. His hand is warm, strong and reassuring. He smells of toothpaste.

"Follow me, folks." Leading them to his office, he invites her to sit on a brown leather sofa. She perches at its edge, shivering at the clamminess of its surface, chilled by the air-conditioning. Will she never grow used to this climate, sticky and warm outside, dry and frigid within?

"OK, little guy, come sit," Montini says, beckoning Tariq to join him on a red floor mat covered with toys. Tariq holds back at first, but within minutes, Montini has him laughing and absorbed. They play a fast-paced game, which Naema can see is allowing the prosthetist to assess her son's reflexes and strength.

"Mrs. Jassim, you have a bright, healthy boy here," Montini announces, springing to his feet with enthusiasm. "He's going to adapt to his new limb quicker than you can say Jack Flash."

What does it mean, Jack Flash? But no matter, this is going well.

After putting Tariq on a scale and measuring his height—three feet five, which Naema converts to meters in her head—Montini leads them to another room, tells Tariq to take off his shorts and, with a flash of toothy smile, leaves.

Tariq is less frightened here. The room looks nothing like a hospital clinic, being small and painted cotton-candy pink. Half of it is occupied by a platform on which a padded white chair is mounted like a throne. A muddy but soothing mix of violin and piano music is piping in from an invisible source, and nobody else is with him but his mama.

Soon someone else does come in, though, another man, this one tall and bronzed, with hair as black as licorice and the polished looks of a game show host. He smells strongly of cologne, a mélange of peppermint, bubblegum and alcohol that makes Naema want to pinch her nose. Like Montini, he's not wearing a white coat, only jeans and a pastel-green shirt rolled up at the sleeves. "Call me Ricky," he tells Tariq with a wink, then looks at her. "Your kid understands English?"

She answers this question yet again while Ricky lifts Tariq onto the white throne and sits below him on a stool. Tariq looks minuscule perched up there, his curls drooping over his brow, his face tight with fresh anxiety. She reaches out to stroke his good leg. "I'll stay right here with you, *ya amar*, don't worry." She sits on the floor beside him.

"So, King Tariq, how d'you like your throne?" Ricky says with another wink. Unwrapping the bandages from Tariq's interrupted thigh, he measures its circumference and length and, with a special pen, draws marks around each of the bumps and twists of his suture. Naema keeps her eyes on Tariq in case he grows afraid again but he only giggles, the pen tickling him. "The pen transfers its ink onto the plaster to help us see exactly how to mold the socket," Ricky explains. He hands Tariq a pair of pantyhose. "I know this seems weird but just pull 'em up nice and snug, OK? They're to protect your delicate parts when I put on the plaster. And don't worry, nothing I'm doing here is gonna hurt."

Naema has to help because Tariq quickly has the hose in a tangle. "Iron Man pants!" he crows.

When Tariq is back on his throne, Ricky brings out a bowl of white bandages soaked in plaster of Paris, which smells of dust and disinfectant. "This is gonna feel awesome." He wraps Tariq's thigh all the way up to his groin.

"Ooh, cold," Tariq squeals in English. "Mushy!"

"Feels funny, huh? Know why we're doing this? To make your new leg fit so good it's as strong as your other one."

"I have two legs today?"

"Not today. But tomorrow, yes."

"Two legs, Mama! And pictures! Iron Man!"

"Pictures, yes," Ricky says. "I can't promise what kind but it'll be something cool, you'll see."

"We have not decided about the pictures," Naema says crisply.

Ricky smiles, his teeth as white as Montini's. "Ma'am, I think maybe you have."

Naema's new phone rings just as she and Tariq are leaving to join Lisa in the waiting room. Not wanting the day marred by the unwelcome news that telephones so often bring, Naema is tempted not to answer, but the thought that it might be *Oum* Ismail with her invitation to dinner or, better yet, a job offer at last, persuades her to fish it out of her purse and peer at the number. Oh. Sergeant Donnell.

What to do? She promised herself never to speak to the man again, but the worry that something might have happened to Hibah makes her realize she must answer whether she wants to or not.

"What is it, Sergeant?" she says coldly.

"It's *Oum* Khalil," he replies, just as Naema feared. "She's having trouble breathing. I checked her with my stethoscope. She has a pretty bad wheeze."

He owns a stethoscope? Why has she not known this all these weeks? Then she remembers the Combat Lifesaver kit she noticed in his old pantry when she was decorating Tariq's birthday cake. If only she had thought to ask for it. "Sergeant, you must take her to the hospital immediately."

"I did—we're there now. But she won't go in."

Naema closes her eyes a moment. "Yes, she is like this about hospitals. Give her the telephone." A murmuring, a rustle, a curse in Hibah's usual querulous tones. "Mama, are you there?"

"Where else would I be? This son of an ass has trapped me in his car. He's kidnapping me! Tell him to take me home right now!"

Naema can hear the wheeze in her voice, the gasp and rattle of clogged lungs. "Don't be silly, Mama. Let him bring you inside the hospital. He says you're very sick."

"I won't go! I don't care if I'm sick. I want to die in my own bed!"

"Mama, please. Think of Tariq. Think of me. Think of what you mean to us. Think of Khalil—would he have wanted his mother to suffer like this? We aren't in war anymore. The hospital will be clean and safe, and the soldier will look after you till I get back. Please, be reasonable."

Naema has to repeat all this many times before Hibah will listen, but at last the old woman begrudgingly relents. "Give the phone back to Sergeant Donnell now," Naema tells her, and after another spate of grumbling, Hibah complies.

"It is all right now," Naema tells him, "but try not to let them separate her from you until she is truly settled. She is very frightened, you understand?"

"Don't worry, I'll stick to her like gum on a shoe."

"And you will relay to me what the doctors, they say?"

"Of course." He pauses, the silence thickening between them. "Naema?" She braces herself for another of his apologies. "Would you mind telling me how it's going with Tariq's leg?"

Her anger at the man is far from vanquished but she does feel she owes him a reply. "It is going well. They will make the leg right here in the clinic. These people, they are most efficient."

"You mean he'll get it tonight?"

"No. But tomorrow, yes, *insh'Allah*."

"My god, that's fantastic! Can I speak with him?"

Naema says nothing for a moment, the distrust still hot within her. Yet she cannot help but be moved by the joy in Jimmy's voice. "You may," she finally says and holds the phone to Tariq's ear.

"Jim-Jim!" he shouts into it. "I get Iron Man leg!"

21

The motel Lisa helped us find before she went home, the least disreputable place within walking distance of the clinic, is a shoebox of a building decorated in the same dull colors I saw in the hospital employment office where I so resoundingly failed. Our room is no different. Curtains like ironed rice. A synthetic bedspread as stiff and brown as cardboard. A carpet the color of dried egg yolk. It makes me miss the scarlets and blues of my house in Al-Karrada, our cozy ottomans and rugs, our tiles in green, cobalt and turquoise. Furthermore, I do not trust the room's odor of air freshener and carpet shampoo, a saccharine mix of chemicals reminiscent of Ricky's cologne. But Tariq is enthralled. "A secret TV!" he calls, opening a dark wooden cabinet. "Tiny bottles!" he exclaims from the bathroom. While I struggle without success to open a window, he hops back and forth with the curtain wand, swishing the curtains open and closed as if they hide a stage.

"Come, my sweet, it's almost dark. Time to find supper," I tell him. "We'll go to a restaurant, just like . . ." I am about to say, "just like we used to with Baba," but stop myself. *No, Khalil*, I whisper to him in my mind, *leave us in peace.*

Edgetown must be named for its location because it sits only a few meters back from the edge of the Hudson River. We easily find a street to lead us there, passing rows of little wooden houses so flimsy and ill-built I marvel that they can stay upright. I have often thought it odd that Americans have built so many of their houses out of wood, as if laying the kindling for an enormous fire. A town like Edgetown, or, for that matter, Slingerlands, would flare up in an instant under just one of this country's own bombs.

Before long, we reach a chain-link fence overlooking the river and, on the far side, Manhattan itself. Threading our fingers through the wire, we press our faces against it to soak in the view, a warm breeze drifting across our skins.

"Awesome!" Tariq exclaims in English, one of Rory's favorite words. He peers at the colors springing across the black water and at the city beyond, its millions of windows pinpricking the night sky. "It's like magic, Mama!"

"Yes, *habibi*, it is." I gaze at the jagged silhouettes of Manhattan's hulking buildings, their weight transformed by the twilight into a mass of black shadows. A vast, imposing bridge—the George Washington, Lisa told me—arcs above us, its reflected lights darting like dragonflies over the river's inky surface.

"Isn't that bridge beautiful, Mama?" Tariq says quietly, gazing up at it.

I rest my hand on his warm little head. "We once had twelve bridges in Baghdad, you know that? They were beautiful, too." I refrain from saying more, not wanting to sadden him, but I remember standing with Khalil on just such a balmy night as this, looking down at the Tigris from the Al-Sarafiya Bridge. That same bridge that was later destroyed by a truck bomb, filling the river with broken history and blood.

"Mama, I'm hungry."

"So am I, *habibi*. Let's eat."

Turning inland, we only have to walk a little way before we find a small Indian restaurant that looks affordable and, best of all, empty of other customers who might stare. Inside, an elegant man with a round, gentle face and a head of luxuriant silver hair greets us, almost bowing in his delight at having any customers at all. I can guess why his restaurant is so empty: it is devoid of air-conditioning and smells powerfully of cardamom, curry and desperation. I feel instantly at home.

We choose a table in the back, where Tariq can prop his crutches in a corner and where we cannot be seen from the window. I've only been to an Indian restaurant once before and am enchanted by this one's unabashed gaudiness. Tables draped in creamy white cloth. Candles nestled inside golden cups. Real linen napkins. Strings of tiny red and green lights blink from every corner, recalling the colors in the river, while portraits of Shiva and Ganesh—names I only know because they are inscribed in large gold script beneath their feet—gaze beatifically down on us from walls covered in tinsel and glitter.

"Mama, is this a palace?" Tariq whispers, looking about in wonder. And a second later, "When I get my Iron Man pictures, I'm going to show Uncle Ugly!"

I smile, having given in on the question of pictures. There, alone with Tariq in that sparkling place, I feel so relaxed that I refuse even to worry about the cost of the motel and this dinner eating up my entire month's public assistance check. Only my contrition over Hibah gnaws at me. How could I, a doctor, have allowed myself to remain so blind to her condition?

Our host reappears to take our orders, recommending lamb, saffron rice and lentils while handing us a basket of naan, a flatbread so like our *samoon* that my eyes sting. He also brings Tariq a free fruit drink with two miniature paper umbrellas poking out of it, one pink, the other yellow, and stops to chat at any excuse. Indian and Iraqi, Hindu and Muslim—we are not natural allies. But in this country, where we are so marked and yet invisible, so resented and yet diminished, I suspect that he is as relieved as I am to find himself in the company of anyone who is not white, American and supercilious.

Back at the motel, after I have unwrapped and washed Tariq's residual limb, a term I much prefer to that unfortunate English word "stump," we cuddle up under the cardboard bedspread to watch a film. I select *The Little Mermaid* from the cable menu in the hope it won't give Tariq nightmares. He is prone to bad dreams if anything reminds him of war, something I've tried to explain to Rory each time he brings over those violent cartoons he seems to think suitable for children.

The film is not violent, but it shocks me, nonetheless. The mermaid is wearing the skimpiest of bikini tops over exaggeratedly pert breasts, while the villainess is painted to look like a brothel madam. I cannot fathom why Americans want their children to see such images, what they are trying to teach.

Tariq leans against me sleepily. "Mama, can we stay in America forever? I love it here."

I have to draw in a long breath before I can answer. "Perhaps we can, my little man. And, maybe soon, *insh'Allah*, we will find a bigger home where we can each have our own rooms. Won't that be nice?"

Tariq shakes his head. "I don't want my own room. I want to stay with Jim-Jim."

I close my eyes. "Let's watch the movie now, *habibi*. We'll talk about that later."

When we return to the clinic early the next morning, Marilyn greets us sunnily, her head bobbing atop her long neck. "This is your big moment!" she says to Tariq, who, even though he has no idea what she means, catches her excitement and grins, all his former fears gone. Striding across the floor, she flings open the door to the blue room as if ushering us into a theater. "Ricky, look who I've got here!" she crows.

Ricky sends us one of his winks. "So, are you ready, King Tariq?" Tariq nods happily. "Let's try on your leg!"

Sitting us on a bench, Ricky picks up the prosthesis, handing it first to me. It looks like the legs I saw stacked in the waiting room, a metal rod attached to a cup on one end and a molded foot on the other, only with a bendable joint at the knee. The foot is at least brown rather than pink, although not the same delicate brown as my son. And, to my dismay, the cup is covered in grinning green frogs.

"No Iron Man," Tariq says in English, his voice dropping.

"No, but you know who these cool frogs are?" Ricky asks.

Tariq shrugs.

Breaking into a squeak, Ricky sings, "T is for Tariq, C is for Cool, L is for Leg, K is for—"

"Kermit!"

I look at them in confusion. Why is Ricky singing in this horrible voice and what is Tariq saying?

"Don't worry, Mrs. Jassim, this is only temporary." Ricky offers me another of his smiles. "Your son needs to practice on this leg for a couple weeks. Then he can come back for adjustments and we'll put on the skin. We'll do a color match in a minute." He turns to Tariq. "All right, big guy, let's try it."

Crouching in front of us, Ricky shows Tariq how to pull on the silicone sleeve that will hold the prosthesis in place by rolling it up his thigh, much as a woman rolls up a stocking. Then he slips on the cup-shaped socket. It fits as snugly as a sock.

"You see this little button here?" Ricky points to a tiny bump on the outside of the cup. "Push that when you want to take the leg off. And hold it down when you fit the leg on. That creates the suction that holds it in place."

I am impressed. No straps or buckles or harnesses. The leg simply stays on by itself.

Once it is attached, Ricky tells Tariq to sit for a time, just to get used to it. "It's hot," Tariq says. "It's hot and heavy, Mama. It doesn't feel like my other leg at all."

"Of course it doesn't, little heart, but don't worry. You'll get used to it."

"OK," Ricky says after a few minutes, "you ready to stand now?" Tariq nods, his eyes solemn. Helping him up, Ricky hands him his crutches. "You'll have to practice getting up and down from chairs. But for now, King Tariq, stand up straight. And walk."

Tariq remains still a long moment, feeling for his balance. Finally, leaning on his crutches, he takes a teetering step. Ricky warned us that because the new leg weighs a little over three pounds, less than Tariq's real one but much more than air, it will feel uncomfortably heavy for some time, as if he is dragging an anchor. Furthermore, a prosthetic foot lacks all the tendons and toes with which we balance, never mind calf muscles, an ankle or a knee, so he might feel as though he is walking on a stilt. Nonetheless, my little boy seems undeterred. With Ricky on one side and me on the other, he sets off slowly down the room.

At first, even with his crutches, his walk is unsteady. Not only does the prosthetic alter his balance, but he is no longer used to moving his left leg and having it execute a step. Nor is he accustomed to feeling the pressure of his own weight on his thigh, let alone having to direct a step by shifting his entire torso rather than using the muscles in his calves, hip and thighs. Yet, even though I doubt he can remember anymore what it was like to walk with two legs, his body clearly does, because soon he is scarcely teetering at all.

Ricky grins. "See that?" he says. "It can take an adult weeks to walk this easily. Kids are amazing."

"Mama, take these." Hobbling over to the parallel bars, Tariq thrusts his crutches at me. "I want to try without them." Grasping a bar in each hand, he turns and slowly sets off, Ricky and I following on either side, close but not touching him.

Again and again, Tariq pulls that heavy leg up and down between the bars, all the way from one end of the room to the other, sweat glistening on his brow and running down the thin stalk of his neck, his arms and good leg trembling with the effort. "Aren't you tired, *habibi*?" I keep asking him. "Don't you want to rest?" He ignores me.

Back and forth he walks with a determination I have never seen in him before, not even when he was learning to use his crutches. He does not talk, he does not cry, he does not look at us. He only clamps his jaw tight and works.

By the time he reaches the end of his tenth lap, he has almost mastered it. A hitch and a swing and he can walk. Step, swing, step, swing. He looks up at me, his face suffused with triumph. "Look, Mama!" Letting go of the bars, he walks back and forth, back and forth, his stride growing stronger with each length of the room. And as he walks, he laughs and laughs and laughs.

Half an hour later, I leave him with Ricky to continue practicing and, after wiping the happy tears from my own eyes, step outside to telephone the soldier.

I intend to ask for news of Hibah but when he answers, I cannot keep my joy to myself. "Tariq, he has his leg! Already he can walk!"

"He can?" The soldier's voice rises in wonder. "My god, that's . . . What's it look like?"

"Oh, it has some dreadful little frog faces all over it. It is quite hideous but he loves it." I wipe my eyes again. "I think perhaps it is something to do with your television?"

"Kermit? I bet it's Kermit."

"Yes, that is what they said. It is very silly. But no matter, they will make a skin later of just the right color and it will cover the frogs. They showed me the swatches, I think you call it? Like when you choose paint for a wall? So many shades of white and pink and brown, Sergeant, like all the people of the world. Tariq, he is so proud!"

"I can't wait to see him. Show me soon as you get back, OK?"

"I shall. Now tell me please, how is *Oum* Khalil?"

I hear him hesitate, which awakens the worry in me again. But all he says is, "There's nothing to tell yet. I just left the hospital and they're still running tests."

"She is not too frightened?"

"Don't think so. She sleeps a lot. And I've been staying with her most of the day."

I am so relieved to hear this that my anger at him is floating beyond my grasp, even as I want to hold onto it. "Tell her we shall come soon and show her Tariq's leg. And Sergeant?" I draw in a breath. "My Tariq, he is so happy. He is the happiest I have seen him since the bomb."

22

Saint Paul's Academy looks exactly as forbidding as I expected a Catholic boys school to look. The gray stone mansion and narrow windows glower down at a yard buzz-cut so short the grass is more brown than green. A blackened brick chapel on the side sags like an exhausted nun under the weight of its oversized steeple. And a cast iron gate looms over the driveway like a guillotine. Any kid here for his first day must be scared shitless.

I've come for a job interview, nothing like driving forklifts with those cabbageheads at Home Depot, but something I badly want for a change: phys. ed. teacher for grades two to eight. So, as I climb out of the car, I try to keep myself on an even keel. No thinking about whether Tariq's new leg will really fulfill its promise. No dwelling on the lies I just told Naema. No fretting over how to tiptoe around all the other landmines surrounding her and Khalil's increasingly problematic mom. And no spinning into darkness over Kate.

Inside, the school is just as forbidding as the outside: oak-paneled walls, marble-floored hallways, polished balustrades, oil portraits of former headmasters snarling down at my head. I look around for priests but see no one except the receptionist, a tiny teenage girl in a moss-green dress who makes me think of the elf I'd imagined driving Tariq's tractor.

"Hi?" she questions as I approach, offering me a pixieish smile. "You're here for the interview with Principal Putnick, right? You can wait there?" She points to a polished wooden bench against the opposite wall, where boys in trouble are presumably sent to await punishment. I sit, feeling like one of those boys myself. Although I dressed for this interview in the required uniform—gray pants, blue tie, navy jacket—I'm far from confident that this will make up for my lack of teaching experience or references. I only hope this Putnick guy won't take me for a fraud or, worse, a perv looking to spend all day with little boys in gym shorts.

The elf returns way before I'm ready and sends me into an office across the hall. Soon as I walk in, the principal jumps up to shake my hand. A small pointy man in glasses with a small pointy face, there's nothing forbidding about him, at least, except maybe the hulking mahogany desk at his back. Taking a chair in front of it, he tells me to sit and faces me with a blinking expression, reminding me of the groundhogs potholing my lawn.

"I'm honored to meet you, Staff Sergeant Donnell," he starts in right away. "I've been reading your résumé—a Bronze Star! The boys will be mighty impressed."

Civilians aren't usually interested in military titles and medals. Most don't even know what they mean. "Are you a veteran, sir?"

"Very astute of you. I was a Marine Corps Captain. Served in Operation Desert Storm."

Covering my surprise that this marmot-like man was a marine, I reach over to shake his hand again. "Honored to meet you, too, sir."

"Now," Putnick says, crossing his little legs and opening a file on his lap. "I see you haven't taught before, so what makes you want to teach now?"

Having expected this question, I've been rehearsing a response for days, but now my mind catapults into confusion, several answers rushing in at once: "I've been playing soccer with this one-legged Iraqi boy and it's been amazing to watch him cope." Instinct tells me to avoid that. "I raised my little brothers practically on my own and I'm good with kids." That opens a whole row of worm cans and doesn't sound like a job qualification anyway. "I really like children and I love exercise." Way too molestery. In near panic, I fall back on the kind of speech I made when I was applying to crawl up the NCO ladder in the army.

"I enjoy teaching teamwork, sir. Being Staff Sergeant was the most satisfying challenge of my life. Most of my soldiers were kids—not as young as the boys in your school, of course, but eighteen, nineteen—and it was my job to keep them fit and disciplined, as well as safe. More importantly, it was my job to teach them to work together as a unit so they could rely on each other in battle. It was incredibly rewarding to see them learn self-discipline and how to work in teams like that. That's why I thought I'd like teaching kids."

I stop. Hope the guy won't think I'm a nutball.

But Putnick is beaming. "I can't imagine a better answer, Staff Sergeant.

That's the whole point of team sports, in my opinion—building camaraderie, cooperation, trust. And discipline, of course, as you say—something we know about in the Corps. You are aware that we have this opening because our former gym teacher suffered a heart attack?" Putnick raises an eyebrow. "The man was at least fifty pounds overweight and drank like a whale. I don't expect that's going to be an issue for you, is it?"

Is Putnick asking if I'm a drunk? Is he going to give me a drug test? The pills and disability rating clatter through my head before I realize that he was joking. "Oh no, sir, I run twelve klicks a day and do five hundred push-ups every morning."

"For God's sake, don't make our boys do that or you'll kill 'em!" Putnick chuckles. "I'm delighted to tell you that you're hired, far as I'm concerned. Tell the truth, I decided that before you came in—only wanted to make sure you weren't a powderbrain. Now all we need is a nod from the board, but I don't anticipate a problem there. Normally, I'd ask for references but your army record speaks to that. So, I'll let you know next week, and at the end of August you'll come in for orientation and a little training. Now, let me give you a copy of your schedule, and we can talk salary and benefits and see if we can come to an agreement."

On the way home, I am soaring. This is the first break I've had since coming back from war, the first time I've met anyone in civilian life who treats me with the respect I got used to in the army. I wish I could tell Kate about it. Crack jokes about how she'll have to listen to *me* griping about students now. I miss her more than ever when I've got good news like this. I miss the simple pleasure of being able to bask in a triumph together.

Before reaching the house, I stop at Price Chopper to buy something special to celebrate the job and Tariq's new leg. Naema just applied to work here, so I glance at the row of cashiers behind the counters, every one of them homegrown and white, wondering how they might treat her, with her scar and her accent. Most are either high school kids or beaten-down divorcées, many from military families, including Cathy Boynton, a girl I kissed once back in ninth grade whose brother died in Iraq. She looks away quickly when she sees me, her blush visible even from the door.

My cell rings just as I'm maneuvering my shopping cart around a stack of toilet paper. I take one look at the number and almost drop the phone while I fumble to answer. "April! Did she call?"

"Yeah. Just now."

"I told you she'd be in touch. Is she OK? What did she say?"

"Nothing. Just that she misses me." Her voice trembles. "She sounded weird, though. Like, sad? I wish she'd come home, y'know?"

Of course I know. "Where'd she call from?"

"Some number I never saw before. It's on my cell—she won't call our landline in case Mom or Dad picks up."

"She didn't say where she is?"

No answer.

"April?"

"Excuse me, I told you to get outta my way!" I turn to see a dumpy old man glaring at me from behind his own shopping cart. I grab it and shove it down the aisle, leaving him to waddle after it, cursing me.

"April? You there?"

"Yeah, sorry. Heard Mom outside my room."

"So, where did Kate say she is?" I ask for the third time. *And is she cheating on me with some backdoor bastard?* I won't let myself ask that.

"I don't remember. Someplace hot. She's teaching water ballet."

"You're kidding."

"No. She's working at some kind of resort. She said it sucks 'cause all these, like, white people are drinking piña coladas in swimming pools while in another country just a few miles away brown people are dying 'cause of some famous earthquake."

"The one in Haiti? Is she in the Dominican Republic?"

"Yeah, that sounds right. I think."

"Can you give me the number?"

Long silence. "I don't know, Jimmy. I feel bad even, like, telling you she called. She made me promise I wouldn't. She says I'm the only person in the world she trusts."

I thought I was the one Kate trusted. "Alright, don't give me the number. But keep it someplace safe so it doesn't get lost. Please?"

"OK."

"And then when you talk to her, will you tell me if she's all right?"

"I don't know if I can, Jimmy. She told me, like, not to call her, ever! She said I gotta wait for her to call me." She falls silent a moment. "Jimmy?"

"Yeah?"

"You think I should, like, tell Mom and Dad about this? She asked me not to."

"Are they scared she's in danger?"

"Only from you."

Damn that sheriff to hell—him and his candied razor blade of a wife, too. "Listen." I try to calm myself. "I feel bad asking you this but don't tell them. It'll only make things worse."

"I think so, too. And Katie'd be so mad if I did."

"But if she calls you again, let me know, will you? And . . . and tell me if you think of any way to make her come back."

"Wish I could. Need to go now. Bye."

At home, while I'm putting away the groceries and the red velvet cake I bought for Tariq, I call Patrick to invite him and Lisa over. I want to tell them about April's news and my job, but more than anything I want Lisa's advice so I can hop a plane to the DR, search every damn resort in the country and bring Kate back for good.

Patrick has something else on his mind, though. "You talked to Rory lately? 'Cause he hasn't shown his ass at home for two nights now and he's not answering his phone."

I tuck my own phone under my chin and shove a pizza into the freezer. "You try calling him at work?"

"Jesus, I'm not a moron. They said he's on vacation."

"He doesn't get vacations. Where's his car at?"

"No idea. One of us should go see if it's at Sue's place but I can't till I get off of work."

I ball up my plastic shopping bags and stuff them under the sink. "You mean you want me to go 'cause I've got nothing-fucking-else to do?"

"Well. Yeah."

"Shit, OK. Listen, you ever talk to him about stealing my OCs?"

"Not yet, no. It's not . . . not the easiest thing to bring up, y'know?"

I roll my eyes. What a chickenshit. "OK, I'll go look for him and collar him about that, too. But you and Lisa are coming over later, right?"

"Yeah, Jimmy. We're coming."

When I reach Sue's place some forty-five minutes later—a small clapboard house tucked behind Cairo's elementary school—I spot Rory's rusty Hyundai right away. It's parked across the road, looking just like him: orange, battered, unwashed. What a lot of hullaballoo over nothing. I knock.

Sue's brother, Tom, answers, looking just as pissed as he did when I returned his motorbike a day and a half late. Short and pumpkin-shaped, with a ratty beard and a balding head, he's wearing plaid pajama bottoms, even though it's two in the afternoon, a stained white undershirt and fuzzy blue slippers. I back away, my military sensibilities offended. I'd like to order the slob to hit the deck right here and beat his face to a hundred.

Tom leans against the doorjamb and yawns, emitting a blast of digested garlic. "You, again. Woke me up. I work night shift, for chrissake. Whaddya want?"

"I'm looking for Rory. He here?"

"Nope." Tom yawns again and scratches his beachball stomach.

"Know where he is?"

"All I know is that when he took off on my bike, he never said goodbye to my sister. Shitty manners, your brother's got."

"Your bike? You mean you lent it to him again?"

"Hell no." Tom combs his fingers through his tangle of beard and sniffs them. "He bought it. 'Night." He slams the door shut.

I stare at its scraped black paint. That bike must have cost at least five grand—probably more, given the likelihood that this blubberbelly ripped Rory off. Rory has nowhere near that kind of money.

Back at the car, I dial his cell again. Still no answer. Goddammit to hell and back. Now I've got two people missing.

"*What*?" Patrick yelps when I give him the news. "That scumbag told me he couldn't even pay his half of our electricity bill this month! Where the hell did he dig up that kinda dough?"

"Seen any strangers coming around lately?"

Patrick takes a beat. "You mean you think he's dealing?"

"How else is a kid of eighteen with no high school diploma and a brain the size of a raisin gonna make five or six grand? Fuck!" I kick my tire. "I should've kept a better eye on him. I'm such a meathead!"

"Jimmy, chill. Lotsa kids deal. Maybe it isn't anything heavy, y'know? Maybe it's just weed."

"Weed, coke, meth, pills, I don't give a shit. It's all illegal and could land his ass in jail. If he doesn't crack himself up first. We need to find him."

"How?"

"I'll ask around. Gas stations, diners, you know. It's not hard to miss a carrot-headed zit-face on a giant red motorbike, is it? You keep calling him." I snap the phone shut and jump into my car. Reconnaissance, corner, capture. I might suck as a brother but this, at least, I know how to do.

I Scream Heaven is nothing but a tumbledown shack at the edge of Route 145, two wind-torn deck umbrellas wobbling out front, its red sign faded and scratched. It's such a pathetic place to work that every time I drive past it, I want to throw a sack over Rory's head and shanghai him into the army.

I park and walk up to the window. Not a soul in sight. "Anyone here?" I stick my head inside. It stinks the same way a freezer stinks when someone spills milk in it and then doesn't defrost it for twenty years. "Hey! How about some service?"

"Hold your lobsters." A door slams in the back and a disheveled, grimy-looking guy with red eyes and a graying two-day beard shuffles up to the window. "We got a sale on chocolate chip," he says with no interest at all. His hands are black under the fingernails and smeared with something that looks like axle grease. "Sugar cone or waffle?"

"I'm looking for Rory Donnell."

The man seems half asleep but he still manages to look startled. "Never heard of him."

"He works here. What d'you mean you've never heard of him?"

The man squints at me with his bloodshot eyes. "Who's asking?"

"I'm his brother. He's been missing three days. I'm just trying to find out if he's OK."

"Brother, huh?" The man looks me up and down, his eyes lingering on my tattoos. "You the soldier?"

"For fuck's sake, just tell me where he is!"

"On vacation. Everybody's entitled to a vacation. Gotta close now." He yanks the metal shutter down in my face.

"Hey!" I bang on it. "I'm not done with you yet!" I hear a car start and turn just in time to see an old Buick shoot out from behind the shack and career down the road.

Shit.

The next step is to search every gas station I can think of in and around Cairo and Catskill, figuring that Tom is not the type to have sold a motorcycle with a full tank. But even though I ask at five different places, I find nobody who can remember seeing either Rory or the bike.

"That's the red Ducati belongs to Tom Offerbach, isn't it?" one old farmer says. "Didn't know he sold it. Huh." That's the closest I come to a clue.

Giving up on the gas stations, I move on to diners and convenience stores, knowing that Rory can't get through much more than an hour without consuming some form of junk food. That leads nowhere, either. Eventually, I turn into a combo gas station-general store on Route 32 with the name of "J&J," which I happen to know stands for Jesus and Janice. Janice is a chunky woman with a hearing problem. Jesus is a life-sized plaster statue standing in front, his head in its obligatory crown of thorns, his chipped white arms stretching out pleadingly toward the gas pumps. A sign propped against his feet reads, *ATM inside. Nuts 50% off.*

I know this place because, along with the milk and candy I used to buy here for my brothers, it sells ammunition and guns. My buddies and I would pick up our hunting supplies here back in the days when I was a civilian and still thought guns were for sport.

"Hey, Janice, how you doin'?"

She looks up from behind the counter, her face round and rosy under a helmet of dyed yellow hair. "It's Jimmy Donnell!" she shouts. "I didn't know you were back, honeypie. Haven't seen you for donkey's years. Looking handsome as ever." She runs her eyes over me with an appreciation I could do without.

"Yeah, been back a few months. You keeping well?"

"I am blessed, thank the Lord. So glad you're home in one piece, sugar. My nephew, he was over there, too, a marine. He isn't in one piece at all." She shakes her head, her mouth pulled tight and sad.

"Sorry to hear that. I'm looking for—"

"Yeah, poor baby, Lord have mercy on him. Came back with an arm gone and a hole in his brain. Twenty-five years old and he can't talk no more, just sits in his wheelchair staring. It's real hard on his wife and kids. My sister, too, bless her heart. Nobody wants their baby to end up like that, do they? But there's a reason for everything, right, honeybun?"

She looks at me, waiting for me to agree.

I push up my glasses and rub my face over and over, hard as I can, needing to wipe it off. Wipe off her words, too.

"Jimmy?" She edges around the counter and peers up into my face. "You OK?" She sounds scared.

I rub some more. But finally I get ahold of myself, put my glasses back on and shove my shaking hands in my pockets to keep them out of trouble.

"Something wrong, honeypie? You look like you're staring right to the bottom of hell."

Ignoring this, I force myself to push out some words. "Remember my brother Rory? Long ginger hair, my height? He's driving a bright red motorbike. Wondered if you've seen him?"

Janice eases back behind her counter, where I guess she feels safer. "'Course I remember Rory. But no, haven't seen him at all. Why, he in some kind of trouble?"

"Hope not. OK, thanks. Gotta go."

She fixes her eyes on me timidly. "They sending you over there again, hon?"

I back out of the store.

"Well, stay safe if they do, the Lord be with you!" she calls after me. "And say hi to Kate!"

In the car, I have to lean my forehead on the steering wheel a long time. I know Janice meant well. But damn.

When the nausea and shaking die down enough, I pull away from Janice and her money-grubbing Jesus to head for a Stewart's I haven't tried yet near the thruway, figuring if I work my way south, I might flush Rory out like a grouse. I also need to buy a big bottle of ginger ale and some Advil—my temples are imploding.

The only people inside are a rumpled truck driver buying a giant bag of popsicles and a gnarly guy at the cash register attached to an iron-gray ponytail. I pay for my soda, down the whole thing on the spot, along with four Advil, then I ask about Rory.

"Tall and pimply with ginger hair, huh?" Ponytail says. "Yeah, I remember him. He was bragging like a kid about his new motorbike. Shiny-ass thing red as a stop sign. He dug my eagle." He holds out a stringy forearm tattooed with a fading eagle and flexes his wrist. A wing ripples.

"Nice. When was he here?"

Ponytail counts out some change while he thinks. "Two, three days ago, maybe? He asked for directions to I-87, even though it's right out the frickin' window." He leans over to look at the combat action badge on my own forearm. "What's that inside the wreath, a dagger?"

"Bayonet."

Pat's already in the house by the time I get home, dirtying up Kate's couch with his oily overalls and sucking manically on a cigarette. "Looks like Rory went down to the city," I tell him. "Get off that couch, you'll stain it."

"What the hell's he doing down there?" He jumps up and squints at me. "You OK? You look kinda green."

I push my hands back into my pockets. They're still shaking and I don't want him to see. "I'm fine. Listen, I went to his dumbass ice cream shack and the whole thing looks shady as hell. I just hope he doesn't get his idiot ass arrested. Does he know anyone in the city?"

"No idea. Damn it to hell. Rory's such a knuckle-dragger." Pat takes another worried suck on his cigarette. "Lisa's coming in a minute. Thought we'd eat out on the deck."

When she arrives, sunny and cute in a yellow dress, I heat up the frozen pizza in the oven while she lays out paper plates and napkins on the deck table and Pat plunders the fridge for beer. "I got a job teaching PE," I tell them as they clean bird poop and leaves off their chairs. I glance at the back apartment, which flanks the right side of the deck. If Naema was home instead of in New Jersey getting Tariq's leg without me, she'd be able to hear every word. "It's at that boy's school in Albany, Saint Paul's."

"The Catholic one? Wow." Lisa looks at me with not-entirely-flattering surprise. No doubt she assumed I was hired as a security guard, the fate of a lot of vets I know.

"Yeah."

"Good for you, Jimmy," she says. "That's so cool."

"I remember that place," Pat drags his chair over to the railing. "Aunt Maureen used to threaten to send me and Rory there whenever she got mad at us. She talked about it like it was some kind of juvie." He glances over at me. "You can be pretty hardass, bro. Sure you got the patience to deal with kids?"

"Shut it, Pat."

The three of us sit in a row then, feet propped up on the railing, beers in hand, gazing out at the meadow stretching across the valley behind the house. A generation ago, this meadow was a cornfield, part of a family farm long since bankrupted, broken up into lots and sold. Now it's filled with weeds and scrappy wildflowers regularly mowed by the neighbor's twelve cows, all clustered at the moment under the shade of an old oak, robotically chewing and staring wet-eyed at the dismal trajectory of their futures. A feeling I know only too well.

I'm not sure why but I can sense an awkwardness in the air, like somebody's hiding something. Maybe it's me.

"I got other news, too," I finally say. "I had to take Tariq's granny to the hospital yesterday. Docs say it looks like pneumonia." This is only half the truth.

The other half is that the doctors diagnosed her as "passively suicidal." In plain words, she's been deliberately starving herself to death.

"Jesus." Lisa looks scared. "Does Naema know about this?"

"She knows the old lady's in the hospital, yeah. But not about the pneumonia. I didn't want to spoil her day with Tariq. I'll tell her when they get back."

"No need, I'll do it. I'm driving down to get them tomorrow."

I don't answer but it burns me up that Lisa will see Tariq on two legs before I do. "Listen," I say next, "I need to tell you something else. April called me today. She finally heard from Kate." I eye Pat and Lisa, but they only look surprised. "Seems like she's working at some resort in the DR. Did you know about that?"

"The DR?" Lisa seems genuinely astonished.

"Yeah. So, I'm going down there to find her. Any ideas where I should start?"

She shakes her head. "I don't know, Jimmy. The DR has dozens of resorts. And . . . well, I'm sorry, but if you chase her like that, you'll probably just make her run even farther. I don't think it's a good idea."

"What is a good idea, then?" I look at her with genuine despair.

"I don't know. Just give her time. I don't understand why she left any more than you do, but if she wants to come back, she will. You just can't force her."

I drop my eyes to a little bubble swelling at the mouth of my beer bottle. "'Least she's in touch with April now," Lisa adds. "That's a good sign, right?"

"Yeah, bro, look on the sunny side," Pat chimes in. "Maybe it means she's thawing. I think Lisa's right. You just need to be patient." Prying off his sneakers and socks, he props his hairy feet back up on the railing. His toenails need cutting.

"You haven't been in touch with her without telling me, have you?" I blurt.

"No, Jimmy, we wouldn't do that." Lisa's round face looks earnest enough to make me believe her. Almost.

"April told me Kate's teaching water ballet," I say then, not wanting to let the subject go.

"Butch little Kate teaching ballet? You're shitting me." Pat chuckles, but then his voice turns wistful. "Damn, I miss her."

The three of us sink back into silence then, staring out at the Helderberg Mountains beyond the meadow, the row of furry green humps that define our horizon. The hot whitish-blue of the sky, which happens to exactly match the color of Kate's eyes, is making me sweat. I notice that the willow down by the stream is already looking sick, its leaves shriveled and pale. A plague of Japanese willow beetles has taken to sucking the life out of it every summer, even though Kate tried everything she could to get rid of them, poisonous and otherwise.

She tromped out there in her cut-off denim overalls and garden gloves to dump ladybugs on the leaves. She painted the trunk with toxins. Sprayed it with pesticides. Even picked off every beetle she could reach and crushed them one by one between her fingernails. Nothing worked.

"Lisa, mind if I go get Naema and Tariq tomorrow instead of you?" I ask.

Lisa studies her knees.

"Fuck it. Never mind." I chug the rest of my beer. "Pizza should be ready." I stand and go inside.

An hour later, we're slumped again in front of the TV, having run out of beer and conversation and needing to escape the heat. The news is on, a bunch of marines tearing around Afghanistan, something I have no desire to see. I've more or less learned to handle backfires and fireworks, if not conversations like the one with Janice, but I still don't do well with war news. I do not, for example, need to watch the camera focus in on the tight pucker of that corporal's mouth. I can read the fear in his face easy as a traffic light.

My phone buzzes. I pull it out of my pocket, expecting Naema or one of my dwindling population of buddies, but I don't recognize the number. I answer with my usual hopeless hope.

"Donnell? It's Sheriff Brady."

I jump up. "Is it Kate? Is she home?"

"She is not home, no. Something's happened."

"Shit, is she hurt?"

"It's not Kate." I hear the man inhale. "It's Rory. He's had an accident. We found him on the thruway near the Catskill exit. An ambulance is taking him to Columbia Memorial in Hudson. He's alive but not in good shape. You might want to get over there."

"Fucking idiot!" I shout, jamming my phone back into my pocket and looking wildly at Pat. "He did it, just like we thought!"

"What?" Pat jumps up, too. "Who did what?"

"Rory. He crashed the motorbike!"

Within minutes, I'm tearing down the thruway at ninety, Pat beside me, Lisa in the back. The full impact of the news has hit me now and it's all I can do not to scream. *God, don't let him be seriously hurt,* I chant in my head. *Please please don't let it be bad.*

Pat's gripping the dashboard. "Fuck, I hope he was wearing his helmet. Fucking fuck fuck. What else did the sheriff say?"

"Just that he's not in good shape."

Lisa says nothing, only reaches forward to squeeze Pat's arm.

Soon as we rush inside the hospital, I spot the sheriff standing with some other troopers by the nurse's station. "Where is he?" I yell at him.

He points to the emergency room. "When you're done in there, Donnell, I need a word with you."

I barely hear him. "We're family," I bark at the nurse as Pat and I run through the doors. But all we can see is a clump of doctors standing around a bed. "What's going on here?" I demand in my sergeant voice. "We're his brothers."

The doctors turn to look at us. And then they move aside.

Rory is drenched in blood. Ribs, arms, legs soaked in it. His eyes are closed and his face so battered I can hardly tell it's him. Pushing aside the doctors, I bend over him. "Rory? Rory, it's Jimmy. Wake up!"

"Excuse me, sir?"

At least he's breathing. But he doesn't look normally asleep and he isn't moving at all.

"Sir?"

I pull my eyes away. A surgeon in green scrubs is looking at me over her mask. "Mr. Donnell, your brother's unconscious. We're taking him in for x-rays. You'll have to wait outside."

I stare down at my hands.

"Mr. Donnell?"

A radio voice filtering through a wall.

"Mr. Donnell?"

Sergeant, I think it best if you wipe.

"Mr. Donnell!"

The boy, he was taken by mistake.

"Jimmy?"

Did we not agree to do no more harm than we must?

"Jimmy, can you hear me?"

I pull up my head. Pat's peering into my face. "Jimmy, you with us?"

"What?"

"Doc says we have to go out to the hallway."

I stare at him a long moment, feeling as near to puking as I did in J&J's. But I remember where I am now—and why.

Once we're in the hallway, the sheriff calls me over, his face grim. He holds out a sheet of paper. "I think you'll want to see this."

"What is it?" I'm in no mood to deal with Sheriff Brady or his crappy flap of paper right now.

"Your brother's under arrest."

"Which brother?" I glare at him.

"Don't play with me. Rory, of course."

"What, for having an accident?"

"Possession with intent to sell. We found a large quantity of marijuana on him."

"Rory's smashed up in a hospital and you're going to *arrest* him? Are you out of your fucking mind?" I grab the sheriff by the shoulders and slam him up against the wall. "You slimy piece of shit!"

"Jimmy, stop!" Pat shouts, rushing at me. Two officers rush at me. Nurses rush at me. Lisa rushes at me. Somebody screams. Somebody else pulls an alarm. But I only keep banging the sheriff against the wall, shouting curses, until arms drag me away, cuff me, throw me to the ground and pin me there.

23

On our final morning in Edgetown, I decide to take advantage of our rare independence by treating Tariq to breakfast at one of the restaurants I've noticed lining the riverbank. An overnight rain has washed away the sticky heat of the last few days, leaving the air refreshingly effervescent—perfect for eating outside. After I help him pull on the pair of summery tan trousers I bought him for this moment, both legs full-length for the first time in years, he follows me slowly. Walking is still hard for him, the leg heavy, the pull of it making his muscles ache. He told me this morning that he hurts all over from yesterday's efforts. Yet seeing him walk free of his crutches feels like watching him fly.

We stop once again to look at the river, so different in the daylight, the sun somersaulting over its surface. I have always loved the way rivers change with every mood of the sky. Wrinkled and brown one day, a smooth jade or glistering sapphire the next. The Euphrates has this quality, sometimes a deep amethyst, sometimes the silver-gray of a snake, sometimes the black of a clouded night. I wonder whether Tariq will ever see the rivers that run through his native land, or if he will grow up so American that he'll be indifferent to his country, maybe even ashamed of it. And there is much to be ashamed of, Iraq being no less cruel, corrupt or violent than anywhere else. It is tempting as an exile to romanticize one's homeland, to paint one's people as blameless victims and one's enemies as monsters. I am guilty of thinking like this myself. But, of course, humans and their politics are never so simple.

At the restaurant, I ask the waiter to give us a table out on the terrace. He nods, winking at Tariq. "Can we have that one, Mama?" Tariq points to a table by the water. "I can see the fishies there." I take his hand, as I have not been able to do for years, and we walk over together.

The waiter, a portly gentleman with a red face and an avuncular manner, pulls out our chairs for us and then leaves to fetch a pitcher of water. He has noticed nothing odd about Tariq, as far as I can tell. All he seems to see is an appealing little boy with curly hair and a happy demeanor. For so long I have waited for this, for the time when Tariq can be seen for who he is and not for what he has lost.

He peers over the edge of the railing. "Hello, fishies! Where are you?"

"What would you like to eat, *habibi*?" I scan the shockingly priced menu. "Sit down, please."

"Jim-Jim bread." He settles gingerly into his seat, struggling with his knee joint a moment, while I order French toast for him and an egg for myself. Leaning back, I tilt my face to the morning sky and send up a silent prayer of gratitude. As the proverb says, "Good things come to those who wait. But better things come to those who work for it."

During that morning's visit to the clinic, Ricky checks Tariq's prosthesis in the room with the throne and tells us that he will need some three months to thoroughly accustom himself to it. "He's learned real quick, though. Like I said, I'm always amazed at how fast kids get used to these things. I've seen children who were born with no legs pick up and run across the room the very first day we fit them."

"Yes, children, they are most adaptable," I agree. "It is not so easy for us adults."

Ricky goes on to explain that Tariq's weight and activity will change the fit of the prosthesis, so it will need adjusting, which is why the clinic won't cover it yet. "Bring him back in two weeks and then we can put on the skin."

"You mean these silly frog faces, we shall have to live with them all this time?"

"I'm afraid so." Ricky chuckles. "Now, make sure you clean his residual limb every night and dry it thoroughly—it's gonna be sitting in silicone all day and it is summertime. And he needs to take it off whenever he can to let his skin breathe and give his body a break."

"Yes, Marilyn, she told me. And in Iraq, I was a pediatrician."

Ricky looks at me with the usual surprise. "Well, in that case, you know what to do. Once we fit the skin, I'll find a clinic nearer to where you live, so you won't have to travel so far for check-ups. And if you can clear it with your insurance, you'll want to get him a second prosthesis with an articulated ankle, so he can run."

I thank him and stand to go. I read about those legs for running and how expensive they are in the brochure from the hospital. I also read that most insurance companies refuse to pay for them because, they insist, running is not "medically necessary" for children. Have these people never watched a child? Or been one themselves?

"What you are doing here, Mr. Ricky, it is a very good career," I tell him as we prepare to leave. "My late husband—he was a doctor also—he and I had planned to open a clinic like this for those wounded by war. It is something I still wish to do."

"Well, you're in the US now, so maybe you will. Land of opportunity, right?" And Ricky grins his bright, American grin.

Back at the motel, we collect our bags and sit in the dim, hummus-colored lobby to wait for Lisa. Entranced by the neon-blue fish tank in the middle of the room, Tariq limps over to it with his new freedom and presses his nose against the glass, watching its exotic inhabitants darting through plumes of bubbles. "Hello, fishies," he says again. How happy he sounds; how it lifts my heart.

A large television screen looms over the room, its channel tuned to CNN. Three young American hikers arrested in Iran. Russian wheat crops destroyed by fire and drought. Fourteen million Pakistanis displaced by floods. United States troops withdrawing from Iraq, leaving its people to piece together the ruins . . .

"Mama?" Tariq hobbles back to me. "When we go to New York City, can we see the giant buildings?"

I pull him into a hug. "We won't be able to miss them, *habibi*. I believe the whole city is made of giant buildings."

"What else will we see?"

"I'm not sure. We can ask Lisa. She'll know where to take us."

When Lisa arrives, however, she is too full of bad news to take us anywhere but home.

24

"Bless us, O Lord, and these Thy gifts which we are about to receive from Thy bounty, through Christ, our Lord. Amen." Sheriff Brady clears his throat and waits in silence at the breakfast table while his wife dishes out the bacon and waffles. "Sally, sit," he commands in the gravelly bass he's developed from forty years of smoking. "I've got something to tell you."

"You sound clogged as a frog this morning, honey. Wish you'd take that expectorant I got you."

"Don't fuss. April, you need to listen, too. Without interrupting, for a change."

April slumps in her seat, her bony teenage legs splayed under the table, and stabs her waffle with a fork. She hates it when her dad acts like a cop in their very own home.

Sending her a warning frown, Sally smooths out her blue skirt and laces her fingers together, which, like her face, are bloated by the medications she swallows every morning to blur her failures with Kate and enable her submission to her husband. She looks around, congratulating herself on the kitchen, which she only just finished redecorating the day before: wallpaper dotted with tiny roses, white ruffled curtains framing the windows, new ivory-colored countertops that shine like polished fingernails. Best of all is the crucifix she found at her church jumble sale, now hanging over the stove, where Jesus can watch her cook.

"Well, what is it, Dan?" She straightens her knife and fork on the white tabletop and looks at her husband expectantly.

Brady rubs his temples. It's taken him two nights of miserable sleep and several bouts of prayer to muster the courage to face his family with this news and yet he still dreads their reaction. He clears his throat and twists the buttons on his uniform.

"Honey, you gonna tell us or not? Or can we just eat?"

"Give me a moment." He clears his throat again. "It's about . . . it's about the Donnell brothers." And then he confesses that two days earlier, his highway patrolmen found Rory lying unconscious on the thruway shoulder, that Rory had a motorcycle helmet but no motorcycle, that the helmet was padded with four fat baggies of marijuana, and that when he, the sheriff, tried to explain all this to Katie's bum of a husband, that same bum attacked him like a rabid raccoon right in front of the sheriff's junior officers. "So now Katie's precious James Donnell is cooling off his very hot heels in Willowglen jail, exactly where he belongs."

"*What*?" April bolts upright in her chair. "Dad, you can't—"

"I told you, be quiet and listen." The sheriff clears his throat for a third time. "Didn't I always say those Donnells were trouble, huh? I can't tell you the number of times I booked their father—DWI, domestic abuse, bar brawls, you name it. If James attacked me like that, imagine what he must have been doing to poor Katie all these years. I'm telling you both, we're keeping that punk away from our daughter for good."

"Dad, I can't believe this! You're such a—"

"April, shush," Sally says. "But oh Dan, I don't know. Jimmy must be under a lot of stress. I mean, poor Rory. How bad is he?" Sally met Rory once, back when Kate and Jimmy were under the illusion that their families might get along, and she can still remember him at twelve, spindly as a carrot, with a bashful, appealing grin.

The sheriff shakes his head. "Last I heard, he was in a coma. Or maybe just unconscious, I'm not sure."

"A *coma*?" April jumps up from the table, knocking her chair onto its back with a clatter. "And you slammed Jimmy in *jail*? I can't believe you, Dad! He needs to be with Rory right now, not locked up in your shitty jailhouse! And why didn't you tell us before? He's been rotting in there for days and days!"

"Only two—well, two plus this morning. He assaulted an officer of the law, April. That's a serious crime. And watch your mouth." But the sheriff's eyes skitter to the floor.

"Dad, Jimmy's family! And he obviously didn't hurt you—you look fine to me. You've always been so unfair to him! You're such a pig!" April storms out of the kitchen.

"April, come back here!"

Sally puts a hand on her husband's arm. "Let her be, honey. This is a shock to us all. Let's just pray for Rory a moment. Let's just bow our heads and pray to Our Lord Jesus to heal him. And then let's eat. The bacon's getting gummy."

As soon as April reaches her bedroom, she locks the door and searches furiously for her phone. Finding it under her pillow—she was whispering into it with her latest boyfriend deep into the night—she flips through her contact numbers and calls.

"White Sands Resort. May I help you?" a man answers in chirpy tones.

"I need to speak to Kate Brady. I think she works there. Can you check, please?"

"Sure, babyheart, give me a second. Hmm, let's see. Brady, Brady, hmm. What a long list! So many B's, you wouldn't believe."

April clenches her teeth.

"Ah, here she is. Oh dear. She's busy at the moment, I'm afraid. Teaching water ballet. Sounds adorable, doesn't it? Can you call back later?"

"No! This is an emergency. I'm her sister. It's a family emergency. I need to talk to her now!" April's voice trembles.

"Oh my, hon, please don't cry. I'll page her right away. Just wait a second." He puts her on hold.

After what feels like fifteen hours of listening to the worst music in the world—whining Hawaiian guitar, hamsterish Bee Gees and a bizarre song about chocolate friends—April hears the soundtrack switch off and her sister's raspy voice on the phone. "April, I told you not to call me. Is there really an emergency?"

"Yes! Rory's in the hospital! And Dad busted Jimmy—he's in jail!"

"What?"

"Rory had a motorbike accident and he's in a coma! And he's in, like, all kinds of trouble!"

April has to repeat this three times before Kate can take it in. "Jesus," she says when she finally understands. "Will he be OK?"

"I don't know. Katie, I'm scared."

"And what did you say about Jimmy?"

April explains that again, too.

"Dad's a fucking bastard! I can't believe this. Get him on the phone."

April unlocks her door and hurtles down the hall to the kitchen. "Dad! Dad!"

"He just left for work, sweetpea, what is it?" Sally turns from the sink.

Without answering, April bolts out of the front door just in time to see her father ducking into his cruise car. "Dad!" He looks up. "It's Katie! You gotta talk to her." She runs over, all flying legs and hair, and shoves her phone at him. "Talk!"

Scrambling out of the car, he grabs the phone. "Katie? Thank the Lord. Where are you? Why haven't you called us?"

"Is it true what April said, Dad? You locked Jimmy in jail when Rory's in a *coma*? What the fuck's the matter with you?"

"I'm not discussing that right now. I want to know where you are."

"You've got to let him out!"

"Katie, your thug of a husband attacked me. When I was in uniform. He's a violent, dangerous man. Is that why you left, sweetheart? Did he do that to you, too?"

"No! You've got it all wrong. You've got *him* all wrong. He's never hurt me in his life."

"I'm sorry, but I don't believe you."

"Dad, this is horseshit. You have to let him out—Rory needs him. You've got to listen to me!"

The sheriff closes his eyes, his love for his daughter pulling painfully at his chest. "If you want me to listen to you, Katie, you're going to have to come home."

25

The morning after our return from Edgetown, Lisa picks us up again from the soldier's house to take us to visit Hibah, and all the way there, Tariq cannot stop talking about Rory. "Where did Aunty Lisa say he is, Mama?" he asks me for the third time, his little face pinched with worry.

"He's in the hospital," I repeat as gently as I can.

"The hospital where we're going now?"

"No. A different one. We're going to see Bibi today, I told you."

"But why is Uncle Rory hurt? You said there are no bombs here." I explain that it wasn't a bomb that hurt Rory but a motorcycle. Tariq thinks this over. "If Uncle Ugly's hurt, can we go see him first and make him better? And then go see Bibi after?"

I translate this for Lisa but she shakes her head. "Rory's not ready for visitors yet, little guy. He needs to rest. But soon as he is, we'll all go together. OK?"

"Mama, do you think he'll like my leg?"

"I'm sure he will, *habibi*."

"Then I want to go soon!"

"When he's ready, we will."

At the hospital, Lisa volunteers to wait downstairs while Tariq and I visit, only two people being allowed to see a patient at one time. We ride an enormous elevator to the Intensive Care Unit on the fourth floor, the two of us sandwiched between three white-coated doctors, their faces set square and stern, and a nurse in green scrubs whose own peaked face is yellowed with exhaustion. Tariq clutches my hand, looking tiny and out of place amongst all these purposeful adults. Once again, I yearn to be one of them, standing there in my own white coat, with my own face set and my own sense of purpose.

When we reach the ICU, a circular room humming with blinking machines and urgency, a nurse at the station in the middle tells us that we can find Hibah behind a flimsy green curtain in the back. Ushering Tariq through, I stand behind him, my hands on his shoulders, freshly shocked by how wasted she looks. Her doctor told me the diagnosis on the phone before we came—the pneumonia, the passive suicide—so now I know the secret that she and the soldier were keeping from me, although that makes me angrier at her than at him. He was only trying to spare me useless anxiety while I was at the clinic with Tariq, but she was acting out of much more selfish reasons—the wish to end her life without my interference. Khalil's mother, once so strident and strong, now so set on giving herself up to death, as if she wants to throw away all our struggles to survive and surrender after all.

"Mama, why doesn't Bibi wake up and look at my leg?" Tariq whispers. "Is she not waking up because she's dead?"

"No, no, she's only asleep, *habibi*."

"But why's she got that tube in her nose?"

"It's giving her oxygen. To help her breathe."

"Bibi can't breathe?" His voice trembles.

"She can now, little moon, don't worry."

We stop talking then, watching her frail body shudder under every breath. Intravenous lines snake from her arms, a tube in her ribs is draining her lungs, a mask is forcing air into her nose. How quickly illness strips us of our essence. Already she bears no resemblance to the forceful, handsome woman I once knew, friend to dignitaries, fierce protectress of her husband and son, antagonist to my own mother and so often to me. Now her cheeks are collapsed, her body caved in, her eyes sunken, their lids so fragile they seem about to crumble away. And gradually, my anger gives way to pity. I, at least, have my son, but she has lost the two people she most loved in the world and so is left with but two choices: To drag herself through the remains of her life stooped under the weight of her grief, as if carrying a sack of stones. Or to relinquish those stones forever and let herself fall free.

We leave the hospital in a somber mood, matched, it so happens, by the weather, gray and oddly chilly for a July afternoon, a cold dribble of rain splatting against our skins.

"Lisa, where is Sergeant Donnell?" I ask as we duck into her car. "I have seen no sign of him since we returned from the clinic."

A slight flush washes over her cheeks. "He . . . he's staying at a hotel in Hudson near Rory's hospital. So he can visit more easily, y'know?"

"I see."

"So, where to now?" she asks. "Home?"

"No, I must visit the refugee office first. You need not stay, thank you. We can take the bus back. I do not wish to keep you any longer."

"No way, Naema." She gives me one of her warm smiles. "I'll hang in the car, do some studying till you're done. I don't need to be at work till six."

Derek is clearly surprised to see us again so soon, although he tries not to show it. "Look at you!" he says to Tariq after we have waited the usual wait. "You've lost your crutches. Where did they go?" He winks at me.

"Not lost. Don't need!" Tariq marches in a circle, grinning up at him.

Ushering us into his chaotic office, Derek hands him the customary lollipop jar and sits behind his desk. Tariq settles onto the floor with the jar on his lap, poking around inside it and naming the various colors and flavors in English as he sucks on his favorite, strawberry. "So what's up?" Derek asks me over his chatter, a phrase that still makes me glance involuntarily at the ceiling. "Has something happened?"

"No. Well, yes. It is only that I wondered if there are any new jobs on your list. I must earn money as soon as possible. Our life, it is becoming an emergency."

He looks worried. "I'm sorry to hear that, *Oum* Tariq. I'm afraid that nothing new has come through since you were last here, but Soft-Tex, that mattress factory I mentioned? They're still hiring, if you want to reconsider that."

I imagine sitting at a bench in the middle of a long row of other immigrant women, our backs humped from bending over our sewing year after year, our eyes dim. Sore fingers, sore necks, sore spines, minds as attenuated as the needles hemming in our lives.

"I will reconsider, yes." Yet it is hard not to think of my work as a doctor, of the lives I once saved.

"I'll give them a call and set you up for an interview then."

"Thank you, Derek." And then I tell him what we say in Arabic of those who are kind: "You, Mr. Derek, have the heart of a child."

On the way out to the rattling elevator, Tariq and I pass a handsome young man standing in the hallway, examining the same photographs I studied on my first visit here all those long weeks ago. Tall and broad-shouldered, his skin coppery brown, he holds himself upright in just the way Sergeant Donnell does. My guess is that he is either a fellow refugee or one of the American do-gooders who show up here on occasion to help people like me find homes or clothes or jobs. I cast him a furtive look and see he is wearing a nametag saying *Louis Martin, Volunteer.* Ah. Even so, the set of his spine tells me that, somewhere in the world, he has been a soldier. I only hope it was not in Iraq.

After he moves away, I look at the photographs again myself. The dazed faces, spent tears, the cracked and skeletal hands reaching out for alms. I wonder what has happened to these people since the pictures were taken. How many have chosen to keep pushing through life carrying that sack of stones, as have I. And how many have chosen to release that weight once and for all, as, it seems, has Hibah.

PART IV

26

April stands entwined in her mother's arms, shivering under the same frigid airport air that welcomed Naema. The sheriff is not with them, having had to report to work, for which April sends up several silent prayers of thanks, but she still feels as though something small and sharp is jumping around inside her stomach.

"I hope Katie manages your dad all right," her mother says, clearly feeling the same. "She won't listen to me, honey, but she listens to you. Try to get her to calm down if she's all steamed up, will you? Lord knows it'll make everything worse if she starts fighting with him again."

April nods, pressing closer to her mother to keep warm. Sally is wearing sensible white pants and a green blouse but April's own waifish body is clad in nothing but her usual skimpy shorts, a pink tank top and flip-flops, fine for the blistering July outside but certainly not for the climate in here. She watches the other people milling about under the fluorescent lights, wondering who they have come to meet. A slim but heavily bearded young man in a bright puce coat pacing outside the Baggage Claim exit. A lone teenage girl who can't stop fiddling with the piercings pimpling her face. An elderly man watching the gate anxiously, looking pasty and rumpled. The last time April can remember being in this airport, she and her parents were cordoned off in a special area with a crowd of other military families, waving homemade welcome signs and little US flags while they waited for their girls and boys to come home from war. And then scanning the faces of those same girls and boys as they filed off the plane to see if they were the person they were before or had come home somebody else altogether.

Katie had looked nothing like herself when she had finally appeared. She had looked as spindly and dead-faced as a puppet. She'd walked like a puppet, too, having passed out and fallen off her guard tower over there and hurt her back. April was only eight at the time but she can still remember how unnerved she was by the change in her sister. How she sensed, even then, that Katie's return would knock their family askew forever.

Sure enough, as soon as they reached home that evening, Katie locked herself in her bedroom, refusing to come out for days or talk to anybody, even April. Their mother was forced to leave trays of food by the door, as though Katie were a prisoner. And then, one afternoon, when the sheriff was at work and Sally busy in her garden, Katie threw open her door and tore into the polished living room, shouting something about faces. "Katie, what's wrong?" April called, running after her. Katie didn't hear. She only looked around in a panic, snatched the sheriff's spare gun out of its hiding place in the mahogany sideboard, flipped off the safety and shot out all the windows one by one. April cowered in the corner, arms over her head, screaming while shards of glass flew around her like arrows, pinging off the porcelain lamps, piercing the brocade curtains, littering the ivory carpet, raining over her like a hail of needles, peppering her skin with tiny dots of blood.

Their parents put Katie away then, in a VA hospital for soldier nutcases. The sheriff drove her there himself, Katie fighting and cursing the whole way. April wasn't allowed to see her for weeks and weeks after that.

Jimmy saved Katie. She used to say that all the time. Maybe because he was the only one of them who knew what had happened to her over in Iraq, so he understood what she needed. Or he did until now.

"There she is!" April shouts, spotting her sister at last: a short, sinewy redhead pushing her way through the airport crowd, a duffel bag slung over one shoulder. Kate has never lost her soldier walk and still wears her hair cut short, the curls bubbling around her head. April thinks her so pretty, with her heart-shaped face and round, pale blue eyes. She doesn't think her sister looks like a soldier at all.

"Katie!" April breaks from her mother's embrace and jumps up and down, waving. "Over here!"

Kate strides up to them, her face deadpan. Without a word, she drops her bag to the floor and wraps April in a strong, tight hug for a long time, Sally hovering eagerly behind them. Kate's body feels short and hard and tense, the only softness her breasts pressed against April's. She smells of swimming pool and suntan lotion, but also of something edgy and metallic.

"How's Rory?" Kate says, letting April go at last. Her voice is as husky as ever, scratchy around the edges, low for someone her size, but it sounds oddly disconnected.

"I don't know, haven't heard." April slides her eyes away, suddenly shy.

"What about Jimmy? Dad let him out yet?"

April shakes her head.

Only then does Kate look over at their mother. "Hey, Mom." The greeting comes out flat and toneless.

"Oh, Katie, honey, thank the Lord Jesus you're back! I've prayed and prayed for this moment." Sally throws her arms around her. "Why didn't you tell us you were safe?" Her voice wobbles.

Kate ignores this, standing limp until her mother lets go. She turns to April. "Where is Dad, anyhow?"

"Work."

Kate studies her a second. "You look mighty cute. Hair's gotten so long."

April blushes, pleased. But she wishes her sister would smile.

"How was the trip, Katie?" their mom says then. "Did it take long?"

"Bus, bus, taxi, plane. Yeah, it took long."

"Your color's great—you picked up a lot of sun. Where were you, honey?"

"Doesn't matter. Let's go."

All the way home, Kate sits in the front, gazing through the side window without saying a word while Sally chatters nervously, her plump neck running with sweat. April watches her sister's profile from the back seat, the jumping creature inside her refusing to stay still. They spin past a tiny wooden post office, the sprawling local YMCA, a chemical factory secure behind a hurricane fence, cornfields, a farm stand, rusting tractors, empty meadows choked with milkweed, thistles and ticks. And along the road, the great vehicular massacre of the upstate countryside: mangled raccoon, flattened squirrel, run-down deer, mutilated chipmunk, a blood-caked bluebird, at least twenty squashed frogs and efts, a bloated porcupine and a smashed possum buzzing with flies.

At the house, Kate pulls her duffel bag from the trunk, scans the immaculately shaven lawn, the geometric flowerbeds, the sheriff's absurd sign and their bland brick of a home, and marches inside. Heading for April's bedroom—her own was converted into a TV den long ago—she kicks open the door and tosses her bag in a corner. Dropping onto the bed, she lies with her arms folded under her head, eyes on the ceiling. April follows her in, closing the door behind her. "Lock it," Kate says. "Don't want Mom poking her nose in."

April does and then stands looking down at her. Kate was always athletic, body lithe, legs and arms sleek with muscle, but now she looks stronger than ever, her biceps swelling like goose eggs under her freckled skin.

"You're getting on my nerves. Sit."

April glances about her room, newly conscious of it with her sister there. She decorated the powder-pink walls with posters of smoky-eyed vampires and Justin Bieber, along with collages of selfies and snapshots of friends, and normally she's proud of it. But now, with Kate lying there all grown up and sad, it only looks stupid and juvenile.

April sits on the end of the bed. "Why are you dressed like that? Aren't you hot?" Her sister is wearing khaki overalls, a grubby white T-shirt, equally grubby white sneakers.

"Had to wear this at work for clean-up detail. Usually, I was in a bikini and dumb little skirt. That's how we had to dress all the time to please the horny customers. Couldn't get on the plane in a bikini, could I?"

"Don't you have any, like, regular clothes?"

"In my bag. All dirty."

"Oh."

April stands to turn on the air-conditioning—the room is suffocating—and then sits back down cross-legged to face her sister, knees sticking out like a grasshopper's. "What are you gonna do, Katie?"

"Wait till Dad comes home and scream his fucking ears off till he lets Jimmy out of jail."

"You planning to see Jimmy?"

Kate keeps her gaze on the ceiling. Her face does look darker than usual, a kind of brownish brick color under the freckles—a redhead's tan—that makes her already light-blue eyes lighter than ever. April notices a few lines at their corners she can't remember seeing before. But then, Kate is twenty-seven now. "Well, are you?"

"Don't know. Need to call Lisa first, find out how Rory's doing." Kate pauses. "Do my laundry, too." Her eyes are still fixed on the ceiling. "You met Naema and her family yet?"

"No. Dad wouldn't let me go to your house after you left—didn't want me to see Jimmy."

"Dad's a fuckhead. Thanks for not giving Jimmy my number, though, sweetie. That must've been hard."

April swallows. "I wish you'd call him, Katie. He's, like, so sad without you."

Kate shifts on the bed. "He hasn't found some new babe?"

"'Course not! You know him better than that." April pokes her sister's leg, angry now. "You don't have any right to be jealous. You're the one who left."

Kate sits up, pushing her back against the wall.

"Why *did* you leave, anyhow?" April pulls her knees to her chest. "And why did you, like, go so far away and stay there so long without telling anyone where you were? And why are you being so weird and mysterious and mean?"

Kate rubs her face. Her nails are bitten to the quick, the cuticles torn and bloodied. "I can't explain it, sweetie. I can only say that I made a mistake once, a bad one, and now because of it, I had to get as far away as I could."

April stares at her. "Why? What did you do?"

Kate tears at a finger with her teeth. But she says nothing.

"You gotta tell me! I mean you, like, left for months and months and you won't even say why? That's not fair!"

"I can't."

"Why not?

"'Cause . . . 'cause it's something you just shouldn't know."

"But you always said you trusted me! That you could tell me stuff you, like, wouldn't tell anyone else." April's voice quivers. "Wasn't that true?"

Kate releases her hand from her mouth. "Of course it's true. Please don't cry."

"Will you tell me then?"

Kate leans her head against the wall and closes her eyes, her pale eyelashes almost invisible. "April, I'm sorry, but I've never told anyone. And I can't tell anyone now." She inhales, her breath catching. "'Specially not you."

27

Welcome to Willowglen Jail Hotel!

We hope you enjoy your stay at this low-cost, intimate boutique situated in beautiful downtown Willowglen. All meals are provided for free and your stay might last longer than you anticipate.

BEDROOMS: EIGHT CELLS IN A CINDERBLOCK BOX.

BED: SHELF BOLTED TO A WALL, MINUS A MATTRESS.

BATHROOM: IN-ROOM LIDLESS METAL TOILET EMITTING ITS OWN SPECIAL PERFUME.

LIGHTING: ONE 9 X 7-INCH RECTANGLE OF WIRE-EMBEDDED GLASS.

DÉCOR: GRAY WALLS. ORANGE BARS.

MENU:

BREAKFAST: PEANUT BUTTER ON STALE BREAD.

LUNCH: PEANUT BUTTER ON STALE BREAD.

DINNER: PEANUT BUTTER ON STALE BREAD.

VIEW: ME.

At least Pat figured out to bring my Ativan. He's come to see me all three nights I've been locked up, and though he never has anything good to tell me about Rory—only that he's still in a coma, the cops are still sniffing around the hospital and the docs know no more than before—he did manage to slip a few foil-wrapped pills through the bars. It wasn't difficult, this being a precinct jail intended for DWIs, hookers and juvies, not sheriff-batterers like me; the guards nothing but bored local cops who'd rather salivate over their sports pages and porn than check up on us "guests" or our visitors. And then I pulled my war hero horseshit on them for good measure, which has kept them somewhat off my back. Although the irony of being a former army prison guard behind bars myself is not lost, at least on me.

Having nothing to read and no glasses anyway—confiscated, along with my belt, shoelaces, phone and the contents of my pockets—the only way I can pass the time is to do endless push-ups on the piss-soaked concrete floor and prowl my cell like a cat in a cage, needled over and over by thoughts I can't shake. How I've screwed up with my brothers—not only Rory, but Pat, too. How I enlisted when they were much too young. The hurt on their faces when I dumped them that first time with Aunt Maureen. The fear on those same faces when I came home, jacked up on violence and heartbreak. Five years of war seeping into my pores, twisting into my veins—what the hell made me think that was the way to raise my brothers?

That must be why Kate left. Not to follow some other loser and not because of the pills or my lack of job, either. But because she's sick and tired of cleaning up the enormous pile of shit I've made of my life.

I look around, trying to find something, anything, to pull me out of my head, which feels like a jar full of snakes eating their own tails. I've discovered that I'm not the kind of person who can handle being locked up like this. It makes me understand in a new way why the Camp Bucca detainees we locked in windowless shipping containers for punishment would throw themselves against the walls till their scalps split.

"Hey, Donnell." A porky officer named Thornton waddles up to my cell. "I got news."

"What? I'm finally seeing the judge I should've seen two days ago?"

Ignoring my question, he unhooks a porcupine of keys from his belt and opens the cell door. "Your lucky day. You're sprung."

Too surprised to speak, I shuffle after his bulging back to the front office, my laceless sneakers trying their best to escape my feet. He squeezes behind the counter and shoves a sheet of paper at me. "Sign for your effects." Sitting down, he reaches behind him for a tray and pushes that across the counter, too. "Check it's all there."

I pick up my stuff, each item sealed inside a separate Ziploc bag like it's evidence for a murder. "That's it? I can leave?"

"Uh-huh. You're free as a bee, far as I know." Thornton yawns, eyes watering, and flips open his newspaper.

Outside, squinting against the flare of the sun, blinding after my dank cell, I take out my phone. I've no idea why I've been released like this but now, at least, I can get to Rory. I'm about to dial Pat when something makes me glance up.

Kate.

She's leaning against her mom's cobalt-blue Kia, arms folded, looking at me without moving. White T-shirt, denim cutoffs, flat sandals and a pair of sunglasses so huge I can hardly see her face. Little and wiry as ever, she still has that halo of curly red hair and those lovely slim legs. I dash at her, pick her up and crush her to my chest.

"Hey, whoa, hey," she splutters, her sunglasses flying to the ground. She wraps her arms around my neck and breaks into tears.

Pat is already at the hospital when we walk in, hovering outside Rory's room in one of his baggy black outfits, chewing a wad of dip in deference to the No Smoking signs, a trick I picked up in the army and was dumb enough to pass onto him. "Hey, Pat," I call. He spins around, the dip bulging out a cheek.

"Kate! Fucking hell, you're back!" He rushes over and hugs her, her head of curls up against his chest. "And you sprung my jailbird bro, I see."

"Yup. Got big daddy to stop being such an asshole." She lets go of him. "How's Rory?"

"Better. He woke up at last—"

"Thank god," I breathe. "When?"

"'Bout an hour ago. But he's in a lot of pain. Docs say he broke a leg, a shoulder and a bunch of ribs. Wrenched his neck and banged up his head, too, right through his helmet." Pat gives Kate another squeeze. "Damn, it's good to see you again. You look amazing."

She does—tan and fit and more freckled than ever. But now that the tears are over, sunglasses pushed back on her head, her face has turned so buttoned-up and blank it scares me. "Thanks," she says. "Can we see him?"

Pat scoots over to a nearby garbage can and spits, returning dipless. "He's gone back to sleep, but sure. He's next to some sorry sucker wrapped up like the Invisible Man."

He leads us down the hall and through a door into a darkened room, where we tiptoe past a guy whose head truly is bandaged up to the eyes. Rory is on the other side of a curtain. His head isn't bandaged but the rest of him is, a cast on his left leg, a brace wrapped around his neck. He looks gruesome, face scraped and bruised, nose swollen again. Eyes blackened and closed. "Jesus," I mutter.

"He's gonna be happy as a dog with two dicks when he sees you," Pat whispers to Kate. "He missed you like hell. We all did."

"I missed you, too. How's Lisa doing?" But even as Kate says this, she sounds robotic. She sounded like that on the way to the hospital, as well, like she'd borrowed her voice from somebody else, so I did most of the talking while she drove, filling her in on Rory's accident and my stint in jail, leaving everything else hanging between us like a fire curtain.

"Lisa's good, thanks," Pat answers. "She's in Albany with Naema, visiting Tariq's grandma in the hospital—they'll be back tonight for dinner, so you can see them then. But hey, I heard you been teaching water ballet? That for real?"

Kate ignores this. "You think we can wait here till Rory wakes up?"

"Don't see why not," I say. "I just need to use the sink a moment." The jail offered no showers and I don't want to stink all over Kate.

Pat perches on the windowsill, his raccoon-tail hair dangling over his eyes, while I strip off my shirt, grab a handful of paper towels and give my top half a whore's bath, the water turning gray with jail scum. Yanking my shirt back on, which is still pretty fragrant, I take the visitor's chair, pulling Kate over to sit beside me on its arm. My worry for Rory is making me sick to my stomach but I'm so high on having her back, I hardly know how to think. Whatever she's done, whatever I did, whoever she did or didn't run off with, all I want to do right now is inhale her so deep into me that she will never, ever be able to disappear again.

"So how'd you break my bro out of jail?" Pat asks her then—we're all still trying to whisper.

"Got Dad to accept that Jimmy's never hurt me. Or him, either, for that matter. But he's sure Rory was run off the road and robbed 'cause of some drug deal gone wrong, and I can't make him change his mind about that."

"Fuck," Pat mutters. "You think Rory's in seriously deep shit then?

"Don't know. Dad's gonna question the crap out of him when he wakes up."

"Maybe he won't slap him with anything too heavy," Pat says, ever the optimist. "I mean, whatever the cops suspect, they only found weed on him, right? Least it wasn't smack or pills."

"You think Rory's on smack?" Kate asks in alarm.

I put my arm around her. "We don't know what he's on. Lots has gone down since you left. You are coming home, right? We need to talk."

She looks away.

Pat is the first to notice Rory open his eyes. Jumping off the windowsill, he rushes over to the bed. "Hey, Rory, you awake?"

Rory blinks. I hold my breath, afraid Rory won't be Rory anymore.

"Am I still in this shithole?" His words are slurred but distinct. "I hate fucking hospitals."

I exhale.

"You need to stay here a while still," Pat tells him. "It's only been a couple hours since you last woke up. How you feeling?"

"Can't feel anything at all. They must've put me on, like, twenty meds. You got rainbows all around your head." Rory squints at him. "Know where my Ducati's at?"

I stand up. "Hey, Rory."

Rory tries to move his head. "Ow! Fuck. Come over where I can see you. I seem to be paralyzed here." He sounds truly frightened.

"You're not, don't worry, bro. It's only a few broken bones and a neck brace." I suppress the urge to ask him what the hell happened to him and why—I'll save the interrogations till he's better. "Looks like your nose is busted for real this time, too, but you'll be fine. Afraid your motorbike's gone, though."

"Gone?" Rory looks so scared it rattles me.

"What's wrong?" I almost ask but decide to leave that till later, as well. "Listen," I say instead, "someone's here to see you. A surprise."

"Is it Nutpea?" He still sounds shaken.

Kate steps into his line of vision. "It's me."

"Kate! At fucking last! Where the hell you been?"

She shakes her head. "It's good to see you, kid. Though I wish it wasn't in this place." And then she's the one to ask. "What happened, you remember?"

"Hell yeah, I remember. Some motherfuckers forced me off the road and tried to kill me, that's what happened." He pauses. "Did the cops find anything on me?"

"Yup. Your weed," Pat answers. "Four sacks of it."

"Nothing else?"

"Not that we know of."

Rory closes his eyes. "Kate, can I talk with you alone a sec?"

I'm both surprised by this and not. Rory has always confided in her more than he ever did in me. Pat and I troop out to the waiting room.

"He's his old self, thank god," Pat says. "Dumb as the back end of a hot dog."

"Yeah. Sounds like he might be mixed up in some heavy shit, though. Jesus, why does Rory always have to be such a fuckup?"

On the way home in her mom's car, Kate at the wheel again, the tension clouds back up between us as thick as ever. Now that my first giddiness over her return is passing, a hundred questions are boiling up in my throat. It's too soon to spit any of them out, though, so I tamp them down for now and ask what she learned from Rory.

"He made me promise not to tell you."

"Kate, come on. He's been dealing out of I Scream Heaven, hasn't he?"

She sighs. "Yup. Oxys and weed. Turns out he's part of a pretty big operation."

"Shit."

"Worse, he's been short-changing the clients and selling the skim-off to his friends." She shifts gears and I notice that her fingers are bitten and torn, just like they were when she ran away from that VA hospital all those years ago. "His boss sent Rory down to the city to do a deal, and that's when he figured out what Rory'd been up to."

"'Course he fucking did. What was Rory thinking?"

"I know. Anyhow, the boss hired somebody to chase him back, and you heard what happened next. Apparently, Rory had a whole load of cash on him. That's what the boss wanted back."

"Why didn't they take the weed, too?"

"He doesn't know for sure, but he figures either they didn't have time or they wanted his dead body to take the rap for them."

I stay quiet a moment, the news soaking into my skin like a spill of gasoline. "How much d'you think your dad knows?" I finally ask.

"No idea." Kate stops at a red light and drums her torn-up fingers on the wheel. "My guess is all he's got is a hunch." The light turns green. "But I'll keep working on him to leave Rory alone. Or at least I'll try."

For the first time in my life, I'm glad to be married to a county sheriff's daughter.

"Still," she says a second later, "even if Dad drops the charges, once Rory's out of the hospital, I think you better send him away from here for a good long time before he really gets himself killed, y'know?"

I pull off my glasses and rub my eyes, which feel dried out and shriveled from lack of sleep and jailtime air. "Yeah. I'm thinking rehab, if we can afford it."

We fall into silence then while I try to stop myself from asking my hundred questions, all of them floating around in the car like toxic bubbles. "I got a new job," I tell her instead. "Or I do if they don't find out about my little vacation." I fill her in on the marmot marine and Saint Paul's. "So we might both be teachers now. What d'you think?" I glance at her, hoping to see her pleased. But she doesn't seem to be listening.

"Who's Nutpea?" is all she says. "And what's the grandma doing in the hospital?"

I explain.

"Does Naema usually eat dinner with you?"

"Not usually, no. Why?"

Kate takes a left too fast. "Pat said they're coming tonight."

"That's 'cause we're going to celebrate. Tariq just got a prosthetic leg, his first ever! He's been on crutches since he was three, Kate, can you imagine?" I glance at her tight little face. Those freckles I love, those blue-gin eyes. She looks miserable. "You don't need to be nervous, babe. Naema's not hostile. Well, she was a little at first but it's better now." I pause, not wanting to sound accusing but needing to anyway. "She was pretty upset that you weren't here when she arrived, though."

Kate hunches her shoulders over the steering wheel and stares straight ahead. But she doesn't say a word.

28

"Jim-Jim, where you?" Tariq calls out the car window the minute Lisa pulls up to the house. Scrambling out, he hobbles as fast as he can across the yard, leaving Lisa and Naema to carry the groceries they just bought into the back apartment. He hoists himself up the porch steps with the help of the banister. "Jim-Jim, you here?"

Hearing his voice, Jimmy hurries out from the kitchen. And there Tariq is, dressed in a blue tracksuit and standing on two legs, as sturdy as any boy who has never seen a bomb. "My god!" Jimmy's voice catches. "Look at you."

"Now I beat you football!" Tariq marches up and down the porch, his curls bouncing. "See?"

An ache blossoms in Jimmy's throat. "Show me those frogs I've been hearing about."

Tariq lifts the left leg of his pants, revealing a metal stalk of a shin and a plastic cup splattered with pictures of Kermit's grinning green face. "Awesome, yes?"

Jimmy nods. "Stupendously awesome."

Kate and Patrick emerge then, wiping their hands on dishtowels. Kate has just thrown away the red velvet cake and other food that rotted during Jimmy's incarceration, while Patrick has been shucking corn and slapping together hamburger patties, the tension emanating from Kate so suffocating he was tempted to jump out the window and run for home. "Holy shit, Tariq, you can walk on that thing?" he exclaims. Kate twists the towel in her hands.

"He sure can," Jimmy says. "Amazing, huh?" But Tariq has stopped paying attention to either him or Patrick and is staring at Kate instead. Dropping his pants leg, he moves over and gazes up into her face.

"Who you?"

She steps back. "I'm Kate. Jimmy's wife?"

Tariq regards her steadily. "Go 'way."

"Tariq!" Jimmy says.

The boy ignores him, his serious eyes fixed on Kate. "Jim-Jim marry Mama and be my Baba. You go 'way."

"That's enough now." Jimmy takes the dishtowel from Kate and hands it to him. "Go with Uncle Pat into the kitchen. He needs your help."

Tariq flashes Kate a last look and then hobbles off after Patrick, already forgetting what he said. Now that he doesn't need crutches, he can carry things, lift things, fetch things. It makes him feel so grown up. It makes him feel strong.

"He didn't mean it, babe," Jimmy says once they're gone. "He just misses his dad."

Kate tears at her cuticles with her teeth.

The second Lisa and Naema appear from around the corner, Lisa gasps. "Kate!" Jumping onto the porch, she hugs Kate long and hard. "Where the hell you been, girl? Thought I'd never see you again!"

Kate says nothing, but she does cling to Lisa for a long time, her eyes closed tight.

Naema backs away on the grass. The last time she saw this soldier-girl, that first year of the war, the girl was armed and in uniform, while Naema was standing in a crowd of civilians, clothes dusty, heart wrung dry. The last time they were enemies.

Only once Lisa and Kate finally break their embrace, still smiling at each other, Lisa's eyes moist, is Naema able to force herself to mount the porch steps and approach. "It is a pleasure to see you again, so far from our initial circumstances," she enunciates carefully, extending her hand. "I am most pleased you have returned."

Kate licks her lips and takes Naema's hand in a limp grasp, only to drop it right away. "Welcome." Her husky voice wavers. "Guess it's a bit late to say that now." Her eyes flit to Naema's scar, which was not there before and which Jimmy neglected to mention. "How is, are you . . . I mean, has it been OK for you here?"

Naema examines this short, redheaded girl she has not seen for so long. That girl, so open and ignorant, has become a woman now, a woman who has clearly lost the protective cover of naivete. But then, much has happened to change them both in these seven long years of war.

"Thank you for asking," is all the answer Naema can think of. She turns to Jimmy, whose face is at least friendly. "What do you think of my Tariq's leg?"

"It's fantastic!" He grins at her. "He's walking so naturally!"

"He is." She smiles back at him. "Tonight, we shall celebrate this and your wife's return, yes? And also, the good news about your brother. Lisa, she told me he is awake and feeling better?"

Jimmy hesitates, thinking of the bad news as well. "Yeah, thank god. I'm sorry *Oum* Khalil can't join us, though."

"Well, perhaps she will in the future, *insh'Allah*. The doctors say she is improving."

"You don't mind that I didn't tell you—?"

"No, no." Naema glances at Kate, who appears to be rooted in place, her freckled face rigid, her eerily pale eyes fixed on the space between Naema and Jimmy.

She doesn't want me here, Naema realizes. *She never did*.

"Let's go around to the deck," Jimmy says to diffuse the moment. "We're having barbecue beef—it's kind of like shawarma? I think you'll like it."

Out in the backyard, Patrick tends to the burgers and corn on the charcoal grill while the others take their seats around the circular table up on the deck. Kate has set it with her old flare: powder-blue tablecloth, yellow napkins, a candelabra of multicolored citronella tealights to fend off mosquitos. Jimmy hopes this effort signals she is home to stay.

"So, Mr. Tariq," he begins while he hands out the food, "when did the doctor say you can get your leg skin?" Only Kate notices how odd this sounds; everyone else is used to such talk by now.

"Two weeks." Tariq grabs a corncob and bites into it, smearing his chin in butter. "I no want skin." He waves the corn in the air. "Keep frogs."

Jimmy explains what they are saying to Kate, who is sitting across the table from him, staring into her lap.

"When I see Uncle Ugly?" Tariq asks then. "I want show him Kermit."

"I could take him in a couple of days, maybe," Lisa says, looking at Naema. "What do you think?"

But Naema is too disturbed by Kate to hear. The more she absorbs Kate's presence—her drawn face, nervous tics, darting eyes—the more vividly she recalls the long days she spent waiting outside Camp Bucca for this same Kate to bring her news, and the more she feels again the devastation of that news when it came.

"Mama." Tariq tugs at her shirt. "Answer."

"Sorry, *habibi*, what is it?" He repeats Lisa's question. Naema turns to Jimmy. "But how does your brother look?"

"Like a horror show."

She rubs Tariq's head. "Uncle Rory still isn't well enough for us to see him yet, little one. But you can come with me to visit Bibi again tomorrow. And then we must take care of some business."

The business, she has just resolved, will be to return to the Resettlement Center yet again and tell Derek that she and her family cannot live with these soldiers for even a week longer. He has to find them a new place. Now.

The rest of the evening is not a success. Patrick tries to fill Rory's shoes by kicking a soccer ball in the yard with Tariq, but as Patrick possesses neither Rory's playfulness nor the boy's affection, Tariq soon grows tired and fretful, saying his leg hurts. Kate sits with her back to the view—the sun splashing flames of salmon pink and neon orange across the sky as it sets—neither eating nor speaking. Lisa flits between her and Naema, telling Kate about the wedding and trying to smooth over something she can't understand. Naema is counting the seconds until she can leave without being discourteous. And Jimmy wants them all to go away so that he can fold Kate into his arms and mend whatever it is that has gone wrong between them.

At last, once the sun is gone and the meal finished, Naema pushes back her chair and stands. "Tariq, it is his bedtime now and he must rest his leg. *Salaam*." Taking him by the hand, she leads him around the corner and out of sight.

"That was sudden," Patrick remarks. Jimmy catches his eye and jerks his head toward the side window of Naema's room.

Lisa stands as well. "I'm pretty beat myself. Pat, let's clean up and go."

"Already?" He follows her as she carries a pile of plates inside. "Can't we stay and booze it up awhile? I thought this was supposed to be a celebration. It's more like a fucking funeral."

Lisa puts her finger on his lips. "It's Kate's first night back, dumbcluck. Use your brain."

After they leave, Jimmy and Kate finish cleaning up in silence, he ferrying the detritus in from outside, she bent over the sink, scrubbing the same plate again and again without realizing it. He tries to ignore this while he brings in the tablecloth and candles but finally can't stand it. "Stop, babe, please." He pulls her away from the sink and draws her to his chest, the familiar curve and dip of her body igniting his desire. "I know it's early but let's go to bed. We can finish this in the morning. We need to talk."

She pushes him off and turns to dry her hands on a dishtowel, making him afraid she'll refuse. But then she nods and follows him upstairs to the bedroom, where they undress without speaking, her back to him. He knows this means no looking, so only glimpses her taut buttocks and runner's thighs before she curtains herself in a white sack of a nightgown he's always considered the opposite of sexy. Laying his glasses on the bedside table, he strips to his undershorts, not wanting to be naked if she isn't. When she lies down, she pulls the covers up to her chin and fixes her gaze on the window, filled now by a full summer moon shrouded in a scarf of cloud.

Jimmy climbs in beside her, longing to wrap his body around hers and claim her again, but restrains himself. He cannot, however, exercise the same restraint over the questions still banking up in him like a storm. "I'm so happy you're back, know that?" he begins, moving as close to her as he dares. "I missed you so bad. It's been hell, Kate. You've got to tell me what's been going on."

She says nothing, so he shoves his glasses back on and sits up to face her. "Listen, just come clean. Did you run off with some fuckface you're dying to get back to?"

"Jimmy." Sitting up as well, she crosses her legs, bunching the nightgown between them. "Be real. I didn't wait for you through all those deployments to fall for someone else when I finally had you back. I can't even imagine wanting anybody but you." She plucks at the sheets. "What about Naema? Something going on with you two?"

"Jesus. Of course not." But he does look away for a second. "That's just little Tariq's fantasy."

Kate scrutinizes him. "She's pretty hot, even with that scar."

Jimmy looks back at her, face open now. "Kate, she's Khalil's widow, for chrissake. She doesn't even like me."

Kate looks at him in surprise. "Oh yes, she does. I could see that clear as day."

"Well, I guess we made our peace, that's all." He strains to see Kate's expression in the moonlight but all he can make out is a tension around her eyes. "So, if it wasn't some other fucker made you run, was it something I did?"

She takes a moment to answer. "No. You didn't do anything. I don't want you blaming yourself, Jimmy."

"What the hell was it, then?" He tries to stop himself from shouting. "And why wouldn't you take my calls—why did you *do* that to me?"

The clouds shift, allowing the moon to slip a pale shaft of light directly over the bed, turning Kate's small face white. "I don't blame you if you're mad," she says quietly. "I would be."

"I'm too relieved to have you back to be mad. I'll get mad later."

She looks down at her lap, picking again at her cuticles, and when she next speaks, her voice quivers. "I'll explain, I promise. It's just not gonna be . . ." She stops.

"Gonna be what?" He's shouting after all.

She tears at another finger. "It's just that I'm not who you think I am. Never have been. I shouldn't have come back." Her voice is shaking more than ever now. "I wouldn't have if it wasn't for Rory, and for Dad locking you up. Now I'm gonna screw over your life more than ever. Naema's, too."

Jimmy wraps his hands over hers to stop her tearing at herself. "Kate, you talked like that at Bucca, remember? After Yvette died? And when you first came home. Don't start again. You know it's bullshit."

"It's not bullshit." She looks directly at him now, her eyes hollowed out by the darkness. "I just pushed all that deep down where I could ignore it. And now it's come back up worse than ever."

"What are you talking about? I don't understand. You've got to tell me!"

She glances away. "I don't know how."

"You have to. You owe it to me. You have to tell me now."

"I know." She pulls her hands out of his and picks at them again.

Jimmy waits, the skin of his heart tightening.

When she speaks again, her voice comes out a whisper. "Remember that day at Bucca when you and the guys called me to beat up that detainee? The one who'd been jerking off and throwing his turds at me every day?"

Of course Jimmy remembers. Kate was up on her tower when the detainee burst out of his tent screaming, tearing at his clothes and pulling his hair out in clumps. The MPs ran over to subdue him, pinned him to the ground and called to her to join them and take her revenge. Jimmy was part of that, too, wanting to give her a chance to fight back, show the bastard and all those other fuckers that they couldn't get away with treating her like shit just 'cause she was a female. "Why, what about him?"

"It was the wrong man."

"What wrong man?"

"He wasn't the jerk-off."

Jimmy leans toward her, afraid now. "What are you saying, Kate?"

She hides her face in her hands. "The MPs had him belly-down on the ground, so I couldn't see who it was . . . I kicked him and stomped him and shoved his mouth into the sand till he couldn't breathe." Her words are barely audible, coming out in little gasps. "He'd just found out that we'd killed his son—that's why he was freaking out. But I didn't see who it was till I picked up his head. I yanked it up by the hair like it was just a sack of potatoes, Jimmy, and that's when I recognized him." She draws in a breath, her hands still hiding her face. "I tried to help him, undo his cuffs, clean him up . . . His mouth was full of dirt, he was choking, covered in blood. But it was too late. The MPs pulled me off him, told me I was a crazy bitch and dragged him away. And then . . . and then he died."

Jimmy stares at her.

"See?"

"No, wait . . ." His words evade him, as though he's chasing them through waist-high water. "That was Naema's dad? Is that what you're telling me?"

"Yes." Kate collapses into a ball, arms clutching her head. "I killed him, Jimmy. I killed Naema's father. That's why I wanted you to hire Khalil, help her family, bring them here after he died. I thought I could face her if we did all that. But I couldn't."

Jimmy slides off the bed and paces the room, door to window, window to door. He paces for so long without speaking that Kate begins to sob. "Jimmy, say something. *Please*?" She is still fetal and hidden.

He climbs back onto the bed and gently sits her up, wiping away her tears with his fingers. "Oh babe, why didn't you tell me about this when it happened?"

"I . . . I was afraid you'd hate me." She is weeping so hard now she can barely speak. "I *knew* you'd hate me. 'Specially later, once you got so close with Khalil."

"But I could've helped you."

"How?"

He strokes her hair. "Because Naema's dad didn't die from that beating. He died of a heart attack weeks later. Khalil told me all about it."

Kate sits up, cheeks slick with tears. "A heart attack?"

"Yes. He was fragile, Kate, broken from the war and grief over his son, and probably the imprisonment too. His heart couldn't take it—he'd had other heart attacks before. It wasn't your fault."

"I beat up a man with a bad heart, a man mourning his kid. That's still killing him, Jimmy."

"You didn't know it was him. You can't blame yourself."

"Then who can I blame?"

"War. The bullshit of it. The way it deforms us all. You know."

A long silence.

"So, you don't hate me for it?" Her voice is tiny.

"Of course I don't."

She studies his face. "Not even deep down where you don't want to admit it?"

"No, Kate." Jimmy takes her hands again. "Listen, we all carry shit from the war. We all did things we can't stand to think about. How do you think I feel about Naema's brother getting shot? Or about Khalil's dying because of me, because I hired him, because I didn't keep my promises? But we can't undo those things, can we? We just have to find a way to live with them."

"How?"

"We'll figure it out. I'll help you. We'll help each other." Wiping the tears from her face once more, he folds her in his arms.

She shivers against his chest. "Should I . . . you think I should tell Naema?"

Are we your path to make yourselves feel better? Your "atonement"? "No. What good would that do her? She can't wash us clean, if that's what you want, and we can't ask her to try. She owes us nothing, Kate. We have to find another way."

Kate picks up his muscled arm, glowing white now in the moonlight, and traces her fingers over the three strands of barbed wire tattooed around his bicep. One to commemorate Camp Bucca. One for Jack Muller. And the last one for Khalil.

"What other way, Jimmy? I don't think there's any way at all."

29

On the evening of our long-awaited dinner with *Oum* Ismail, Tariq and I dress as well as our wardrobes permit—he in a little blue jacket and his tan trousers, I in a long black skirt and white blouse—and wait in front of the house to be fetched. Tariq leans against me, chattering about Iron Man, but soon stops and looks up at me, his face grave. "Mama, will the little girls there like me?"

I know why he is asking. He has not found a single playmate here in America, and since he lost his leg, his interactions with other children have never been easy. "I'm sure they will, *ya amar*, don't worry." Yet I am worried myself, not only for him but because, even with Kate Brady's return, I am still living with soldiers and still in fear of how I might be judged.

The car pulls up at exactly the time arranged, a dented gray sedan obviously far from new. Mustapha sits behind the wheel; his sister Yasmin beside him, her dark eyes and aquiline nose set off by a royal-blue hijab, under which her hair is piled into an elegant mound. I feel a pang of new anxiety. Will they be offended by my not wearing hijab in their house? I never did at home—or not until America's war empowered conservative imams and I was forced to cover myself. Yet if I were to wear one now, it would proclaim me more pious than I am, thus rendering me a hypocrite. For a moment, I wish I had never accepted this complicated invitation at all.

Mustapha climbs out to greet us, his square face breaking into a smile, his teeth white but crooked, his eyes hidden behind sunglasses. He is shorter than I remember, not much taller than I, but his wide shoulders and impeccable beige suit emanate solidity. "It's a pleasure to see you again," he says. "And this is Tariq, if I remember?" He bends down and shakes Tariq's hand.

"You see anything different about me, Uncle?" Tariq asks, standing with his legs apart, hands on his hips.

Mustapha straightens up and regards him thoughtfully. "No crutches?"

"Right!" Tariq pulls up his trouser leg. "Kermit!"

This turns out to be the theme of the evening. As soon as we arrive at *Oum* and *Abu* Ismail's apartment, Tariq ignores all the manners I have painstakingly taught him and accosts everyone, young and old alike, to demand that they admire his frogs. I do not know whether to be proud or mortified, for he is behaving more like an unruly American child than the well-bred Iraqi I have taught him to be. Yet it does help to dispel our initial awkwardness.

The two small girls present are immediately fascinated by Tariq, which is lucky because when he first sees them and bursts into a stream of boasts about all the extraordinary feats his leg can perform, only a fraction of which are true, the girls look at him blankly. It turns out that neither of them can understand Arabic anymore. "They were so young when we came here," explains their mother, Saba, the Rasheed family's eldest daughter, who was not at the Refugee Center when the rest of us met and who, to my relief, is also without hijab. "And once they started school, they refused to respond to anything but English."

"I fear this may be the case for Tariq as well," I reply, thinking of my conversation with Lisa. Tariq switches to English and soon the children are off in a bedroom, playing.

Oum and *Abu* Ismail live in a housing development on the edge of Albany, every building an exact red brick replica of its neighbor. Their second-floor apartment is new and basic, the rooms nothing more than a collection of white boxes. Yet the couple has enlivened it with wall hangings and rugs from home, much as I have in the soldier's house. They even have a display of intricately decorated ceramics arranged on a bookshelf.

"My husband used to be an importer at home," *Oum* Ismail tells me, picking up a white bowl painted with delicate spirals of flowers and vines in periwinkle blue. "We had a beautiful shop of the loveliest bowls and plates. Not only from Iraq, but Turkish ones like this—the pattern here is called Golden Horn—as well as Syrian, Tunisian, Egyptian, Moroccan, Persian—oh, the list was long, wasn't it, Nezar?"

Her husband, sitting silently in an armchair by the window, shakes his handsome silver head. "Please, Derifa, let's not talk of the past."

But, of course, we do. Throughout the long evening, from the tasting of olives at the start through the multi-coursed meal *Oum* Ismail serves us at her cramped oval table, the past seeps into our conversation like blood through a bandage. *Oum* and *Abu* Ismail, I learn, lost all three of their sons to the war, leaving the devastated couple with no children at all. Their eldest, Ismail, was killed by American bullets, as was his brother, Ahmed. The youngest, Sinan, was captured and beheaded, either by a militia or a gang of ordinary criminals, no one ever knew which. How *Oum* Ismail manages to smile at Tariq and be so welcoming to us in the wake of such devastation, I cannot fathom. Were I to lose Tariq, I would never be able to bear the sight of a child again.

The Rasheed family, too, has taken its blows. Like me, Saba was widowed by a militia's bomb, leaving her girls fatherless. Zahara and Yasmin both lost their fiancés in the war, one shot by US soldiers, the other disappeared. And Mustapha, who was indeed an interpreter for the Americans, was captured and tortured by Muqtada's army for his efforts, only managing to escape in the maelstrom of a mortar attack. Yet I am shocked by none of these stories. I know so many like them. No, what shocks me is something else entirely, something I only learn later.

When it is time for dinner, I am directed to sit beside Mustapha, an obvious move on somebody's part to matchmake, whether his own, his mother's or *Oum* Ismail's, I don't know. This renders me stiff with self-consciousness, which Mustapha does his best to ameliorate. He asks after Hibah's health, where Tariq was fitted with his leg, and for my impressions of America. He even draws from me the history of Khalil, Zaki and my parents. But as we converse, I come to feel that I am talking to two people at once: a polished conversationalist on the surface and an entirely different man beneath, peering at me guardedly from deep within his eyes. A man hiding wounds far more devastating than any I have heard about here.

"Tell me, if you don't mind," I say to him at one point, "what work are you doing now?" He remains silent for so long that I speak again. "I'm sorry if that was intrusive, I didn't . . ."

"No, no, it's all right." He gazes back at me, the deadness of his expression chilling. "I haven't found a good job yet. Nobody here seems to want my skills as a translator or an engineer." He smiles wryly. "I work in a factory making window shades and blinds. *Abu* Ismail works there as well."

I look at my silver-haired host in dismay. "How long did it take you both to find this work?"

And this is the news that shocks me. "Ten months. My mother took eight months to find hers—she's a cashier in a supermarket. My father, eleven. He works in the stockroom at Walmart, which is hard on the back at his age." I glance at Mustapha's father, elderly, worn and thin. "At home, my mother was an engineer like me, my father a professor of linguistics. And, as I said, I was employed by the United States Army. But here, all this means nothing." And for the first time, I hear bitterness in his voice—the bitterness of a man betrayed.

At the end of the evening, Mustapha drives us home with Yasmin, our chaperone, in the back beside Tariq, Mustapha having insisted that I sit up front with him. Tariq is so exhausted from his long hours of playing that he falls asleep on Yasmin's lap. By the time we reach the main road out of Albany, she is asleep as well. Or pretending to be.

"I hope you enjoyed yourself," Mustapha says, driving so slowly I could pass him at a jog.

"I did." And I am speaking the truth. "We've been here for nearly three months but, aside from my brief encounters with *Oum* Ismail, I've seen nothing of our countrymen until tonight."

"Yes, it's a lonely business being an exile. I, at least, have my family, or what remains of it. Forgive me for saying this, but I'm sure you miss your parents very much." He knows better, I notice, than to mention how I must miss my husband.

"I do." Folding my hands on my lap, I look out into the summer darkness, waiting for the subject to pass.

"Do you mind my asking for your father's name? You mentioned that he was a poet as well as a professor?"

"Halim Mohanammad al-Jubur. Yes, he published several books of poetry."

"Ah, yes, I remember. I used to read his work as a student. He was a brave man, may Allah grant him mercy. His poetry moved me very much."

I say nothing, suspecting Mustapha of flattery. Then he adds, "Let me see if I can recall," and he recites,

Where lives justice,
When every side has its angels and demons
And every coin two faces?
One face, freedom,
The other, death.

"You like that poem?" I ask.

"Yes, it meant so much to me when I was young. Someone speaking the truth for a change."

"It's part of the poem that got my father arrested and tortured."

Fearing that I have been overly revealing, I turn again to look outside. But Mustapha replies, "Saddam did much to wound us. It tears at my heart," and I feel, for the moment, relieved.

I roll down the window, the car lacking air-conditioning, and over the warm breeze and hum of tires listen to the melodious throb of crickets and the piping of what I have learned are tree frogs. "These American nights are so noisy," I murmur.

"Everything about America is noisy."

We chuckle and drive on in silence. But it is a comfortable silence, not the strained one of earlier in the evening. I am able to relax now, having survived the dinner without feeling condemned. Mustapha's mother made me nervous—I caught her scrutinizing me more than once—but otherwise I felt accepted enough. Perhaps our shared predicament will finally allow us to overcome our grudges and suspicions. Perhaps.

"I wonder," I say aloud.

"You wonder what?" We are speaking quietly so as not to wake the sleepers in the back.

"I wonder if it will get any easier being here. Being away. Being alone."

"I think it will. We adjust, we adapt; it's the human thing to do. But being alone, isn't that the essential condition of exile? A man without a nation, who is he but a man alone? And an Iraqi without Iraq, can he—or she—even be Iraqi anymore?"

"There's no such thing as being Iraqi now," I answer. "We all feel this, don't we? War has split our country into pieces the way a hammer shatters a melon. Now we're no longer Iraqi first, but Sunni or Shi'a, Kurdish or Arab, Muslim or Jewish or Christian . . . We long for unity but there is no unity. We are longing for nothing but a dream, don't you think?" I turn to look at Mustapha, needing him to drop his defenses and give me an honest answer—to show his true self, that second self I see hiding behind his eyes. I want a sincere interaction with him, one that will alleviate the very loneliness he just said is inevitable. The line of Baba's poem comes back to me: *To survive is to live in a prison of solitude.* I so want this not to be true.

"Yes, you're right," Mustapha says, and for a moment he does sound less guarded. "But I can't bear to believe it."

We have reached Sugarhill Road by now, having driven for much longer than necessary. Mustapha pulls up to the house and switches off the engine. "Thank you so much for your company." He offers me a tentative smile. "I hope my sisters and I can become your friends."

I feel myself blush. "I would like that, yes." I turn to wake Tariq.

"May I . . ." Mustapha clears his throat. "Please, do not take this wrong, *Oum* Tariq, but may I telephone you?"

Later that night, after I have washed and dried Tariq's suture and put him to bed, I step onto the back porch to listen again to the orchestra of insects and rush of the stream hidden by the night. Fireflies are cavorting and a light breeze fingers my hair, but I am intent on other matters now, a new determination hardening in my breast. I will not wait for ten or eleven months to find work, as Mustapha and those others did. Nor will I depend upon the flimsy promises of Lisa, as kind as she is. No, tomorrow I shall return to Derek, accept the seamstress job at Soft-Tex and sign a lease for any apartment he can find for us, no matter where it is or what it is like. Soon, Tariq will be in school, I will be free to work and, once Hibah recovers, she can look after him while I take classes at night in medicine. The first three months of our exile in America have almost passed. The time has come for yet another beginning.

I say a silent goodnight to the fireflies and go inside. Upstairs, I presume, the American soldiers are lying asleep in each other's arms, their pampered hearts untroubled. Here, the room is hushed but for the whisper of Tariq's breathing. His prosthetic leg stands in a corner, casting a faint shadow in the moonlight. I move over to his bed, gazing down at his little face, his future stretching unknown before him, as mine stretches before me.

I bend to kiss him, whispering the words of the very last poem my father wrote before his death:

Rest from the running now, my child,
And sleep while you can.
We have wars to lose
And wars to win.
Sleep, before the vultures come,
And wake only for the honey.

AUTHOR'S NOTE

President George W. Bush's 2003 war against Iraq is almost forgotten today, even though it is now widely recognized as having been unnecessary and unjustified in any way, and as having destabilized the Middle East so deeply that the repercussions have lasted ever since. Nonetheless, the fact remains that this war killed some one million Iraqis, widowed two million women, and orphaned at least a million children, according to Physicians for Social Responsibility and others. Over four million Iraqis were displaced, either within or without the country, meaning that one in five people were, like Naema and her family, forced from their homes. Meanwhile, thousands of interpreters and their families were killed or tortured for working for Americans, while the US has turned its back on its promise to rescue most of them by bringing them here as refugees. Naema's family represent the lucky few. Iraq has never fully recovered from our devastation.

In the light of the government's refusal to help, several private organizations have worked long and hard to rescue not only Iraqi interpreters but also those in our other war in Afghanistan. I particularly commend The International Refugee Assistance Project (IRAP) at refugeerights.org, and No One Left Behind at nooneleft.org. For those interested in also helping wounded, starving, or displaced Palestinians, I recommend the International Network for Aid Relief and Assistance (INARA) at inara.org, and the United Nations aid organization, UNRWA, at www.unrwa.org.

ACKNOWLEDGMENTS

This novel, *The Soldier's House*, is the middle volume of a trilogy I call *Reparation* about the 2003–2011 American war on Iraq, a trilogy I wrote out of the years of research I put into my nonfiction book, *The Lonely Soldier: The Private War of Women Serving in Iraq*. The first volume of the trilogy is *Sand Queen*, which takes place in 2003, the year the US invaded Iraq; then comes this one, set in 2010 while the war was still going on; and, finally, *Wolf Season*, set in 2014, after President Obama had withdrawn American troops.

I would never have been able to bring any of these novels to life without the Iraqi citizens and American veterans who gave me their time and trust. In particular, I wish to thank Abbas al-Shukur, Nour al-Khal, Hala Alazzawi, Hiba Alsaffar, Mohanad Alobaide, Yasir Mohammed Abbas, Captain John Ryan, Major Jason Faler, Specialist Laura Naylor and Specialist Mickiela Montoya. I also thank Dunia Kamal and Eyad Awwadawnan for their wisdom about their native city of Damascus, Syria; as well as Zainab Chaudhry and Susan Davies, who were working tirelessly to help refugees in and around Albany at the time this novel is set, and who helped me find Iraqis to interview. This book would never have been born without all of your help.

The Soldier's House also owes inspiration to several Iraqi poets. The line, "A mother weaving a shroud for the dead man in her womb," was suggested by the poem, "When I was torn by war," in *The Baghdad Blues* by Sinan Antoon (Harbor Mountain Press, 2007). I was also inspired by Adil Abdullah's poem "The Prey," in *Flowers of Flame: Unheard Voices of Iraq* (Michigan State University Press, 2008). I found the epigraph from "My Soul" by Omar al-Jaffal, trans. Eman Morsi (2014) cited in "'We live with death': Iraqi Poets on Loss,

Grief and Hope," by Manuel Langendorf, *Middle East Eye* magazine, 4 January 2017. And I took the epigraph from "San Diego (On a Rainy Day)," by Lamea Abbas Amara, trans. Mike Maggio with Natalie Handal, from *The Poetry of Arab Women*, edited by Natalie Handal (New York: Interlink, 2001), 79.

The other secret ingredient to this novel were the residencies at which I was able to write undisturbed while surrounded by peace and beauty: Yaddo, The Virginia Center for the Creative Arts, Blue Mountain Center, I-Park Foundation, Ragdale Foundation, Ucross Foundation, the Tyrone Guthrie Centre in Ireland, the Caprara family of Palazzo Rinaldi in Italy, and Moulin à Nef in Auvillar, France.

I also want to express heartfelt thanks to my agent, Jennifer Lyons, for her support and efforts on my behalf; and to my writer friends Rebecca Stowe, Cara Hoffman, Ru Marshall and Yvonne Latty, who read early versions of my manuscript with insight and perspicuity; to Masha Hamilton and Ellie Siegel-Warren, who so generously read later drafts with care and skill; and to Eyad Awwadawnan, again, for all matters Arabic. A special mention goes to Steven Attewell, whom I have known since he was a baby, for his medical knowledge and help with Tariq's predicament and prosthetics. Steven died much too young and much too tragically in 2024, at the age of only forty.

And finally, eternal gratitude to my family: my children, Emma and Simon, and my grandson, Iggy, who continue to teach me the tenderness of parenthood, so essential to this novel. And to Stephen O'Connor, companion, editor and writer extraordinaire who always believed in this story. I thank you all.

—HB 2026

Biographical Note

Helen Benedict has been writing about refugees and war for many years, both in her recent novels, *The Good Deed*, a finalist for the 2025 Dayton Literary Peace Prize; *Wolf Season*; and *Sand Queen*, and in her nonfiction books, *Map of Hope and Sorrow: Stories of Refugees Trapped in Greece*, and *The Lonely Soldier: The Private War of Women Serving in Iraq*. Benedict has also received the 2021 PEN/Jean Stein Grant for Literary Oral History, the Ida B. Wells Award for Bravery in Journalism, and the James Aronson Award for Social Justice Journalism, among other awards for her fiction and nonfiction. Widely published as a journalist and essayist, her writings inspired a class action suit against the Pentagon on behalf of those sexually assaulted in the military, and the 2012 Oscar-nominated documentary, *The Invisible War*. She is a professor at Columbia University in New York. Her work can be found at www.helenbenedict.com.